Modern Day
Gypsy

Kelly,
Happy Flying
& el colo know you!
GYPSY BROWN

BEAVER'S POND
PRESS
Edina, MN

ISBN 10: 1592982813
ISBN 13: 9781592982816

Library of Congress Control Number: 2010922155

Printed in the United States of America
First Printing: 2010

121110090854321

Cover and interior design by Tiffany Laschinger

BEAVER'S POND
PRESS

Beaver's Pond Press, Inc.
7104 Ohms Lane, Suite 101
Edina, MN 55439-2129
(952) 829-8818
www.BeaversPondPress.com

To order, visit www.BeaversPondBooks.com. Reseller discounts available.

Contents

Prologue

Preface (prĕ-f`ĭs) A preliminary statement.

What is my introduction to others when I encounter them? I like to believe that I exude the qualities of a sincere and trustworthy individual, and I also believe that karma plays a large part in how my life will turn out. For instance, if you are a kind and giving individual, your life will be a blessed one. However, if you are evil and selfish, then you will face many unpleasant consequences. Most of the time, I stay on the right side of the law, but there are times when the wind blows and pushes me gradually to the left, and for these times when I lack responsibility in my judgment, I know there is a penalty.

My name is Gypsy Moon, and I really do receive great pleasure in pleasing people. I donate to charities, perform volunteer work in my community, and rescue pets. However, my endorphins go crazy when I experience naughty behavior no matter if it's my committing the act or some random person I observe. For example,

---

one time when I was eight, our family went to the drive-in theater just as we had several other times before to see a PG-rated movie. I asked mom if I could go to the bathroom, and of course she agreed. But instead of heading to the snack stand area where the restrooms were located, I jumped the cable fence and snuck into the adjoining theater to peek at the R-rated movie playing on the other screen. My parents thought I was drinking too much soda pop that night, and each time I came back from the restroom they would say I missed the best part of the show. That was only the beginning of my unmanageable childhood.

White lies you may call it; my mom called it tampering with your karma, which may explain why later on during that week I got caught looking at my father's dirty magazines and my mom put me on punishment for the rest of the month, meaning that I wasn't allowed to go to the next family drive-in excursion, that it was my karma balancing out.

Karma (kär-mə) The effects of a person's action.

As we were growing up, my sister and I were watched very closely by my parents. My father believed little girls had to act and respond in a non-confrontational manner at all times, and in addition Mom made sure we looked like the well-behaved trophy children that Dad assumed we were, and we dressed the part, too. This may be the reason why I love watching others do things I was never allowed to do. I'm not sure if the karma method works this way, but I'm supposing because of Dad suppressing my desires that my karma has been forever affected and altered. I fit somewhere in between being blessed for all my good deeds and paying dire consequences for my indiscretions.

I feel my father is liable. If I had been allowed to flutter about just a bit in my early years, I don't believe the rush that I get from misbehaving would be so strong, and Mom knew I was a defiant free spirit. I could see it in her eyes every time we had the big girl talk. She knew she wasn't getting through to me. Mom didn't want me to be like the preacher's daughter, the one that goes boy crazy every time she's away from home. Mom's way of avoiding this from happening to me was to occasionally pick me up early from elementary school, and we'd spend the rest of the day playing hooky at the airport watching the planes take off and land. She believed that these breaks would help curb my rebelliousness, but it seems to have only encouraged my devious behavior, and shockingly enough it shows up later in my adult relationships. Some of my non-suspicious boyfriends had no idea the kinds of mind games I was trained to play, which of course I learned from my mom; after all, she was the one who went behind Dad's back and pulled me out of class, insisting that I was never to tell anyone that I skipped school.

So when should I expect the results of my harmful conduct to surface? As a teenager I think I stayed out of trouble well enough, which was good, but Nina and I carried fake IDs and went to the bar every weekend. What line of attack should I prepare for? My first love was into religion as was his entire family, but I specifically chose a boyfriend whose religion was unacceptable by my family. See where I'm going?

Aura (òr-ə) A distinctive quality.

Life has been rewarding for me. Therefore, my aura must not be all that bad. I manage a special yet cautious friendship with my best friend Nina and close relationships with a few others I consider dependable, but my question is this . . . when is it going to be my turn to obtain the dream job, to go on a vacation that makes me smile, and to be granted an incredible soul mate to love and treasure? Where do I fit in this karmic equation, or is there a place for me at all, maybe outside of the parameters? I know I'm not the greatest person, my ex will attest to that, but I'm not the nastiest either.

Okay, so actually I have ended up with the dream vacation and the dream job, but the soul mate situation has yet to surface. Plus, with the dream job comes a lot of madness—police officer madness, NBA madness, pilot madness—and when I say madness

I'm speaking of the extreme excitement, the confusion, and the agitation of companionship, all of which I find appetizing. If I try to simplify my life and take the men out of my karmic equation, what would life be like for me? I have always counted on the male species to provide the madness I have come to enjoy.

I always thought I would end up being with my exact opposite to provide the balance the universe prescribes. Nevertheless, I'm falling for a man who knows how to play mind games better than my mother and me put together, the ultimate brain teaser. He's so skilled at dishonesty I don't know why I'm considering accepting his proposal other than I imagine he may be the soul mate I have been searching for. If it wasn't for my best friend Nina stealing my last boyfriend and in return saving me from the heartache of being used and tricked, I would almost be inclined to ask her for advice on this one. She said it was in the plan from the beginning, taking his attention away from me and all. How else would she have me believe in her and doubt him when exposing his escapades?

Disloyal (dis-'loi ' əl) 1. Lacking loyalty. 2. Nina.

Part I

The Pre-flight

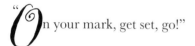

CHAPTER 1

Family

"On your mark, get set, go!"

My best friend Nina and I were racing to the corner of the next block to see who would win the Evil Knevil bike-racing event for the day. We were going downhill, and because I weighed two-and-a-half pounds more than Nina, I was ahead by a fraction. The small hill ended just past the fast-approaching Fuller boys' house. If I planned on keeping the lead, I needed to start pedaling feverishly. My braided ponytail was bouncing up and down against the back of my head, and I could feel Nina's presence as she gained way, disrupting my airflow. I didn't dare look back, knowing that in the millisecond it took to twist my neck to the right and map Nina's location, I would lose not only momentum but also my aerodynamicness. I could smell hints of Nina's Poison perfume in the wind as she inched her way beside me. I watched in horror through my peripheral as Nina sprinted past me down the driveway.

"I won." Nina declared her victory wearing her hand-me-down jeans.

"You cheated. We were supposed to stay on the sidewalk," I declared back.

"You went down the Fuller boys' driveway, too, Gypsy!"

"So, you did it first, cheater." I had on my Gloria Vanderbilt denim jeans, which should have automatically made me the winner.

My sister Melody came speeding down the sidewalk on her older-model Huffy, slightly out of breath.

"Dang, Gypsy! You almost got hit by that car. I'm going to tell Mommy," she huffed.

"No, please don't tell, Melody. I'll let you ride my bike home if you promise not to tell."

"Let's trade bikes now," Melody sang. "And you have to do the dishes for me tonight after dinner. Then I won't tell."

Blackmail. I'll take it. "Okay, cross your heart and hope to die." I made my sister draw two imaginary lines over her heart in the form of a cross to seal the deal.

Growing up in the 1990s on Linwood Avenue, I roamed the entire neighborhood, which spanned four square blocks. It was not only my playground but also the place where I earned my given name, Gypsy. Custard Elementary School was located across the bridge from our house, and the third year that I attended Custard I was nominated best dressed in my class, mostly for my trendy style and changing looks so often, giving the students something to gossip about. I thought back then that Linwood was the place I wanted to spend the rest of my days. Life was simple for Nina, Melody, and me, we spent most of the summers on our bicycles chasing time. After eating breakfast and watching cartoons, we hopped on our Huffy bikes and wouldn't return home for hours. Nina and I often had to talk my goody-two-shoes sister into riding to other neighborhoods to check out the boys, and every Sunday afternoon we rode by Sears three miles down the road to see the new dresses on display in the window.

Next to Nina, the Fuller boys were my best friends. They were twins but looked nothing alike. One fat, one skinny. One short, one tall. One dark-skinned, one light-skinned. The fat, short, dark one was my running buddy. He played Barbie with me, and I played trucks with him. Nina befriended the skinny, tall, light one. The two of them played spin the bottle behind the big oak tree in the alley.

Our parents had no worries when we were out and about. They knew that once the streetlights came on we would be sitting on the porch cracking jokes or playing jacks. We were well-behaved girls. Besides that, the neighborhood had Gertrude living across the street. We hated mean, old Gertrude and her cataract eyes peering through those burnt orange curtains, spying on us. Each summer morning, we saw the slow movement of her heavy drapery pushing apart. On some days, when we were brave enough to stare back, we could make out silver-blue hair wrapped in pink sponge curlers twitching from left to right, right to left as though watching a tennis match, with us neighborhood kids being the ball. Scratchy, her dusty cat, sat on the bay window sill, hissing, helping the old woman stay alert to our comings and goings.

Gertrude wasn't the only nuisance on the block. Nina's mom also contributed extra challenges to our pre-teen lifestyles, making it hard to maintain our goal of not having any disappointing stories getting back to Daddy. If by chance the two of us did misbehave, Nina's mom was allowed to discipline us, then send us home where we'd receive further punishment from my mother, mostly a good talking to, at which point Melody would always fold and tell Mom everything was all my idea.

There was plenty to keep us occupied during the summer breaks. Playing basketball with the Fuller boys in the back alley behind our three-bedroom bungalow was one of my favorite activities. Mr. Harper, a retired sanitation engineer, kept our alley well maintained from noon until the *Sally Jessie Raphael Show* came on. Mr. Harper swept, rinsed down, and gathered any debris that threatened our precious alley. He also checked the grass level of each resident's backyard, making sure every house on the street met the standards of the block club.

The gang (Melody, Nina, the Fuller boys, and I) went for bike rides near the train tracks to catch tadpoles. We climbed trees to pick berries. Oftentimes, Nina would climb in her Sunday school dress. On sunny days we played hide-and-go-seek, and to my dismay on gray, rainy days, we gathered in the basement in front of the mirror to summon Mrs. Meriwether. Whenever we played that ghoulish boogieman game, we swore up and down that her image became visible after reciting "Mrs. Meriwether appear" three times while standing nervously in the darkness surrounding the wall-mounted mirror and holding hands, watching, waiting. We were never allowed to play Mrs. Meriwether in the basement, and even though Dad punished us twice before for playing, we continued to take chances on getting caught because the gang loved that dreadful game and they would be furious with me if I told my mother, and knowing Mom and her angelic spirit, she most certainly would ban such a devil-ridden sport.

On rare nights when I'd got totally spooked, I would ask to sleep with my parents, and on rarer nights Mom would actually give in.

"Please, please, please can I sleep with you tonight?"

"Why don't you want to sleep in your own bed, Gypsy?" Mom would ask.

"Because, Melody keeps blowing candles and stinking up the room."

"Your sister is lactose intolerant; milk gives her gas."

"Well, I'm scared. Melody said because it's Friday the thirteenth something bad is going to happen to me."

"It's Thursday the twelfth."

"Mommmmm."

"Judy, let the girl fall asleep. I'll put her to bed later."

Thank you, Daddy. He always had my back. I knew I was secretly his favorite.

My father worked long hours for the City of Detroit and financially provided the family with plush living quarters. Mom stayed home to take care of the household, which included Tundra, the dog. Daddy's hard work allowed Mom to take us on regular shopping excursions for lace dresses. Seeing that we were not allowed to wear pants except on Saturdays, we needed a constant supply of dresses. On every other weekend Daddy treated our family to the drive-in theater to see a newly released movie in his restored black Lincoln Continental with the white convertible top. Mom and Daddy sat in the front seat and we two girls sat in the back, outfitted in our girlie powder pink pajamas printed with white sheep and golden moons floating through blue clouds. Melody toted along the prickly feather pillow encased in white, and I carried the pink fuzzy blanket with green carpet lint stuck to it from our spare room and a box of Junior Mints to share.

"Mommy, Gypsy wants to be a pilot. She told me so." Melody's big mouth ratted on me as she stuck her head over the bench.

"Oh, Gypsy, you love to play dress up. Pilots don't get to wear dresses. Only stewardesses are garmented in stunning outfits and high-heeled shoes." Mom turned to speak over the headrest waving her arms in a grand gesture. She knows me well. I didn't want to be spruced up in trousers like a boy. Yuck.

". . . and mom, I want to be a housewife like you." Melody smiled at Mom as she continued to lean forward. There she goes again, staying on the safe side of approval. Double yuck.

"Sit back, big head. The movie is beginning, and you're blocking my view." I could see the screen clearly; I just wanted her to sit back and shut her big mouth.

This is how it went every weekend, with Mom giving us guidance and Daddy sitting and listening, wearing a pleasant smile and enjoying his family.

By the end of my pre-teens, Melody and I managed our relationship well: I'd mess up, she'd get bribe money from me, I'd slip up, she'd get my bike, I'd screw-up, she'd get the night off from washing dishes. Melody was there to see it all and to cipher from each of my disobedient actions. Stopping her from running and telling Daddy on me became a full-time job, and one that didn't pay well either. One morning I had knocked Mr. Harper's trashcans over by mistake while practicing riding my bike, trying to perfect my Evil Knevil jump. Melody rushed home ahead of me to inform my par-

Knevil jump. Melody rushed home ahead of me to inform my parents before I even had a chance to trip her or run her off of the road with my Huffy. By the time I rose up from the ground and dusted the gravel off my new pink Adidas track suit, Melody was halfway up the block, turning into our backyard from the alley.

"Daddy, Daddy, guess what Gypsy did now!"

Gertrude popped out of the kitchen in anger. "Melody, please keep your voice down. Your mother is on the phone."

"Where's my daddy? I need to tell him something."

I had dashed into the kitchen right behind Melody and saw Mom sitting with her elbows perched on the white wooden table, pressing the palms of her hands firmly against her reddened eyes.

"Don't believe her, Mom. Melody's telling a story."

"Mom, what happened?" Melody bellowed.

"Mom, don't worry, and anyway I didn't knock them over on purpose."

"Be quiet, Gypsy! Mom, what happened?" Melody repeated.

"Yeah, Mom, what's wrong?"

"I said be quiet please, Gypsy."

"You be quiet."

Mean old Gertrude walked into the kitchen and picked up the telephone receiver that was lying on the floor next to Mom's bunny slippers.

"Both of you, be quiet and go to your room. Your mother will be in to speak to you in a minute," Gertrude softly said. "Understand me?"

"Okay," Melody said. "Why is Mom crying?"

"Please go to your room. Your mother will be in to explain." Gertrude's voice remained soft but firm.

"Okay but don't keep us waiting long," I said as I watched my mother's body give way to the shakes.

"Close your mouth, Gypsy," Melody ordered.

"You close yours, ugly."

"You're ugly."

"Girls. Go to your room now," Gertrude demanded. "Your mother received some very bad news and as soon as she's able she will be in to speak with both of you."

Old Gertrude came into our bedroom that evening to deliver the heartache instead of Mom. Gertrude sat on the edge of my bed and spoke to us with great concern in her voice.

"I have terrible news," Gertrude said.

"Is Mommy dying?" I asked.

Gertrude looked at me and said, "No, worse."

I focused on her face and asked, "Did Tundra die?"

Mean old Gertrude rolled her eyes and informed us that my father had been robbed on his way to work and shot in the head, but she assured me that Tundra the dog was still alive. Gertrude rose up from my bed and asked us not to disturb my mother with our bickering, for she had been disturbed enough for the day.

That was the first big blow to our young lives, and by some strong force of nature, Daddy's death became the resurrection of Melody's life.

My mom was five months pregnant at the time, and four months after that we found ourselves rushing to Memorial Hospital. My grandmother, G-ma, was a retired nurse, and she came to the rescue after receiving a call from Mom telling her that her water had broke. It was late Saturday, about seven. G-ma gathered Melody and me up and insisted that we ride to the hospital in our pajamas so we could be present for the baby's birth. The emergency entrance was quiet. It was New Year's Eve, and most of the staff had already left for the evening, except for those who must not have had families and chose to work for the holiday pay. G-ma dropped us off at the entrance and had me locate a wheelchair for Mom while she parked the car. Normally there were wheelchair pushers available waiting to escort the patients into the hospital for a tip, but not that night. That night was different.

The sky seemed to be constipated as it crackled and spattered rain against the big panes of the hospital windows. It had been threatening to rain all day, and soon rain was pouring down and sweeping the streets. The air smelled of humid cold. Cars were speeding through the icy streets leaving widowed water in their wakes. My body was stiff as I resisted the chill and pushed the heavy wheelchair up to the reception desk.

"Mom, how are you feeling?" Melody asked as she held Mom's hand.

"I'm in pain, baby, but that's part of labor."

"Mrs. Moon," the receptionist called out. "We are ready to take you back now."

"Gypsy, stay here and wait for Grandma. Melody, you come with me to the examining room."

"Dang. Why does Melody get to go?" I said under my breath. "Well, okay then."

Mom was in control even when there is no controlling this type of situation. I sat in the waiting room for ten minutes before G-ma came bursting into the lobby, her gray curls stuck against her wet face and her soaked dusting gown adhering to the bandage wrapped around her left knee from the spill she had when trying to clean out her attic the week before.

"Where is your mother?" G-ma insisted.

"The lady took her to the back. She told me to wait here for you."

"Is the doctor here yet?"

"I don't know. Only Melody was allowed in the back."

"Wait here, Gypsy. I'm going to find out if the doctor is here."

"Can you make Melody come out and wait in the lobby with me?" I stood up to follow her. "G-ma!"

"Wait right here, I said. I'll send her out." G-ma shuffled to the information desk to get her desired results, and like Mom she was successful. The receptionist rose from her cushioned chair and escorted G-ma through the sliding glass doors.

Forty-five minutes later a pale-faced Melody appeared in the lobby dressed in white paper.

"Is it a girl?" I jumped around Melody, anticipating the good news.

"Yeah, but . . ."

"What does she look like?"

"A baby, Gypsy. Something's wrong with Mom . . ."

"What kind of answer is that, a baby, who does she resemble?"

I paused to take a closer look at Melody. "Why do you have on paper clothes?"

"The nurse had me put it on. I told you something's not right with Mommy."

I stopped jumping and studied Melody's sincere eyes, the same eyes that comforted me when I cried on the playground after the kids laughed at me for peeing in my pants, the eyes that helped me not be afraid to sleep with my legs hanging out from under the covers because Mrs. Meriwether was waiting to yank me under the bed, the eyes that focused on Nina and back to me when asked whose outfit was the prettiest between the two, the eyes that would almost always choose mine. The eyes I grew to trust were now alerting me to pay attention; her eyes were demanding that I get serious. My own eyes began to tear, and through my blurry vision I could see a pleasant, familiar figure approaching. I blinked back the burning tears and recognized G-ma's wet clothing.

"Girls, the doctor is going to allow the two of you to visit your mother but only for a few minutes."

"Yay! I get to see the baby." I hopped around in excitement, rejoicing until those Pepsi-colored eyes found me again, gazing at me, reminding me to settle down.

"Hi, Mommy." My heart crushed at the sight of the multiple tubes attached to the major pulse points of Mom's body.

"Hmmm," weak and distressed, Mom attempted to communicate. "Hi, baby."

"Mom, I'll look after Gypsy until you return home," Melody's take-charge voice sounded as strong as the other women in our family.

"I can take care of myself . . ." I started before Melody's distraught eyes silenced me again.

"Girls, I called your Aunt Mary," G-ma said. "She's on her way to the hospital to pick you up and take you to my house. I'll stay here with your mother and call you when she wakes up."

"We don't want to go," I whined.

"Do as I say. Your mother needs rest."

"Yes ma'am," Melody said, grabbing my hand and giving it a squeeze.

"Yes ma'am," I bowed my head and recited.

The nurse had been frantic the whole time we were in the hospital room, in and out, in and out, looking at Mom's chart, checking her pulse, all the while avoiding eye contact. When Aunt Mary finally picked us up, the nurse looked relieved. Aunt Mary kissed mom's drunken forehead goodnight and whisked us away in her blue minivan to G-ma's house where four of my cousins, the same age as Melody and me, and six adults were waiting. The kids played board games and sang church songs while I watched the adults huddle in groups, whispering to each other and making numerous phone calls. It seemed as if it were a soap opera unfolding in real time.

When the phone rang at midnight, Aunt Mary answered. Her mouth tightened and her shiny eyes reddened. A powerful earthquake seemed to have erupted. Aunt Mary handed the phone to her husband as she settled into G-ma's rustic arm chair. The other kids were still playing, but I watched my uncle's expression change as he obtained information about Mom's condition from the inept doctors.

I sensed ghastly information coming forth. The temperature inside of my body rose, and chances of my surviving any more bad news were practically nil. This unavoidable catastrophe would be the second major disaster in my life in less than a year, and I felt incapable of handling additional volumes of emotions in such a short time frame.

I continued to listen as my uncle received the news announcing the death of my mother nearly three hours after the quake had struck. Though the doctor was remorseful and apologized for the delay in notifying the family that we had lost our loved one, one fact still remained unanswered. Why had he concealed for hours the truth about Mom's death? I felt all those involved in the cover-up ought to go to jail for their actions and never be able to work in a hospital again. I hated doctors. All of them.

The thought alone of Mom dying was way too harsh. That and the possibility of my being at fault for her death because of my slight misbehaving was even harsher. I didn't really mean it when I wished her dead for punishing me when I stole that candy bar from the corner store. Mom made me return it and apologize to Mr. Seaton for stealing from his store. I would do anything to take those words back. I would do anything to get my mother back.

The ground beneath my feet started shaking, and I buckled, overwhelmed by the doctor's inability to sufficiently help my mom. I began to hyperventilate; I called on God for help.

"God, please help! The rest of my life is completely ruined!"

Mothers actually die?

I ran out of the house and into the cold, freezing darkness of the evil night, rain beating on my unprotected back making me quiver, unprotected like the fragile leaves against the wind that lashed through the trees. This was the equivalent of manslaughter. I could hardly withstand the collateral damage the doctors had put upon me.

I thought about everything as I ran through the winter streets. *Mother died on the delivery table at Memorial Hospital. New Year's Eve. Doctor wanted to get home early. New Year's with his family.* Meanwhile Mommy was left on the delivery table with the attending nurse at 11:27 p.m., where she hemorrhaged to her death. Happy New Year. My childhood had ended. At the naive age of thirteen, I didn't know mothers could die! Cease to exist?! I hate all doctors.

G-ma came out of retirement to care for me, my older sister Melody, and my youngest sister, Kathryn, a newborn infant. Grandma refused to name Kathryn by her aura as my mother did with Melody and me. Instead she stayed generic so it was left up to us to give her a nickname that suited her. Because of her sneaky nature we settled on Kat. Somehow by default she managed to receive a name to complement her spirit anyway, the way mom would have liked. G-ma also tried to maintain major pieces from the lifestyle we had prior to Mom's death by moving into our home, which allowed me to continue attending my middle school and Melody to stay at Redford High School. We both were on the honor roll, and the sacrifices that G-ma made helped us continue to flourish despite our horrific past.

Melody and I were unrelenting, and we rebelled against G-ma, despite her every effort to keep normalcy in our life. Dr. Sike, the psychiatrist G-ma had us visit, said it was usual behavior for teenagers in our situation to act out against those closest to them, especially toward the caregiver, and that it would take a lot of time and patience for us to adjust to life without our mom. G-ma understood and was extremely loving. She knew about *patients* because she had had plenty in her lifetime.

I was in the eighth grade at Cerveny Middle School. Redford High was in the very near future. One day near the end of the school year, I asked for a pass to go to the lavatory. Mrs. Richards, our history teacher, had given Tracey permission to go eight minutes earlier and she hadn't returned. I pleaded with Mrs. Richards to not make me wait for Tracey's return, stating that it was an emergency and I couldn't hold it any longer. I didn't want to relive that pee-pee-girl playground moment. I begged until I received the pass to the bathroom and ran down the gray hall so fast past the purple lockers and into the girls' bathroom that I bumped right into Tracey Brown and Marion Lipscomb.

"Watch it!" Marion yelled. "Oh it's you, Gypsy. Why didn't you and your mom come to the parent-teacher conference yesterday?"

"My mother has been sick lately," I responded.

"No, she's not."

"Yes, she is."

"No, she's not, she's dead isn't she, Tracey?"

"Yeah, we heard she died!" Tracey said proudly.

"No, she's not. She's sick!" I yelled.

"Mrs. Richards announced to the whole class that your mother died trying to have a baby." Tracey proclaimed.

"What business is it of yours? I hate you, both of you nosy instigators!"

Sickened by Tracey and Marion's pleased smiles, I opened the bathroom door, slamming it hard against the wall, and ran back down the hallway, away from Marion and Tracey and away from the rest of the classroom full of snickering students. I ran out the door into the welcoming arms of the mean city streets.

The whole school had heard about my mother's death, but still I denied her passing to my classmates. I was embarrassed not to have a mother and didn't want people feeling sorry for me. After that day, in which I ran home crying, G-ma arranged for me to stay out of school for the remainder of the semester. All I was required to do was complete the last two weeks of homework G-ma had fetched for me from my teachers. I couldn't wait to put all this behind me and begin a second new life in high school, focused on being the best dressed in my class, wishing desperately that Tracey and Marion would attend Henry Ford High and not my school of choice, Redford High.

Melody and I were absolutely devastated but we manned-up as my father would have said. Even as destruction came at us full force and took both parents, we stood strong, determined to enjoy life, hoping that our parents' spirits were satisfied by how brave we had become. Mom would especially admire my new, improved fashion sense I acquired from the three-week camp G-ma let me attend at the Fashion Institute of America over the summer.

With the exception of not having parents, Melody and I turned out to be relatively typical young adults. When Daddy was killed earlier in my first life, Mom had a hard time adjusting to his death. My sister and I wanted to make life as easy as possible for my widowed mom, and our way of doing that was to man-up and not speak another word about Daddy. We never mentioned his name again ever, all the way up to Mom's own death.

CHAPTER 2

Ultimate Betrayal

*D*uring my first year at Redford High School, I met my true love, Ali. He was perhaps the most sought-after freshman in the class because of his exotic features and alluring hazel eyes. Even though he wore unflattering Converse tennis shoes, he still had girls standing by their lockers between bells waiting for him to pass by just so they could ogle him. I caught his attention one day when I walked into our classroom wearing a tracksuit with high-heeled shoes. I looked chic and kicked off a new trend for that spring season at Redford High School. Together we made history during our senior year. Ali proposed to me, and for the first time in Redford's forty years of recordkeeping, the homecoming king and queen were engaged to be married.

Though Ali and I were opposites, my being a prissy fashion plate didn't interfere at all with Ali's reputation for being a rugged Chuck Taylor, tennis-shoe-wearing football player. He loved my daring fashion statements but could care less about his own appearance. G-ma was extremely tough on him. She never allowed Ali and me to sit on the front porch alone. She never wanted me to get involved with any boy who lacked guidance, used curse words, or didn't attend church.

Every Saturday morning, G-ma would be at City Temple Seventh Day Adventist Church seated in the front row clutching her Bible to her chest, saying amen and nodding in agreement with the preachings of the minister. I sat directly beside her, nodding off to sleep.

My grandmother petitioned the court and obtained custody of us after the terrible loss of my mother. My parents' estate helped with the financial woes of raising an infant and two females entering adulthood. Well, my woes, anyway; Melody and Kat didn't cost much. Melody easily adapted to the new frugal lifestyle my grandmother forced upon us. I wanted to move away from home so badly I was willing to do just about anything short of wearing army fatigues as a fashion statement to get away from G-ma's parental control. I wanted to travel and learn the ways of the world on my own, without my dear G-ma's influence.

After I graduated from high school at the top of my class, G-ma pressured me to enroll into Madonna University's Fashion Merchandising program. G-ma said it was important to have a formal education and that if I was living under her roof I must attend college, even though it was my parents' roof that we were all living under. She also proposed that I get a part-time job so that I could begin learning how to budget my money. Now that my life was my own, seventeen and grown, I sought employment where Nina worked at Hudson's department store and accepted an offer for a position as a catalog model. My work schedule balanced well with my college courses during the week, and on the weekends Nina and I hung out at the nightclubs. Before hitting the bar with our fake IDs, Nina and I shopped at the outlet malls for sporty outfits to wear to Danny's nightclub, and being the responsible adult that G-ma was sure I was not, I incorporated my fashion merchandising homework with my night excursions and completed many of my mandatory assignments on these shopping sprees, which made the trips to the mall even more of a priority.

During the whole time of working and going to school, Ali and

I were romancing and virtually inseparable, except for the times I was with Nina. We walked through the state park hand in hand, picnicked by the riverfront at midnight, and enjoyed winter afternoon naps with the bedroom window cracked as we snuggled under down-filled comforters. Ali often picked me up from school to make certain we spent quality time together before my evening curfew.

On one particular day, we journeyed to the science museum to experience a bit of art and to take in the human exhibit. Ali and I found it funny that the volunteers sat around doing nothing except smelling of menthol rubbing cream while the fragile security guards, looking as though the wind could knock them over, hobbled through the echoing halls of the museum disciplining the middle-school children who were touring the hands-on exhibit and instructing them to keep their hands off of the displays. Ali and I seemed to be the only two in the building not wearing diapers or in need of a motorized wheelchair. As we studied the human exhibit, we began to get excited. I wanted to touch the naked remains myself. We couldn't stand it any longer. The nude bodies turned us on so much we skipped catching the bus and caught a taxi back to Ali's house to do our own exploring. Even though it wasn't Saturday, we still took a chance.

Usually on Saturdays I snuck out of Sabbath School and caught the bus over to Ali's house. His parents worked on the weekend at the Chrysler plant, so we played husband and wife. Once fully trained in the romance department, we moved on to sexual studies. Ali was the boy I lost my virginity to. He introduced me to oral sex. He showed me how to French kiss. I watched my first pornographic movie with Ali. He located my G-spot and taught me about orgasms. Everything sexual Ali took upon himself to make sure I experienced.

One evening on a typical Saturday night, hours after my valuable Ali time, I was feeling intensely sexual. I talked Nina into skipping our usual shopping at the mall and coming with me to a new local club called Playmates. The venue advertised an amateur night all-male review, and I was eager to get there early so I could be chosen to help judge the striptease contest. I walked in ahead of

Nina who was straggling close behind, complaining about not having a new outfit to wear, stopping to fix her tattered straps on a bra that she should have replaced long ago, stopping to check the worn heel on her shoe, stopping to see if her slip was showing, stopping, stopping, stopping. I was beginning to lose my patience when Nina stopped dead in her tracks and tapped me on my shoulder.

"What now, Nina?"

"I thought you might want to know something."

"What?"

"If you're going to have an attitude like that then we can turn around and leave."

"You know I'm looking forward to being a judge tonight so I won't be leaving, Nina."

"Apologize then."

"Apologize for what?"

"Your funky attitude."

"Okay, I'm sorry you feel I have a funky attitude."

"You're forgiven. Now look over there."

"Look at what?"

"Over there."

Nina's index finger was pointing to the middle of the club. My gaze followed her pointer finger, and to my alarm I discovered Ali approaching the center platform where the contest was being held.

"Ladies, welcome to the stage our next contestant, Indian Feather." The emcee sounded like an announcer introducing a pro-wrestler to the ring instead of an inexperienced ex–high school football player. Ali stood glimmering in a blue-and-white thong that was illuminated under the black lights. He wore navy suede chaps with tan fringes hanging down the sides, rendering his oiled butt and well-developed legs to the crowd as he spun around and did a tensed muscle trick with his butt cheeks. Over his chest, he wore an unbuttoned sleeveless vest that was being yanked off by a young bachelorette in a netted veil. He didn't look much like an amateur at all.

"What the?" My mouth hung open at the sight of the obese women assembled around the stage. My first protective thought would have given Indian Feather, with his mystifying hazel eyes, an excuse of being an exhibitionist. There pranced my ravishing man with an assured expression fixed on his face, stripping off his costume while swinging his wavy hair and gyrating his muscular body for the hordes of horny women. But reality muscled its way into my thoughts, and I was devastated. Ali was, in my mind, being a cheater. *How could he do this to me? To us?* Even though I kept hidden the fact that I attended these male review shows, Ali's secret was much worse than mine, defiantly concealing his liaison and allowing other women to view what I considered for my eyes only, him in his micro-briefs.

"Nina, what should I do?" My eyes were tearing up, but I was determined not to cry. I won't cry.

"Go and snatch him down from there. That's your man!" Nina demanded.

"Okay, my man. That's my man. Good plan." I began marching to the stage ready to claim my prize until I remembered I was wearing my forbidden outfit, the super-sexy sarong Ali had purchased for me in Florida while on spring break. The same piece of material Ali later chastised me for wearing in front of the senior class during our weeklong stay at the Hyatt resort in Daytona Beach. Before I could retrace my steps, he spotted me.

Ali leisurely picked up his dollar bills and departed the dais after his set was over and waltzed toward me. He halted inches away from my face.

"Gypsy, why are you here? You need to go home."

"What! Wait a minute. Why am I here?"

"This is not the kind of environment I want my fiancée frequenting."

"Fiancée? Here we go again, are you serious this time Ali? Are you saying that you're ready to commit now?"

"Yes, baby girl. Go home, put on your pajamas, and do some soul searching. Think hard about our relationship, and consider if you are ready to marry me."

"I've been ready. But how is it that you feel it's okay to dance?"

"Shhh. I have to go back to work now. Think about it. I'll call you later."

"Going back to work? Don't you think we should discuss this some more?"

"I'm due back on stage. We'll talk later."

Ali was asking me to think about becoming the proper housewife his Islamic religion called for, a wife he could be proud to present to his parents. Together we would produce many Muslim male grandchildren, and Ali's father would finally look at Ali with pride. My mind was spinning with excitement even though Ali decided to re-propose long after he first proposed to me in high school and after he got caught shaking it up dancing around in his underwear and only after his routine was completed. He concluded by informing me that he'd call after he got off *work*.

"Way to delude! Proposing to me in a strip club. Humph."

"Girl, what are you going to do?" Nina said as she witnessed the entire exchange.

"What do you mean?"

"Nothing about his deception bothers you? You're just going to go home and begin making arrangements to spend the rest of your life with a . . ."

"With a what, Nina?" I looked crossly at my best friend, cutting her off before she said something she wouldn't be able to take back.

"I'm saying, you should think about the situation. I know you want to get out of the house, but at what price?"

"Nina, Ali is my high school sweetheart. We've been engaged for over a year. How romantic and endearing to be able to say 'I married my first love.' Besides, I would be a hypocrite if I were to express negative feelings against his dancing. I'm here to observe the art and so are you, Ms. Judgmental." An innocent smile came across my face as I watched Nina's eyes dart downward once she realized I was right.

"Well, why do we have to leave?" Nina questioned.

"Because."

"Because what?"

"Because I don't want you looking at my half-naked boyfriend." *Why does she always have to challenge me?*

"I'm not interested in your boyfriend. I want to see the grand finale."

"Well then, I don't want to look at Indian Feather parading around naked. It makes me jealous. Besides, my maid of honor is supposed to support me and my decisions."

"Maid of honor! Me?"

"Yes, I want you to be my maid of honor."

"Oh my God Gyps, your maid of honor."

"Again, yes Nina."

"If that's the case, come on, let's go. We have a wedding to plan!" Nina became animated and ushered me toward the exit. "We need to get started on the color scheme."

Subsequent to forgiving him, Ali was hired for the evening shift at Playmates and I began attending his shows on Fridays and Saturdays. Afterward we would go to Denny's for breakfast then drive back to his place. At his apartment, we watched devil movies like *Rosemary's Baby, The Omen,* and *The Exorcist*; we ate ice cream out of the container; and we fell asleep with the night light on. Indian Feather didn't particularly embrace the being-exploited-by-women concept. After a few months of shaking his tail feathers, he traded them in for handcuffs and a flashlight. Like his parents, Ali worked security, the late shift at the Chrysler plant on Jefferson Avenue. The uniforms were horrid, flat front polyester trousers featuring back pockets with button and buttonhole closure. The waist was cut high and had darts for shaping, but wearing the unisex uniform pants paid the bills and covered Ali's body. Of course after Ali stopped dancing, I was forbidden from entering any establishment that endorsed sexual freedom, including Hooters. This was really beginning to suck.

Our relationship appeared to grow, and the more I confided in Ali and the closer my heart felt to him, the more he began to pull away. I was doing all I could to make him open up to me, but he still insisted on being mysterious. I almost hired a private detective to follow him around until he approached me and told me he had decided to join the Air Force. He said he wanted more out of life and this opportunity would allow him to better care for the two of us. Leaving me behind would be the reality of the situation, but Ali couldn't stomach the idea of my being available for someone else to govern. Per his insistence, we shuffled to the justice of the peace and solidified our union. I officially became his property.

Honestly, I felt like I was living my sister Melody's dream, the controlled housewife who honors and obeys her noble husband, who by the way, after graduating high school went to perform missionary work around the sphere, which was my dream, globetrotting. When Daddy was killed, Melody swore she wouldn't rely on a man like Mom had for survivorship. My other dream of having a big, glamorous wedding, dressed in a long, white, flowing gown with a beaded bodice and lace trim and a diamond tiara was dead, along with my dream of being a stewardess or an actress. Heck, the only dream of mine that did manifest was the marriage, and what a sucky marriage it was with my new husband leaving for the military without me.

Ali and I were married at age eighteen, and to keep the spiritual peace between the two families, G-ma had to humble herself and accept their religious differences. She welcomed Ali with open arms and considered him an addition to the family.

Eight weeks later, Ali packed his belongings and was ready to be shipped off to the service a determined man, one who vowed to support his new family. The actual day Ali did leave for the Middle East, I felt a little guilty for wishing he'd vanish sooner. In the weeks since he had finished boot camp, he continued calling with unreasonable requests like, "Gypsy, can you fly to Chicago and pick up my passport from the passport agency for me?" I was so tired of his demands that I was ready to send that man off to defend his country myself.

Once he was gone I became distraught and needed to apply my energies to positive thinking. I considered reorganizing the apartment furniture or shopping for miscellaneous gadgets again, but those thoughts didn't fulfill me. This time I wanted to do something for others instead of my normal self-serving healing methods. Because I was feeling abandoned, I didn't believe shopping would work. Instead, I started cleaning out Ali's closet of all his belongings and began joining my closet with his to create one huge California closet, and through this action I had a grand idea . . .

I decided I should release my many fancy dresses from the confines of the cardboard wardrobe closets in our basement storage unit and donate all the old clothes I hadn't worn to the local Salvation Army. The community could even hold an auction and use the proceeds to feed the starving children around the world. The idea was perfect. Volunteer work, feeding the poor, and self-fulfillment would be accomplished in one gesture, pure genius. Any guilt I had felt for willing Ali away was replaced with newfound pride.

As soon as Ali's plane left American soil, Nina called to say she was coming over to the apartment to supposedly cheer me up. She was glad Ali had left because she felt he didn't belong in my life, even though she had appeared delighted to be my witness at the courthouse when Ali and I exchanged vows. I think she was mostly excited about the new gowns. She couldn't wait to come and divulge a secret she wasn't able to reveal while Ali and I were living together.

"Nina, what kind of drama have you created now?"

"I didn't *create* drama. It appeared."

"What is it? Tell me."

"The traffic sucks, but I'm almost there," Nina said.

"Grr. I hate when you do this." Nina won't tell me over the phone this dire secret. She requested that a couple of peach-flavored martinis be waiting for her arrival because this scandal was huge.

"Okay, so what is it?!" I bombarded Nina at the front door.

"Dang. Where's my martini?"

"Ugh. Here, take mine. Now what?"

"This is what." Nina handed me a letter addressed to Ali.

"What is this and where did you get it from?" I asked, stepping aside so Nina could enter.

"Just open it up and read it!"

I sniffed the perfume-scented envelope addressed to Ali, took the purple stationery out, and began speed reading the first paragraph:

My dearest Indian Feather, the last two months have been fulfilling . . .
. . . sorry for the false alarm . . .
. . . please find it in your heart to forgive me; I wasn't trying to trap you
. . .

"Who gave this to you?" My root beer–colored eyes fixed on the letter.

"Licorice. She's an exotic dancer." Nina answered after taking a sip of her used martini.

"She gave this letter to you?"

"Uh hum. I met her a while back when I was waitressing at the Dollhouse."

"Yeah, I'd forgotten about that. You've gone through so many jobs."

"Yep. She knew we frequented Playmates, but she didn't know about you and Ali."

"Are the two of you friends?" I questioned already knowing the answer.

"No." Nina looked at me with a slick smile. "You're supposed to always keep your enemies close."

"Okay and?"

"She talked constantly about everything. When she started bragging about this guy who danced at Playmates she was dating, I began paying attention."

"But why give you the letter?"

"Oh right. She gave it to me to give to Ali, she said he had forbidden her from attending any of his performances. She used the word *forbidden*, Gypsy."

"Like Ali uses. He had forbidden me from visiting you at your last job at the casino." I looked up from the scented letter. "Why didn't you show this to me sooner?"

"Oh please, you would have stayed with Ali regardless. I'd probably be banned from hanging out at the apartment or exiled from your life altogether by Ali."

"No, that's not true. He likes you."

"Yes, it is true. And no, he doesn't like me."

"Okay, so he doesn't but you could have given this to me sooner."

"I'm giving it to you now, besides I haven't had it that long."

"Better late than never, huh?"

"Exactly."

I stared at Nina, knowing she was right, hating myself for not being strong, hating myself for not standing up to Ali, hating the way I married so quickly just to escape G-ma's grasp, and hating that Nina was enjoying being right.

CHAPTER 3

Girlfriends

*A*li and I had been married for eleven months. We kept our relationship together by making video calls and emailing each other, but we hardly ever had a decent telephone conversation, which concerned me. And when I received a letter by messenger from the Air Force, I began to panic. I was so bothered by the appearance alone of the manila envelope sitting on the mantel and the horrible news it may contain that I picked up the phone and dialed Nina's number and asked her to come over. She had been my life support through the Ali cheating ordeal, and she made inappropriate jokes only occasionally, usually suggesting that I remain optimistic about my marriage, concentrate on his one good quality— engineering—and look forward to his return home in a body bag. I was afraid to read the letter alone in my apartment. The last time I saw a certified letter come to the house was when my dad was killed and the City of Detroit sent Mom his personal records by messenger. Mom read the contents, and after seeing Dad's death certificate for the first time, she passed out, right in front of Melody and me.

"Hi sweetie." Nina stopped to study me. "What's wrong? Why the boo-boo face?"

"Nina, I received this certified letter from Ali today. It has a military return address from the Middle East."

"That's fitting, seeing that he is in the military. Open it up."

"Or it could be from the air force informing me of my husband's death. You open it." I handed the letter to Nina.

"You would be so lucky. I'm sure they have different procedures for death notices." Nina's steady hands began to unseal the envelope. "Okay, brace yourself."

"Wait!" My imagination was reeling.

"What, Gyps?"

"What if he's requesting a divorce?"

"Again, you would be so lucky. He sends you a monthly allowance. He wouldn't voluntarily send checks if he wanted a divorce."

"Maybe he's coming home." I give a hopeful look.

"He would have phoned, Gyps. Let's just open the letter." Nina's voice was saturated with impatience.

"Okay, okay." I put my hands over my eyes. "Open it."

Silence. Why is there silence? I removed my hands to inspect the situation. Nina's face was frozen. Damn.

"What? Tell me!"

"Here, Gypsy. You read it." Nina handed me the letter.

My dearest Gypsy, when we gathered in front of the Grand Sheik, I vowed to take care of you . . .

"Oh my God. It is a break-up letter." My right hand pressed against my chest, attempting to hold my rapidly beating heart intact.

"Keep reading, Gyps."

I am proud to have you as my first wife, and I will continue to provide for your needs . . .

"First wife?" I stared at Nina for answers. She bowed her curly head and looked up at me with an expression that said "keep reading" as her eyes pointed to the letter that now burned in my hands.

As you know, in the Muslim religion we are allowed more than one partner. I am writing to inform you of my intentions to take on a second wife. Her name is Makah, and her family has made arrangements for the nuptials to be exchanged next month. Please know that I love you and this new union by no means will jeopardize our current relationship. I have enclosed instructions for you . . .

"What the hell? This fool believes I'm going to sit around and participate in his harem?" I balled up the letter in the tightest ball I could muster.

"Sweetie, I don't know what to say other than I told you so." Nina looked at me through sympathetic eyes. "You want to go to Playmates and have some drinks?"

"That's the last place I want to go. Let's go to the Dollhouse, your old place of employment. I won't have to be bothered by men there. Let the female dancers keep the losers busy. That's what they're there for anyway, right?"

"If nothing else, we could find that hussy, Licorice. You have to see what Ali was cheating on you with."

"Yeah, Nina, good plan!"

"I still have clout there. Maybe I can get us in for free."

"If not just ask if you can have your old job back."

"Yeah, right, like I want to be a barmaid again."

It was Thursday night, and we decided to find Licorice at the newly remoldeled Dollhouse. The outside almost looked like a library with its innocent columns positioned on each side of the oversized lavender double-door entryway. Nina walked ahead of me as if she owned the place and opened one of the heavy doors. The club was dark and intimate. Huge doll faces with wide almond-shaped eyes and feathery eyelashes glowed against the black felt walls. Neon pink lighting flashed over the black and lime green overstuffed booths, exposing glimpses of the men as they lustfully watched the model-perfect women spread eagle on the stage, gently tucking dollar bills into the garter belts strapped around their thighs. Nina located a vacant booth near the back. It didn't have a good view of the entertainment, but it was adjacent to the bar and steps away from the powder room. This simple action of selecting the ideal seat was the unofficial marking of our territory. Licorice didn't show up for work, but we decided to stay and have a couple of drinks to drown my sorrow.

Once or twice a month we visited the Dollhouse, and with each voyage to the saloon we began to have more fun than the last time. Nina and I like to glamour dress in our sexy outfits and often met at our favorite booth in the back corner near the dressing room. It started out as the place to sit so Nina could point out Licorice to me; then later the owner of the Dollhouse established reserved seating for us because it brought in good business. He said some of his customers came specifically on Thursdays with the anticipation of seeing our girly crew gathered in the corner dressed in our Diana Ross attire. Imagine that—men coming to a strip joint to see dressed women.

Licorice didn't work every Thursday, but when she did and Nina and I happened to be in attendance, we would make snide comments about how the skin above her navel lacked elasticity, probably from too many aborted pregnancies, or how her costume of choice never correctly conveyed the Jezebel she truly was. We always ragged on her appearance; the poor girl never had a hint that she was being torn to pieces by two of the most popular female patrons in the bar. But soon, gatherings at the gentlemen's club became less about Licorice and somehow morphed into a sorority-type hangout. I invited other friends to join us in our bi-weekly girls' night out (GNO), and it wasn't long before the drink-yourself-out-of-depression nights turned into inspire-your-girl-into-happiness martini gab fests. Most often we met up on the third Thursday of each month (though Nina and I would come more frequently), and one of the GNO members was required to choose an item from her life, something that needed improving, accepting, or introducing into the present lifestyle to bring to the affair. After the item had been presented, each friend gave an opinion or advice on how to reach a desired goal, and being that we were seated next to the dressing room, the dancers themselves began to gravitate to our booth to join in on the GNO topic of the day.

The dancers had plenty of experience with various men, and they told us that a lot of problems arose from having *too* many dealings with them, like when the girlfriends or wives of some of their customers go the bar to confront them instead of confronting their own boyfriends or husbands. Who would have thought these dancers would share such intimate details about their dealings? In any event, we rotated every third Thursday so that each member would get a chance to shine and tell about what's going on in their lives. And tonight is my turn . . .

"Hi, ladies. I'm late again, but wait 'til you see what I have in my purse."

"I can't wait. You sounded so excited on the phone," Miyuki, my next door neighbor, interjected. She had a certain savoir-faire about her, and I was eager to hear her comments on the chocolate morsel I had tucked in the side pocket of my Coach hobo bag.

"Patience, patience, my little one, for I have with me tonight a fabulous proclamation."

"Gypsy, stop with the acting, will you? There are no talent scouts in here." Sheila, my classmate from Madonna University, so rudely reminded me.

"Okay, but first I want everyone to keep an open mind." I pulled out a paper square from my handbag and unfolded it. Sheila and Miyuki both had puzzled expressions on their faces, but Nina wore a wide, knowing grin.

"Here it is, my new life, ladies. I am bored with my sedentary lifestyle and I want a change of venue. I feel the need for a fresher, more breathable atmosphere. I'd like to have new characters in my existence, something different to fill the spectacular void I've been feeling since I lost my parents."

"Gyps, remember what you said your mom told you in private?" Nina asked.

"Yeah, listen to this, guys. My mom once said to me, 'Baby,

your aura is exuberant and you should follow your adventurous side, pursue acting, go fly a plane; girls can be pilots, too.' She also advised me to consider being a fashion model—she assumed the models got to keep all those dresses. 'Most of all,' she said, 'remember the law of attraction, like attracts like. Stay positive, and you will receive positive results.'" I ended my speech with a bow and sat down beside Sheila, and the girls started laughing.

"What's so funny? I pour my heart out, and you guys laugh at me? I asked you to keep an open mind."

"No, Gyps, we're not laughing at you. It's your imitation. Your voice sounds more like my deceased grandpa's voice, a husky cigar-smoking and whiskey-drinking, full of phlegm voice," Nina said.

I giggled too after Nina's explanation and held up high a picture of an airline stewardess with a white toothy smile. She wore a tailored blue uniform skirt suit with a starched, white, buttoned-up shirt. On top of her short blond-bob haircut sat an upside-down boat of a hat. Her manicured red-painted nails presented a placard that read:

Islander Air

- Interviewing individuals to fill 40 air hostess positions for seasonal flying
- Candidates must be flexible and willing to relocate
- Prior customer-service experience preferred
- High school diploma required
- Must be at least 18 years
- Open house held at the airport Marriott
- Monday at 10 a.m., 2 p.m., 6 p.m.
- Please bring your resume

"I have decided I'm going to go for it. I have talked about it for years, and now is my chance." I paused to make sure I had everyone's attention. "I am going to be an airline stewardess."

"When did you come up with this idea?" Nina asked.

"I had been looking through the classifieds for weeks, coming across this same reoccurring ad for Islander Air. I had never heard of them before and was looking for more of a major airline to apply to like American or United or even Delta, hoping they would be hiring soon and placing ads in the paper."

"So why didn't you put in an application with them?" Nina suggested.

"They are not hiring, or at least they haven't been advertising. So then I figured since I had zero experience I should consider Islander, get my feet wet, use them as a stepping stone, and later transfer to American or United. The legacy airlines probably would prefer that I had previous flying experience anyway. Don't you think?"

"I think that's great. Where do we sign up?" Nina asked.

"Funny, Nina. You don't sign up. They have these cattle calls where on-the-spot interviews are held, and you're hired from that point." I passed the ad around the table for everyone to see and accepted feedback from all the girls.

The evening was perfect. I stood up in front of my crew and made an inaugural speech headlining my new goals, first in English, then in Spanish with Sheila's help. I was still practicing my third language with Miyuki as my coach, so I skipped the Japanese version. I explained, mostly in English, the details of my career choice and why there was no other profession I would consider without experiencing the life of an air hostess first—not even acting. We proclaimed the night "Gypsy Afresh," and every third Thursday after that received an appropriate title matching the feel of the presenter.

The following Monday, I called Nina and asked her to accompany me to the interview session for moral support. She was quite curious and asked many questions about the position, so I began telling her more about Islander Air and how they fly from September to April with the summers off, which is perfection for me—I liked to save my summers for vacationing. Well, I'd start vacationing in the summer *if* I got the job. Nina agreed to come with me and said she would meet me at my apartment after she made a quick wardrobe change.

Nina showed up to my apartment complex twenty minutes earlier than necessary, her hair nicely pulled up into a professional bun.

"Hola amigo, bienvenidos a mi casa." I welcomed Nina in perfect Spanish and made a "please enter" gesture.

"You're such a show-off. Did you just invite me into your home?" my one-language friend spat.

"Yes, I did. Why are you dressed up?"

"Oh, I decided I want to be an air hostess, too." Nina looked down at her glossy leather pumps. "You're not the only one who wants to travel."

"You never mentioned this before." I was bewildered. Nina had never stopped trying to one-up me ever since grammar school. I also knew she admired me a lot so I guess I shouldn't get annoyed.

"I'm mentioning it now. Besides you said they had several positions to fill. Let's go."

"Whatever!" Oh, but I was annoyed. "I'll drive."

Reluctantly, I handed over the newspaper ad to Nina so she could familiarize herself with what Islander Air was looking for in a candidate. We walked out of my apartment both dressed in navy business suits, mine more on the trendier side of fashion. Nina and I got into my Mustang and drove to the Marriott at metro airport. I was ready to begin yet another life.

"Thank you for coming to the open house today, ladies and gentlemen. We appreciate your patience during the interview and selection process. We have chosen ten of you to invite to training. If we do not announce your name, please exit through the doors located in the rear of the room. Those candidates called, please stay behind as we have further instructions for you. Thank you everyone for considering Islander Air. The names are as follows: Summer Knight, Maria Lopez, Ashley Walker, Teshe Vessel, Byron Williams, Dion Bradley, Gypsy Moon, Tracey Morgan, Michelle Strong, and Anthony Browne. Again, if we did not call your name, please exit through the rear doors."

Livid, Nina rose from her seat and stalked out of the interview session without saying a word to me, without acknowledging my victory or giving me any kind of praise. Humph.

Flight attendant training was a magnificent three-week working vacation in Las Vegas at a hotel near Las Vegas Boulevard. The resort was in the middle of renovations and had no casino nor restaurant and sold no liquor. However, this had no bearing on the fun we were determined to squeeze out of Sin City.

Class began at eight in the morning and continued until five in the evening. Lunch was provided daily. We also received two fifteen-minute breaks and a per diem. Each candidate was assigned a roommate, but we were allowed to switch and choose from all of the unfamiliar faces which person we preferred to reside with for the next twenty-one days. The days were long. A yellow bus picked us up each morning and deposited our group of hopefuls on the steps of University of Nevada Las Vegas for nine hours of training before returning and shuttling us back to the Royal Resort. The nights were as long as the days, studying in clusters for hours in the hospitality suite. Then after mastering the lesson of the day, we'd scamper to our dusty rooms to change clothes and meet at the stage bar across the street at Circus Circus to celebrate. Repeat fourteen more times and graduation was granted to the survivors.

We promised our flight attendant trainers the following:

1. We dutifully will arm our door and prepare to evacuate in the case of an emergency.

2. We will not read magazines while sitting at our jump seat during takeoff.

3. We will remain completely aware of our surroundings.

4. We will be ready and willing in the case of an unexpected landing to help the passengers down the aircraft slide and assemble them in small groups on the tarmac, away from the engines of the plane, of course.

----

5. We will not drink alcohol twelve hours prior to reporting for work, and never will we participate in any recreational drug use.

Hopefully everything we prepared for in training actually would work in real life the way the company has it written in the manual. But if by chance the airplane didn't lose an engine or crash, or if any of the other emergency procedures we learned about never happen, then we shall serve the passengers a hot meal and a thirst-quenching drink during a normal operating flight, just like we were trained.

At graduation, our instructors awarded the initial flight assignment to the class. My roommate, Summer, and I became very close during training and had requested to fly our first trip together. When it came our turn to hear the destination bestowed upon us, Summer and I jumped in delight. Cancun, Mexico. Here we come!

"Gypsy, this place is gorgeous. Look how beautiful Cancun is," Summer's sweet voice syruply said.

"Yeah, can you believe this is what we will be doing for a living? Flying to striking islands, toting passengers around, or is this a country? Well anyway, visiting diverse regions toting passengers. I'm so glad you're here to share it with me. My friend Nina would have loved it, too."

"I think it's a country. Do you have the layover hotel information?"

"Yeah, there should be a hired van for us somewhere holding an Islander Air sign."

"Oh, oh. There it is over there. Look see." Summer pointed.

"Come on. Hurry up and get your bags," I shouted as I raced toward the white van.

"I'm right behind you Gyps, I can hear the beach calling our names!"

"I know, I can't wait to answer the call."

Giddy, we trotted toward the Mexican driver and presented

our company identification badges. After studying our IDs the driver loaded our bags into the van and drove us to our hotel.

"Welcome to Cancun, ladies. If during your stay you find you need additional transportation, here's my business card." The van driver searched his pockets and held out a stack of flimsy rectangular pieces of computer paper.

"Er, what is there to do on a Tuesday night here?" I found myself speaking slowly and enunciating every word even though the driver spoke near-perfect English.

"Big Daddy's bikini party is the most talked-about event among the tourists." The van driver gave a sour smirk while trying to unstick his homemade business cards.

"Do people really wear their swimsuits?" Summer questioned.

"That is an entrance requirement. Here, my number is on the back of the card." The driver had finally managed to pry apart the thin paper squares and handed one to Summer.

"Thank you. I'll keep this handy in my purse. Gypsy, can you tip him, please?"

"Oh, right. Here you go, sir, and thanks." I paid the man and grabbed my two bags.

Our modest guest room at the Melia had two double beds just like our recently abandoned home in Las Vegas. In a rush to get out and explore, I peered through the second-floor window to examine the view. Unlike our hotel in the desert, this resort was surrounded by an ocean of blue currents swirling around ready to invigorate the bodies settling into its abundance. We quickly changed out of our uniforms and into one-piece bathing suits. Summer walked down the stairs ahead of me to the lobby and made a left turn at the beach café sign. Now standing outside on the hardwood floor of the hotel's deck, I began to experience imagery overload: water flushing over the palms, sugar-white breathtaking crescent beaches, and infinity pools promising pleasure, escape, and beauty, making me aware of my absolute need for

----

its soothing, void-filling companionship and breaking my heart knowing soon we would have to part. This is what I do for a living, traveling. I love my job!

Summer stood there next to me on the deck in apparent awe of the magnificent scenery. "Who is that?" Summer asked.

"Who?"

"That guy waving at us, who is he?"

"I dunno. Go and see."

"You go."

"I'm not curious," I said. "I'm going this way so I can watch the volleyball game."

"Oh yeah, that's a good spot. Save me a lounge chair while I go get us a couple of towels."

"You better hurry up, they look like they're almost finished."

I walked over to the inviting sun-drenched area where three couples were ending their volleyball match and summoned the beach attendant to set up a large umbrella and two chairs in the newly vacant spot. Our spot on the beach was nearer to the water than any of the other sunbathers, and it was the perfect location to catch some UV rays. Since it appears that I missed the live entertainment provided by the volleyball players, I decided to watch Summer as she returned with a blue-and-white striped beach towel wrapped around her waist and another one folded over her forearm. She handed the folded towel to the attendant to place on my lounging chair and proceeded to unwrap her body from the confines of her own towel. Summer seductively bent over and flaunted her slender glutes as she draped the terry cloth material across her lounge chair. She was loving the attention she was getting from all of the onlookers, mostly from the waitstaff delivering drinks to the patrons. And out of nowhere, a hand appeared, intercepting the transaction and ending Summer's little performance.

"Let me introduce myself." The beach bum who had waved at us earlier was standing in our sun. "My name is Adam Wright."

"Hi, I'm Summer, and this is my friend Gypsy."

"Is this your first time here?"

"Yes. Both of ours," Summer replied.

"Well, let me be the first to welcome you."

"Too late, Adam. Our van driver beat you to it," I said.

"Well, let me be the first to buy you a drink."

"Now you're talking," I said. "Grab a chair."

"You're funny, what did you say your name was again?"

"I didn't, she actually told you that my name is Gypsy. Gypsy Moon."

"Welcome drinks for my new friends Summer and Gypsy," Adam said to the waiter as he passed by with his tray in his hand. "What would you like, ladies?"

"Something island-y please." Summer answered.

"Two specials, please, Alexander."

After we finished a few drinks with Adam, Summer and I toured the area, shopped, had dinner at a sleepy little restaurant downtown, then made our way back to the hotel to change into our evening bikinis. The talk of Big Daddy's was buzzing around the strip all afternoon. Snippets of conversations included a professional soccer team from the Pacific in town and some of the players being invited as special guests to the club. Summer had great expectations for Big Daddy's. She loved soccer players.

"Summer, are you coming out of that bathroom anytime soon?" I was completely dressed in my red, white, and blue two-piece bikini—proud sponsor of team USA.

"One more minute. I'm looking for the VIP card Adam gave us."

"You put it in the same compartment of your purse as the van driver's card."

"Right. Okay, one more minute."

"Five . . . four . . . three . . . two . . . I'm walking out the door. You better come on."

"Here I come. Here I come."

"Did you call the van driver yet?"

"No, can you call him? I need time to add a little more eye shadow."

"Where's your purse?"

"In here with me."

I opened the bathroom door and walked in to find Summer dressed in boy shorts and a tankini. "Is that what you're wearing?"

"You like?"

"I don't like."

"Why?"

"It's just . . ."

"It's what?"

"Old. Two, three seasons old. I have something that will look great on you. Stay right here."

"Great. Don't call the driver until after I wash my face. I'm sure with my wardrobe change I'll have to redo my shadow."

"Even without a wardrobe change, it would be necessary to recall that blue eye shadow."

The line outside Big Daddy's was long. I recognized a few sun-kissed faces from the beach, but everyone else looked like they may have been locals. Flashing lights overhead were shining down on the six-foot bouncers who were swollen in the doorway and resisting the wave of partygoers waiting to get in. The wind of the hot, humid night air was blowing through the heads of curls and gently lifting a few flirty skirts, giving the guys in line a sneak preview of some of the trendiest bikini prints available this season. Summer was pushing her way to the front of the line, gripping the gold VIP card in her tiny fist that entitled us to immediate carousing access into the club.

"First cause of action is to find Adam the Great," Summer said.

"Yeah, he seems to be the city's power source."

"And with the clout that comes with this VIP card, anything is possible," Summer beamed.

"It's about to begin. Excuse me, sir." I got the attention of one of the half-dozen inflated bouncers. "Do you know if Adam Wright is here yet?"

The bouncer grunted and motioned with his grand head in the direction of the bar.

"Ahh, thanks," I said and copied the gesture. "Come on, Summer. I see him by the bar dressed in all white."

"Welcome, ladies. You made it."

"Yes, we did. Thanks for the VIP status," Summer said.

"Yeah, Adam. We'll accept this kind of welcome anytime," I chimed in.

"You guys have excellent timing. My friend Joey here is a lousy drinking buddy. He's lost four dares in a row to my one."

"So you only had one shot of tequila thus far?" I questioned.

"Oh, I get it. Joey keeps losing and has to drink a shot with each loss. Are you sure he's not losing on purpose?"

"Shhh." A buzzed Joey pressed his finger against his rosy lips to hush Summer.

"Ladies, want to play Truth or Dare?" Adam asked.

"Sure," Summer responded. "I'll go first."

"All right, truth or dare?" Adam said.

"Truth."

"Truth, huh? When you first saw me at the beach today, did you consider having sex with me?"

"I need a shot just to consider that question."

Joey perked up at Summer's words, tended to his duty as guest bar tender, and poured four shots of tequila and slid them across the bar—two for Summer and two for me.

"Yes and no," Summer said and drank one of her shots.

"Hey, I didn't get any questions wrong yet," I protested as I slid my tequila shots back across the bar to Joey.

"I challenge you to drink both shots back to back," Joey dared.

"Oh, I can satisfy that dare." I raised one of my shot glasses to my lips and tilted my head back. "There. It's gone."

"That's a good girl," Adam commended. "Now the other one."

"Okay, but I dare you to drink two shots to my every one, Adam." I raised the stakes and downed my second shot.

"Bet." Adam grabbed Summer's last shot and gulped it with ease.

"Hey," Summer faked. "That was mine."

"Don't worry," Joey rescued. "There's plenty more where that came from." He lined up five more shot glasses and began pouring. "Drink up!"

"Salud." I handed Adam and Summer each a shot glass, and we raised them up in the air. "Cheers." Summer swallowed her second shot and grimaced.

"Gypsy, I dare you to dirty dance with Adam," Joey said, trying to escalate the game to a higher level.

"Oh, I'll take that dare, too." I looped my arm through Adam's and pulled him toward the dance floor. "We'll be back."

All evening long, Summer was huddled up in the corner with a pseudo cop Adam had introduced her to and I spent most of the night following Adam around the club, watching as he pranked people. He convinced several girls to reveal their breasts to him by telling them that he was the owner of the club and would have them thrown out if they didn't comply with his request. He even had me approach one lonely guy standing near the ladies' room who had been taking quick peeks in as the door opened and closed. Adam said he had seen the guy before and said it would be a riot if I pretended to be a lady of the night and propositioned him. Upon Adam's persistence I walked up to the guy and whispered into his ear, telling him how interested the two of us would be if he agreed to accompany us tonight, pointing at Summer across the way. I told the bathroom stalker that the two of us were working together and that he could get two for the price of one if he was willing to come back to our hotel room.

I winked at Adam and informed the bathroom stalker that Adam was our John and insisted that the man had to complete the money transfer with Adam before we were allowed to leave. The bathroom stalker gave me a broad smile as he walked away from me toward Adam, which made me giggle in surprise. I couldn't believe someone would fall for such a flagrant lie. When he reached Adam, I escaped to where Summer and pseudo cop were seated to fill her in on our prank. Summer was lazily resting her head on the shoulder of pseudo cop when I walked up, and he invited me to join them. I sat down on the other side of him and used his free shoulder as my pillow. I had planned on warning Summer about the bathroom stalker guy, but my mind was hazy from the multiple shots of tequila and I drifted off into the twilight zone before I could utter a word.

Like spam, unpleasant scenes invaded my sleepy head and popped open mini-scenes from the night.

. . . Topless women, lots of them.

. . . Tequila shots, lots of them.

. . . Popping bubbles and dancing bodies, lots of them.

I clicked the close button of my mind to shut down the unwanted scenes, and all except the last and most damaging site disappeared. My new friend Adam, who had started out pleasant and witty, shifted during the night into a real-life villain, and no power button existed to make him go away. When I opened my eyes, bartender Joey, pseudo cop, the bathroom stalker, and Adam were standing over us, insisting that Summer and I leave the club.

"Ladies, put your hands behind your back," pseudo cop said.

"Ken, stop playing," Summer laughed.

"Put your hands behind your back." Pseudo cop flashed a police badge.

Adam and bathroom stalker walked up behind us, and the stalker guy flashed his own badge. "You are both under arrest."

"What? Adam, tell them it was a joke," I pleaded.

"Gypsy and Summer, these are my friends from the station. Prostitution is against the law, and you violated that law."

"Ladies, you're coming with us down to the station," stalker guy persisted.

"Adam, quit fucking playing and tell them the truth!" I said.

"I don't know what you're talking about. Are you resisting arrest?"

"No, I'm not under arrest. Come on, Summer. Let's get out of here."

I snatched Summer up from the cushioned bench and tried to

push the bathroom stalker guy out of the way when he grabbed my arms and handcuffed me. Pseudo cop followed suit and handcuffed Summer, and the three of them escorted us to the door. As we were being ushered from the club to the police station, I realized why I couldn't close that last site in my mind: This was really happening. We were being arrested.

If it weren't for Adam knowing the police chief, we would probably have spent the night in a Mexican prison eating cold quesadillas and drinking unfiltered water. However, if it weren't for Adam and his twisted sense of humor taking the joke playing to the extreme, we would not have been arrested in the first place. It was so humiliating walking out of the packed club handcuffed in front of the soccer team listening to the players thank Adam for getting us, the undercover prostitutes, out of the club. They said the last thing they needed was to be caught socializing with a couple of hookers after winning the soccer game. The proud winners wanted to keep their image clean and celebrate without any controversy and return the trophy home to their country.

In exchange for our release, Summer and I had to promise Adam that we would continue to be his friends. He even took a picture of us behind bars as an added security measure in case we tried to renege on our agreement.

I promised myself to never, never, never drink again. Take that back, never would I ever drink tequila again. No, never would I drink tequila with frat boys again. Ever. They seem to have mastered the technique of being unfeeling, drunken manipulators who take pleasure in humiliating women.

I can't stand Adam, and neither can Summer. We can't believe he actually managed to graduate from college magna cum laude. Jerk!

Part II

The Layover

CHAPTER 4

Island Fever

The agent greeting the plane opens the door to the aircraft and in rushes the warm, humid island air of the Bahamas. She recites her welcoming announcement in a soft Bahamian accent. Her voice, just above a whisper, makes me relax immediately, as if I were already lying on Cable Beach next to the ocean listening to mellowing waves and smelling the salty air. We arrive on a bright Wednesday morning to an awaiting band playing Calypso music in the customs area of the terminal. The weather is a perfect eighty-five degrees, and the sun is beaming against a soft baby blue sky. I locate my regular driver, Anthony, waiting for me at the passenger pick-up area in a plain white van with script adhesive lettering across the top of the windshield and the air conditioner turned on full blast.

"Anthony, can you turn off the air, please? I would prefer to have the windows down."

"No problem, mon."

"Thank you, sir."

For the past eight months, I have been attending college part time and enjoying my job as an air hostess for Islander Air full time. We only have four routes:

- Detroit to Nassau/Nassau to Detroit
- Detroit to Cancun/Cancun to Detroit
- Chicago to Nassau/Nassau to Chicago
- Chicago to Cancun/Cancun to Chicago

Each layover is twelve hours long, after which I'm back on the last flight of the day to Detroit or Chicago. I fly this Nassau trip three times a week, and this is my second trip so far.

"Here we are again Ms. Moon, the Radisson Cable Beach Resort."

"Thank you, Anthony. Will you be picking me up tonight or Marion?"

"Yes, my wife will drive you back tonight. I don't know why she insists that I pick you up from the airport and she drop you off." Anthony looks at me through the rearview mirror as he speaks to me. "But she is the boss. Enjoy your stay."

I pay the fare and exit the van, smiling to myself. I know exactly why Marion stipulates to her husband these special transportation arrangements. I check into my standard first-floor, ocean-view room with the double beds and begin my ritual:

- toss my leather Tumi briefcase on the extra bed
- wash the makeup from my face
- change into a thong bikini (better than the Brazilian cut for tanning)
- grab Hawaiian-themed beach towel and matching Hawaiian water bottle
- go out the sliding glass doors and onto the beach, ready to claim my favorite spot near the wave runners.

My lounge chair is already set up for me next to a blue umbrella and a small, white fold-up table to sit my new *Shape* magazine on. Rachel, the barmaid, must have arranged this for me. I usually leave my fitness magazines or the latest issue of *People* when I'm finished reading them on the table for Rachel to show my appreciation for saving my spot. Over by the poolside the band is playing dance hall music. It is close enough for me to hear the rhythm but far enough not to disturb my reading, and here comes my favorite islander.

"Hi, Alfred. What time are we going on the wave runner today?"

"Welcome back, Gypsy. How about after the morning rush but before lunch time? I have a new mom-and-pop restaurant I want to take you to."

"Okay, come and get me when you're ready. I'll be right here getting some sun."

"I always can find you right here. I'll be back."

Alfred is one of the wave runner operators on the beach who actually owns his equipment. I often dream of Alfred becoming a successful entrepreneur, and I imagine that he has come to my rescue and we cruise away to paradise on a huge fifty-foot yacht and he's bearing gifts from all around the world. I like the heroic type of entrepreneurs who pay off the balance on my maxed-out credit cards, or the ones who take me on amazing vacations and glamorous shopping sprees. I like Alfred especially; I see potential in him.

I have learned how to camouflage my feelings whenever I'm around him from one of my favorite episodes of *Star Trek: The Next Generation*, where Captain Jean Luke Picard uses a cloaking device to make the starship invisible and undetectable by enemy vessels. I use the same strategy with Alfred.

"Gypsy, are you awake?"

"Hey Alfred. I must have dozed off."

"Come, let's take the wave runner over to Paradise Island."

"Okay," seems my dreams are coming true. "Where is your ship—um, I mean wave runner. You know I'm not riding without a life vest on, right?"

"Yes, I know. When will you learn to trust me?"

"Not today. I'm wearing this life vest nice and tight."

I hop on the back of Alfred's electric blue wave runner, and we push off from the shore and into the blue of the Atlantic. The sun is kissing the tops of our shoulders, making them nice and tan. As we zig-zag through the watery playground, sporadic sprays from the wave runner give a refreshing relief to our burning skin just when it feels like our smoldering shoulders may combust from the heat. An ocean liner passes by about a mile away and creates a wake of determined waves that Alfred decides to challenge. He says that being a native Bahamian and swimming in the ocean every day of his life gives him a sureness that he can vie with any wave, even these forceful, boat-rocking waves.

"The bigger the better," he says.

"The bigger the better, huh?" I repeat.

"Yep. Watch this . . ."

The cool water is smacking hard against the wave runner, causing us to deviate from Alfred's desired course and causing me to forget about that bigger-better statement Alfred made that I so wanted to ponder.

Out here the water is so deep that the color appears navy. I'm a little afraid at this point, and I try to scream but my vocal cords are betraying me. Meanwhile, Alfred is unaware of my fear. He's like a kid in his own hydrosphere, jumping waves, doing 360s, and turning backward on the seat. This is quite a frightening experience but also a little thrilling as it gives me a chance to grab hold of Alfred's brawny body. Feeling my breasts pressed against Alfred's powerful back and my arms wrapped tightly around his waist may be a false sense of security, but who can think about drowning when you've got a Mandingo between your legs?

A couple of yards in front of us I see land forming and much too soon we reach our journey's end, a small, uninhabited island that Alfred has nicknamed Paradise.

"Alfred, this is not *the* Paradise Island."

"No, but it is paradise. Look, just over there in the water is a drop off of thirty feet. Come, let's jump in."

"You really love the water, don't you?"

"Don't be afraid, Gypsy, you won't drown on my watch."

"Okay, but I'm keeping on my life vest." And a cool bath isn't such a bad idea either.

I trust Alfred's uncontested ability to swim and save me if needed, but now that he's not sitting between my legs anymore I can concentrate on the reality of the situation—I don't know how to swim.

The sand on this island is a pale pink and the water has a blue hue, but the closer we walk to the shore the more it appears like clear drinking water. I reach our resting spot before Alfred and watch him as he stabilizes the wave runner. When he finishes, he walks toward me through the resisting waters and I see him in a way I've never envisioned before. What emerges from the aquatic is the blessed one, a fully developed grown man, defined muscles, slender waist, and an enormous, lengthy manfulness extending toward his mid-thigh. I watch as the water glistens against his sable skin, and I feel hibernating desires awakening within my universe. This man has a slight swagger to his walk, and he's totally unaware of how sexy I find him. However, I must continue to conceal my lust for Alfred until I know for sure he's not married nor engaged. I haven't yet worked up the nerve to ask him about his status, probably because I don't want to ruin the intrigue. What I do hope and pray for is that once Alfred jumps into the thirty-feet-deep water he will resurface sans his swim trunks. If I am exposed to some nakedness, it may pique my interest enough to ask him out on a date.

"Go on Alfred, you first!"

"Don't chicken out on me, Gypsy."

"I won't, I just have to see you jump in first."

"No, we go in together." Alfred grabs my arm and pulls me back towards the water.

"Okay wait, stop. Let me get my breathing together."

"No, you're stalling. Now come on, you can depend on me for sure."

"Okay, okay." Breathe, remember to b-r-e-a-t-h-e.

Our provocative dip is just that, provocative. Alfred jumps

into the drop off and I follow. After minutes (maybe seconds) of being suspended under water, I realize that I can't find my way back up to the surface. My kicking is doing little to spring me upward, and I dare not attempt to scream again. I feel Alfred's large hands as he wraps them around the indentations of my waist, which makes me calm down and stop kicking in his security. When we resurface, Alfred still with his trunks on, I drape one arm around his neck and take off my useless life vest with the other. Alfred looks surprised by my action of trust and lays me on my back. He supports me on his outstretched arms while I float, and he smiles at the response my nipples give to the feel of the cool water. Instinctively, Alfred nibbles at the protruding fabric of my bikini top and a soft sigh escapes his lips. I look into his yearning eyes and find the answer to the question I have been avoiding.

We play in the water for a while longer before hopping back on the wave runner to go to the Radisson, and we make arrangements to have lunch at the new mom-and-pop place later after Alfred has finished his afternoon shift on the ocean. I know for sure this time I caught his attention, and I'm curious to see how this adventure will play out at the restaurant.

Anyway, I need a little time away from him before we go out to eat so that I can regroup and play the hard-to-get role. I slipped a bit earlier today and I need to wait until I know what's really going on with his love life before I let him play with the goods. Plus, I need extra time to make myself gorgeous for him. My bikini did the trick on the water, and I have just the right outfit to render me irresistible on land.

Lunch at this mom-and-pop's is rumored to be simple yet delicious, and I'm feeling as though it is a special occasion for me and Alfred. I ordered a conch salad with bits of habanera peppers, the fresh grouper with rice, and a cold island-brewed Kalik beer. I rush through my feeding so that I will have more time to spend with Alfred, which is proving to be a moot point. Alfred isn't sitting down to eat with me. Instead, he has disappeared into the kitchen and is socializing with the working members of the family-owned

and -operated establishment—the daughter, to be exact. I guess my
outfit isn't so irresistible after all. From what I can hear through
the giggles in the back kitchen, Alfred is making plans to meet with
them later in the evening for happy hour at some place called Native. And despite the fact that it sounds like I am invited to accompany Alfred, I feel frustrated and a bit reluctant. I was sure we were
going to spend this time more wisely, getting to know each other.
Isn't that what a lunch date is for? However, I will accept the offer. I
haven't yet experienced the Bahamas nightlife or, in this case, pre-
night life, and I don't want to waste the opportunity because of some
silly misunderstanding.

After our late lunch I return to my hotel room with a full belly
and full with excitement to be going out on the island. Normally my
twelve-hour stays consist of me flying in at 9:00 am, shuttling to the
hotel, laying out, eating, and shuttling back out by 9:00 pm, never leaving the resort once.

It's now around five and Alfred's friend is chauffeuring us to
Club Native in his taxicab. The evening sky is illuminating a romantic hue, and Alfred is sitting close to me in the backseat with
his arm draped around the headrest. Alfred had the driver pick me
up early to supposedly do a little sightseeing before hitting Native. I
hope this is really a way of making up for the busted lunch date and
Alfred's way of spending more time with me off of the water.

On our way to Native, we drive through dingy neighborhoods
with shabby homes and encounter several stray mangy dogs lying
around in driveways and in the street. Our cab driver has to constantly blow his horn at the sleeping dogs to separate them as we
approach, but they return to the middle of the street and continue
sleeping once we pass by. Strange. I have never come across such
a thing before. The dogs at home choose a lawn or maybe a stoop
to sleep on, but these scabby dogs seem to view cars as something
to share the road with rather than the dangerous vehicles they are.
Dumb dogs.

We pass by an old fisherman's village where Alfred and I get out
of the car to observe the transaction between the men and women.

Some are selecting fish to be cleaned and packed to take home to their families, others are having the fish fried on the spot and eating their meals on the curb. Many of the people here don't seem to notice me and Alfred walking around, but I feel particularly out of place wearing my white strappy sandals in the dirt, and I urge Alfred to return to the car.

We ride through a pitch-black alleyway to the back entrance of this hole-in-the-wall of a club. The lantern above the crooked Native sign has been broken for some time; there are no glass fragments littered on the ground beneath the skylight. The outside of this one-story bar is infested with wild vegetation. Some areas have such excessive growth that it would be quite possible to hide a corpse. If I were to judge on looks alone, which I don't, but if I did I would presume that Club Native is capable of intimidating a motorcycle rider or even make a pro boxer a little nervous to enter. With so many random people standing around smoking and passing around a sweet-smelling substance wrapped in cigar paper, and numerous stray dogs roaming about, I am reluctant to go into the unknown.

"Dang, Alfred, I hope your communication skills are as good as your swimming."

"No problem, mon, it's cool."

"Where's the security . . . er, I mean the other exits, I mean entrances?"

"No worries, mon. The club is safe," Alfred says and enters the bar.

"Okay, wait up. Don't leave me out here."

"Gypsy, you're always chicken."

"I'm not chicken, I'm cautious."

"Follow me, for the second time today. And trust me for once, will you?"

"Okay." B-r-e-a-t-h-e.

I put my trust in Alfred again and follow him into the dimly lit club. Inside, wall-to-wall Bahamians are dancing to pure vibrant underground reggae beats that penetrate through the body, the type of music that makes me want to do the nasty dance. The floor is crowded with exceptionally shapely women grinding with Adonis-like men and the scantily dressed waitresses keep the drinks flowing. I trail behind Alfred down the narrow path he creates through the sea of bodies. It isn't really a path as it is a liability, moving against this ocean of tensed muscles, curvaceous rear ends, and bulging biceps.

The crowd is packed tight, beyond capacity. I'm sure the fire marshal would have the place shut down if this club were located in the States. To keep from getting separated, I seize the opportunity to touch Alfred's body again. I rest the palm of my hand on his lower back above his tight ass. I feel him flinch. I suspect he likes the tingle from our connection the same as I do. Alfred is leading us to the dance floor, which is a suitable occasion for me to press up against his body without his being suspicious of my motives. The bass from the subwoofers resonating through my soul is doing a job on my hormones, and I notice that everyone in the house is affected by the seductive tones too, which may explain why each female appears to have the disposition of a tigress and the males seem wolf-like, on the prowl.

We stop at the edge of the dance floor and, being the socializer that he is, Alfred removes my hand from his back and disappears into the crowd. Alfred has abandoned me once again, and I'm left standing on the edge of the dance floor alone, watching the flirtatious movements in the room. My eyes are drawn toward one of the most desirable males I have ever laid eyes on. Though his physique is not as chiseled as Alfred's, he is model perfect just the same. I find myself watching intently, staring blatantly, nearly stalking his every move as he takes ownership of the dance floor. The mystery man's moves are extremely controlled, like a sensei. His body is disciplined, conveying what his mind transmits, and though he is dancing with a blurred figure, his movements are definitely speaking to me.

Alfred appears again behind me with a fruity drink in his hand. I assume it is for me and take it from him without hesitation.

"Who is that, Alfred?"

"That is Mark, the prime minister's son. I'll be right back, Gypsy. My girl is here, and I want you to meet her."

"What?" I answer, slightly distracted.

"Stay right here, I'll be back."

"What girl?"

Alfred disappears again, and I turn back to continue viewing the vision on the dance floor. Prime minister's son is whispering into his dance partner's ear and looking toward me. She fixes her eyes in my direction, smiles, and then walks away, leaving the son on the dance floor alone. He motions for me to join him and fill the now-empty spot next to him on the dance floor. I look at him, and then I make an exaggerated look down toward the fruity drink in my hand, look back up at the son, and shake my head no. Sheepishly, he smiles and walks over to the edge of the dance floor where I am, and now the tall, dark-skinned, dreadlocked Bahamian with a thick accent stands before me.

"Hello, Americon woman. What brings you to Native?"

"Er, Alfred, actually."

"Whattis your name?"

"Um, Gypsy."

"Welcome, um Gypsy. Mi name is Mark. Where did your Alfred go?"

"He is not my Alfred, and he went to meet his *girl*."

"He left the beautiful lady alone?"

"I'm a big girl. I can take care of myself."

"Well, would the big girl like to dance?"

"Yes, I would."

"This way please."

"As you wish. Mark, is it?"

"Yes, um Gypsy."

He takes my hand and guides me to the middle of the floor. I'm hoping that he will dance with me the same way he danced with the blurred figure, very sensually. As I masquerade around the dance floor with Mark in my short Simply Vera skirt, I imagine Alfred's sweaty flesh sticking to my exposed abdomen and thighs instead of the son's. The man with his arms fastened around my body is a spicy and potent specimen, and he's dancing like a sexy Spaniard, but I have a fixation with Alfred. Where is he anyway, and who is this *girl* he wants me to meet? My eyes examine the club in search of Alfred, but the lighting is too dim to make out faces. The fruity drink has begun to take effect, and I can barely see over Mark's broad shoulders.

I begin to loosen up and become more captivated by Mark's alluring moves, and our dance elevates to a more seductive level. We dirty dance, the same way Adam showed me how in Mexico, and it doesn't take long for me to let go of my inhibitions. I'm feeling swirly and sexy like how I was with Adam, as if I'm back on the tequila shots. This is where I remain for several songs until I spot Alfred and *girl* leaning against the bar.

With a slight and unexpected jerk, I immediately withdraw from the son's arms. I make up some foolish, asinine excuse and abruptly exit the floor. Hurriedly, I head in the direction of the bar to inspect the situation. Alfred and *girl* (whose best feature is the well-maintained mustache above her thin lip, she's about a .5 on the looks meter) were speaking to one another with their faces so close I thought they may converge and become Siamese twins. Anxiously I advance toward the bar.

"Alfred. I was looking all over for you."

"Oh, Gypsy, I want you to meet my girl, Chelsea. Chelsea, this is Gypsy."

"Your girl?" How come I didn't get a title?

"Yes, my girlfriend," Alfred states with affirmation.

"Nice to meet you, Chelsea." I place a phony smile on my face.

"My pleasure," Chelsea replies.

She scrutinized me from head to toe, starting first at my plump red lips. Her eyes lower and hesitate around my 34Cs. After blinking several times and pursing her lips, she directs her gaze south to the narrowness of my waistline, hovers around the curves of my hips, and finishes at my Jimmy Choo strappy sandals. I can't decipher if her look is that of disapproval or jealousy.

"I have to use the toilet," Chelsea mumbles as she pushes past Alfred and swims like a mermaid to the restroom. Jackpot! She's jealous.

"Gypsy!" The prime minister's son emerges through the bodies of the deep. "You want to dance again?"

"Yeah, mon," I answer in my newly learned lingo. "Alfred, are you going to be ready to leave soon? Unfortunately, I still have to fly tonight."

"When Chelsea comes from the toilet I will be ready." Alfred appears bothered.

"Okay, come on, Mark. Let's get one more dance in." Suddenly, I am in a really good mood. I detect some animosity in Alfred's voice, and I'm wishing that my dancing with Mark is the source of his anger, but truthfully I believe it's because Chelsea is upset.

When Chelsea returns from the ladies' room, Alfred comes to retrieve me from the dance floor, and together we drive back to the Radisson in Chelsea's Wrangler in silence. I can't get out of that car fast enough. Chelsea says she looks forward to seeing me again, and I say me too, but neither one of us means it. I jump out of the back seat and sprint to my hotel room, almost forgetting that I had four-inch heels on.

Inside of my room, as I'm briskly walking around gathering my things and packing my bags, I grab my beloved Hawaiian-themed towel off of the bathroom clothesline. My towel was with me and Summer when we got locked up in that Mexican jail. They let me take it into the cell, and we used it to sit on so our clothes wouldn't get dirty. I walk toward the door and stop just short of exiting when I hear my hotel room phone ringing.

"Hello."

"Hello, Ms. Gypsy. I wish you well on your travels to America."

"Oh, hey Mark. Okay, I'll make sure to give you a call when I return."

"When will that be?"

"Um, on Friday? Yeah, I'll be back on Friday."

"Good to know. Take care my love."

"Um. Okay. Bye."

Before leaving Native, I told Mark the name of the hotel I was staying in. I'm usually in the same room each trip and I told him it was okay if he phoned me, I just didn't expect a call so soon. Marion is outside waiting to drive me back to the airport so I have to rush Mark off the phone. I absolutely cannot be late for my flight. My friends and I are having girls' night out on Thursday, and I refuse to miss the fun.

"Hi, Marion."

"Hello, Ms. Lady. Did you enjoy your stay?"

"It was a promising trip. Do you remember when I told you about the wave runner operator guy? Well, turns out he has a girl-friend."

"Oh, too bad for you." Marion looks at me through the rearview mirror.

"Yeah, so anyway I met the prime minister's son, Mark. I'm sure you know who I'm talking about, right?"

"Yeah, mon," Marion replies. "Well-to-do family."

"Okay, so after I met Alfred's girlfriend, I decided to make the best of the night and hook up with Mark."

"The two of you, what you say . . . huuked up?" Marion's eyes widen.

I laugh. "Don't ever try to say that again, Marion. No, we didn't hook up like that. We exchanged numbers. Hopefully in two days I can tell you more."

"Oh, I understand. Nice to have options, huh?"

"Very nice, Marion."

Marion lives through my stories. She has been married for two decades and looks forward to hearing what she considers my fantasy-like lifestyle.

I arrive in Detroit at 11:45 pm, and after a slight hold up in customs, I find Kat and Nina outside like clockwork waiting in my Mustang at international arrivals for my return. Nina came with Kat to pick me up from work tonight because she has alternate plans with some guy and she will be unable to attend girls' night out. She wants to get the details from my encounters in the Baha-mas first before her date and before the rest of the girls hear about it. I'm happy to oblige. Thanks to Nina and her connections, my girlfriends and I have tickets to the Detroit Pistons basketball game when they play the Los Angeles Lakers next week and our seats are in the first tier. Nina's sitting in floor seats though, with the wives of the coaching staff. She's dating one of the assistant coaches these days.

We all seem to have great personal lives, and Thursday is the day we get together to share some of our relationship stories. Gathering at the gentlemen's club provides us with the luxury of anonymity because the exotic dancers are there entertaining the men, keeping them and their y-chromosomes occupied while we chat. We couldn't have chosen a better spot for avoiding the unwanted attention from men at a bar.

I'm late for the meeting but I'm determined to make it there before tonight's topic: *Men with Money* gets juicy. The dancers get a kick out of our discussions. After their stage appearances and in between working the room, some of them come by our booth to join in the conversation. That hussy Licorice comes around for the discussion sessions too. Nina never told her about my relationship with Ali so she doesn't know who I am. I agreed with Nina on not informing her, it was Ali and I who had a commitment. Licorice had nothing to do with it and to my knowledge she didn't even know Ali was a philanderer. I have a new life now and I don't like focusing on the unpleasant memories by dredging up the cheating ways of Ali. And I just know speaking his horrid name will only bring the bad energy from that relationship with him into my present life. Besides, Licorice usually has good advice on Keeping Your Man Satisfied topics, and surprisingly Barbie, the youngest dancer, has extraordinary advice on money issues.

By default Kat decides to join the group for the first time ever, but only because I have been complaining the whole way from the airport about having to drop her off and missing out on the evening. And Nina even cancelled her date.

We walk in the gentlemen's club eager to begin our late night. Miyuki is sitting at our booth talking on her cell phone and hangs up as we approach the table.

"Girls, we have to lower our voices to keep from distracting the patrons from the real entertainment."

"Where is everyone?" I ask Miyuki. "And why are those men sitting at our regular booth?"

"In the dressing room. Licorice suggested that we take the meeting to the back tonight to keep the curious George's from listening. It's unusually busy here tonight."

"Licorice? Who made her house mom?"

"Get over it, Gyps. She's just trying to be nice."

"First she steals my husband's affection, and now she's taking my friends."

"No, she's not. We still love you. But she does have better advice than you, I have to admit."

"I know and so what. Sometimes the old feelings come back, and I can't help but get upset."

"Well, I want to see this home-wrecker!" Kat interjects.

"Follow me, Kat. I'll point her out to you. She'll be the one with the saggy stomach." Nina laughs and the three of us follow behind Miyuki as she leads the way into the dancers' dressing room.

TGIF. I'm on my customary flight back to the Bahamas, and I am very much looking forward to spending time with the son this evening. I asked another air hostess to work the flight back for me so I will have more time to spend on the island. She owes me a favor from that one time when her son was ill and she didn't want to call off of work because she had used all of her sick calls and was trying to avoid getting put on a discipline level 3, the final level before getting fired.

I'm hoping that Anthony is parked in his normal spot waiting for me with the windows down and the air conditioner off this time. I'm so ready to get to my room and start primping for my visit with the son I can hardly stand myself. I'll start by the poolside, relaxing and getting some much-needed sun, have a glass of wine to put me in Mellowville, and view the scenery, watching as the eye candy stride by. I love my life.

"Hey, Ant!"

"Yeah, mon. These are for you." Anthony hands me a dozen pink roses.

"They're beautiful. Is this box of candy for me, too? Who are they from?"

"Don't know. Read the card that's attached."

"Oh yeah. Right. You can give the chocolate to your wife Anthony; I'm dieting."

"Again, you're already too skinny."

"Oh, that's sweet of you to say. I see why Marion holds on to you."

I remove the card from the tiny envelope and begin reading the typed letters:

Please have dinner with me tonight. Mark

How thoughtful, he remembered that I was flying in today. Looks like he did a little homework to find out who my driver is too, the little stalker.

We pull up to the Radisson. I hand Anthony the candy back after taking a piece, and ask him to please tell Marion I will call her later. On my way to my room, I stop in the lobby to check my messages. I'm hoping that one of the six I receive is from Alfred about our ride on the water. I see Mark has left a couple of messages as I continue to search through the small stack of memo notes handed to me by a new girl working at the front desk. She programs my room key card and directs me to my standard ocean-view room. As I approach the corridor to my room, Joanne, the maid, is just finishing cleaning my room, and good thing too because I can't manage opening the door with my key card. My arms are too full with gifts from Mark. I toss my Tumi luggage on the extra bed and pick up the phone to make an appointment with the hotel's spa for a bikini wax, and then call Mark to thank him for the astrology book and flowers. Oh and the candy too, although I re-gifted the chocolate to Marion.

Today is another beautiful day on the island, and I refuse to miss a drop of sunshine. I grab my beach towel and open the sliding glass door. Yay! To my delight and as I expect, Alfred's sexy ass is sitting near his wave runner looking, well . . . lengthy, actually.

"Hey, Alfred." I normally hide my devilish thoughts, but this

time my high-pitched voice may have given away how delighted I
am to see him.

"Gypsy, want to go for a ride?"

"Yeah." You bet I do!

"Jump on."

"Okay, hold on one second."

"Where are you going?"

"You know where."

I grab a life vest and climb on the back of his wave runner,
and Alfred starts the motor. Feeling the vibration from the engine
between my legs and holding on to Alfred's super-tight body is
intense. I tighten my thighs against Alfred to hold my body steady.
The anxiety between us is thick, and we start off riding smoothly.
After minutes of unruffled waters, Alfred finds where the deep
waves to ride are and we begin to bounce around. With each
wave, I get shuffled and manage to bounce closer to Alfred. I sense
he doesn't mind but rather enjoys our innocent outing, and I believe he sought after a more turbulent ride for the purpose of this
sexual tension we are experiencing. After I get comfortable and
recover from the last wave we hit, another huge pipe comes along
and capsizes our wave runner. It's so large that the surfers try to
take their surf boards out to catch this wave. My bikini-clad body
swings sideways into the chilly water, and all I can see on my way
down into the depths is Alfred's white teeth. After that everything
becomes an underwater adventure. A school of tiny fish teases me
as they swim by, no doubt feeling empowered by the fact that life
vests are unnecessary in their world. Kicking and swatting the fish
away, I'm beginning to run out of air. I see my hero, Alfred, has
popped up out of the water just as I resurfaced, bobbing around
with my life vest on, hyperventilating.

"Help me back to the wave runner, Alfred." I gasp for air, not
realizing my life vest is doing its job of keeping me afloat.

"No worries, grab hold to me."

"Come and get me, please."

"I'm right here. Try to relax," Alfred instructs with the same
smirk he wore while I was drowning just minutes ago.

"It's hard to relax when you're busy dying."

"Gypsy, you will be fine. Here, let me help you up."

Alfred lifts me and I wrap my legs around his waist. I can feel his enormous, slightly hard manhood pressing against me as he rests my body on his and carries me to the wave runner. I hold tighter, closer, trying to get a better idea, a better feel of him. The wave runner isn't far. In fact, it is in very close reach but Alfred is prolonging the save, slowly fighting the current and enjoying the sensation we have created. I will keep my legs wrapped tightly around his waist for the next sixty minutes if I have to, pretending to be shaken by the fall, or until the unwanted likeliness of reaching the wave runner becomes reality and the lascivious behavior is over.

Alfred raises me up onto the seat without saying a word. Somewhere between lifting me and placing me on the wave runner, his mood has changed and he quietly reclaims his position between my legs and guides us back to the beach.

Even though I enjoy the flirtation between Alfred and myself, I am not interested in destroying my karma or Alfred's relationship with his .5 girlfriend. Okay, that's a lie, well not the karma part, but I would like it if Alfred desired me and showed some sign of yielding. This is killing me to have to pretend not to want him. Besides, he watched me as I danced that night with Mark. He studied our every move, and, after talking to the girls, I believe the look on his face was the look of envy, not of concern for his *girl*.

"Back on land safely. How are you feeling?" Alfred asks with no clear sign of submission.

"Good, thanks Alfred."

"Well, have a good layover."

"I plan to do just that."

"And remember to grab your towel off of the beach."

"Will I be seeing you later?"

"I'll call you."

He is so stubborn. I walk away after giving him a hug and kissing his lush lips and re-enter my room through the sliding glass doors. I still have an hour before my bikini wax appointment so I call the spa and ask if I can come in early for a mani/pedi. The attendant said she will pencil me in but I need to hurry if I don't want to lose my new spot, so I take a quick shower and rush to the spa to begin my retreat. Mark called while I was on the water with Alfred and left a message for me to be ready at 6:00. I still have enough time to get super appealing for tonight's date. I'm wearing the sexiest dress ever made: short, low-cut, clingy, and skin tone. I was hoping to model it for Alfred, but since he's not being sociable anymore Mark will get the visual treat. Whenever I'm in the islands, I feel uninhibited and tend to wear daring outfits like this one. This dress is so seductive I've never gathered enough nerve to wear it at home in the States, not even to girls' night out.

Mark picks me up at six sharp. The sun is beginning to set as we drive in his Jeep to the south shore where his home is located on a private beach. Inside we are greeted by his maid Bridgett, standing next to a dramatic mahogany staircase. Bridgett escorts us across the marble floor through an art studio and gallery to an intimate library where we sit and converse under hand-painted ceilings before being summoned to the formal dining room for dinner.

Inside the nearly 6,000-square-foot villa is a full staff waiting to serve. Chef Jean prepared an Asian-fusion meal, a selection of quail grilled with Thai spices, crab spring rolls, and shrimp satay. The meal is presented like artwork, and I sit savoring the last delicious bite when Mark suggests we retire to the veranda.

Outside Mark has more pink roses waiting for me on the deck. We relax and enjoy dessert and sip on Goombay Smash rum cocktails with freshly grated nutmeg floating on top. Mark lights a Cuban cigar and watches as the masseuse he hired massages my feet. (Thankfully I had a pedicure earlier today.) The property has true island flair. For instance, there's a swimming pool set amid flowering plants and fruit trees and hammocks in the garden next to the wooden gazebo. We sit discussing politics, and the prime minister's son tells me that he wants to follow in his dad's footsteps, and that he is actively looking for his first lady. Me, a first lady. I look around and I allow my mind to wander. I picture what it would be like to live in such a charming home and have a waitstaff. I come to the conclusion that I can easily adjust to this island living.

"Mark, your house is absolutely gorgeous!"

"I can say the same for you."

"Feel free to."

"Does that go for the rest of the evening as well?"

"Only if I can have the run of the house."

"Good, that blends well with our discussion tonight."

"Really? You were serious about that?"

"Yes, Gypsy. I never joke."

"Wow. We hardly know one another."

"I live life by instincts, and I trust you do the same?"

"Well, not always. What else do you have planned?"

"Did you bring your swimsuit, Ms. Gypsy?"

"Yes sir, as you instructed."

"Good, here comes mi boat. The captain will take us on a silent moonlight cruise. You have an offer to consider. You can enjoy the night air. It will help you clear your mind."

"Let's hope so. I could use a lucid brain. I guess everyone could. By the way, Mark, are there any life vests on your boat?"

"Yes, of course. No worries mon."

"No worries huh?" Again with the no worries.

The evening was absolutely delightful. Mark treated me like a princess and I returned to my hotel slightly buzzed and feeling elated. I could easily adjust to this lifestyle . . . easily. As I enter my room I notice the red message light blinking on the phone, but I ignore it and proceed to open my sliding glass door. I walk toward the beach to view the bright full moon against the blackened sky and to wallow in my offer to be a princess. To my surprise, I find Alfred sitting near where the wave runners are normally parked during the day, looking passionate and lost.

"Hey, Alfred. What's up?"

"Hey, Gypsy."

"What's up? Why the boo-boo face?"

"Me and Chelsea fell out tonight."

"What? She broke up with you?"

"No mon, I with her. She kept ragging on me about that night at Native."

"Oh." I manage to sound somewhat compassionate. "What did she say?"

"She thinks I am mesmerized by you."

"Humph, she does, does she?"

"Yes, she does."

"Alfred, why don't you come to my room so we can have a drink? And talk."

"Yeah mon."

He follows behind me into the room and sits on the extra bed, next to my luggage, and he's looking sexy as ever.

"Look, Alfred, I have to admit—I can't get you off of my mind. You barge into my daily thoughts, and I'm finding it impossible not to have some type of physical contact with you, even if it is simply touching your back."

"Aaah, Chelsea said you were sweet on me. I told her it wasn't so, but she spoke something about a woman's intuition."

"Yeah, women can sense these things. But Alfred I must be honest . . ."

Now sexy Alfred has changed positions and is lying across the bed, staring at me wolf-like. I can't seem to find the proper words to communicate my desires and decide instead to act on my instincts, like Mark suggested.

I walk over to the nightstand to subtly remove a magnum condom from the top drawer. Alfred lies there seemingly moved by my sultry evening wear, and encouraged by the attention I seductively drop the spaghetti straps of my dress off both shoulders, slide the thirty-percent spandex nude-color fabric over my ample breasts, pull the snug-fitting garment around my guitar-shaped hips, and step out of the confines of my fave dress and expose to Alfred my tanned body. Feeling empowered, I climb on top of him wearing nothing but my string bikini bottoms and a questionable look. Alfred opens my hand and removes the condom. He looks at it as if it were a foreign object.

"I'm leaving tomorrow, Alfred. My company's contract has expired, and I won't be returning to the Bahamas any time soon."

Alfred continues staring at me with the look of both disappointment and relief on his face.

"You don't have any Magnum XLs, Gypsy? This one is for average size men."

I smile, enough said … it's on.

Alfred strips off my bikini bottoms and strokes his enlarged penis simultaneously. I watch with excitement as Alfred's firm and mannish hands fumble with the condom wrapper. I hover above him, waiting, giving him an extraordinary view of my womanliness. Once the condom is free of the packaging, Alfred slides it down his own package, and the latex clings tight and snug around Alfred's thick mass. I lower myself down onto his sexual power and feel the heated thickness of his organ. It has a fleshiness that gives me an extreme sensory experience. The throbbing, pulsating delightfulness of his strokes makes me shutter uncontrollably. Alfred is very capable of sending me into sexual intoxication at this point, and being aware of my response to his stimuli, he masterfully and tenderly massages my G-spot with his experienced tool, and I deliver to him a stream of sexual relief that cascades down his shaft and puddles. I gyrate my hips rapidly to provoke an eruption from Alfred, and finally after multiple segments of performing remarkable acts throughout the evening, Alfred erupts like a volcano.

Making sure that I enjoy my stay on his lovely island, Alfred holds me in his strong arms all night long and stays with me until early dawn, until the dark sky forms that thin line of glowing yellow streak across the horizon and announces the new day.

When the prime minister's son calls the next evening, I inform him that although I am flattered, I will not be auditioning for the role of first lady. I wish I could transfer his affection to my sister Melody; she always wanted to do the housewife thing.

Marion is waiting outside to drive me to the airport and to hear about whatever she thinks has happened with Mark, who I again had to rush off of the phone so I wouldn't be late for work.

Alfred has already departed and left a now empty three-pack of Magnum condom wrappers lying on the floor and one satisfied air hostess on the extra bed.

"Hi Marion, guess what!"

"The prime minister's son wants your hand in marriage?"

"Humph. I stayed the night with Alfred."

"I thought you had a date with the son?"

"I did and I had a wonderful evening with Mark, but I had a remarkable night with Alfred."

"Oh, tell me about it," Marion mumbles as she snacks on her box of re-gifted chocolates.

On the drive to the airport, I fill Marion in on all the details. She makes a joke-saying that my passengers will get excellent service from me tonight thanks to the superb service I received from Alfred last night. I laugh and promise to keep in touch with her forever. To think her husband wonders why she insists on driving me back to the airport, if he only knew.

I am looking forward to my three-hour flight back to Detroit. I wish I could relive, better yet, set my mental digital video recorder and rewind the sex-educed festival featuring Alfred and his lengthy partner from last night. I'd love to just sit on the jump seat of the airplane and reminisce, but I can't. Instead I have to try to concentrate on work and my first-class passenger Mr. Osteen, who is carrying on about his brokerage firm in downtown Chicago and something about my house-sitting his condo on Michigan Avenue six months out the year while he's on the road traveling. Mr. Osteen is one of my regular passengers. I had been complaining to him on previous flights about how small my apartment is and how I was looking to move into a more spacious place. I do love Chicago. Maybe I'll get his business card and take a look at his condo next time I'm in the Windy City. Maybe, after my service is done, what I would really like to do is go back and sit on the jump seat in the galley and hide from the passengers for a while and push the resume button on my mental digital video recorder so I can finish last night's episode.

Hmmph, would be nice but somehow instead of remembering Alfred, my mind keeps shifting to my friend Nina and how much more fun and adventurous this job could be if she would have been chosen to fly for Islander Air, too. Think of the great layovers we could have shared. Islander is planning to hire again for the new eight-month contract scheduled to begin next season with service to Barbados, and I can put in a good word on Nina's behalf now that I am a seasoned stewardess. I trust I have some influence on the selection of new candidates being hired. Together, Nina and I can make a lot of new friends in Barbados, if not the kind of friendship the two of us have then definitely a friend like Alfred, with his unique talents, because leaving and thinking about never returning to Paradise Island gives me a bit of a fever. I'm going to miss the Bahamas!

CHAPTER 5

Misplaced Trust

"*I* think your boyfriend's gay."

"He's metro-sexual, not gay!" I am frustrated with Nina's constant accusations.

"Why doesn't he take you out to a dinner show or just a regular movie?"

"He happens to be the sole owner of his very own business. You know he doesn't have enough hours in his business day for extracurricular activities." I jut out my chin with pride.

"Then why don't you two get engaged or have some type of formal commitment?"

"Hello. You know why, Nina."

"Because he's gay."

"Okay, I'm done." Nina's words offend me so I turn my back to her.

Although I absolutely love my charming lifestyle and the freedom I have to get up and fly to any part of the country, or any country for that matter, at a moment's notice, I sometimes can't

----

stand some of my relationships, like my friendship with Nina. Nina is persistent in her quest to make my life miserable. She has been annoying ever since I told her that I declined Islander Air's offer. Islander called a week ago and asked if I would be returning for the fall flight schedule, which included a new route as well as the old destinations:

- Detroit-Nassau/Nassau-Detroit

- Chicago-Nassau/Nassau-Chicago

- Chicago-Cancun/Cancun-Chicago

- Detroit-Barbados/Barbados-Detroit

- Chicago-Barbados/Barbados-Chicago

The lady on the other end of the phone seemed excited to be offering me the vacant spot as she waited patiently for me to accept the position. Is it my fault I grew weary with Islander Air's monotonous four routes? Nina believes it is. She's jealous because she wanted that air hostess position badly. She feels I tossed a great opportunity away, and her way of dealing with that frustration is to egg me on about Michael, my newest boyfriend. I don't know who was more upset by my decision, Nina or the lady on the other end of the phone. She hung up on me when I responded, "No, thank you. I'm going back to college to finish my degree."

I walk away from Nina and jump into my Lexus GS, heading toward downtown, preferring to spend time with Michael.

Thankfully, Ali supports my decision to return to Madonna University and graduate first and look for work later. He has taken on the financial responsibility of maintaining my lifestyle. Ali pays the rent on my downtown loft. He recently purchased me my new car, and he's keeping his word by paying for my college tuition. How sweet is it that my husband who has another wife in some foreign country and doesn't care to know any specifics about my secondary relationship is actually honoring portions of our nuptials, probably out of guilt, but at least he is supporting me, his first wife. I must remember to credit that to his account. In the interim, I'll continue withdrawing from Ali's checking account the money necessary to maintain the standard of living I have become accustomed to.

When I finally realized that Ali's vision of a happy home differed from mine, it was too late—he had already decided to leave me and venture off to the Middle East to enjoy a life of bigamy. I was devastated. Ali wanted kids. I never dreamt of giving birth—too painful. He wanted to live in a home with a white picket fence—I like lofts. He wanted to go to the pound to rescue a dog—I wanted a hairless Chinese Crested from a breeder. However, I did want the marriage part of the deal—just us two in a condominium, taking trips and traveling the world to visit new societies. This was my ideal marriage, not the multiple wives living on a polygamy farm with our incest children cleaning up after an untrained dog version he had in mind.

When my divorce papers were filed, I surged forward in my hunt for the perfect man, someone like my daddy. For months I thought my free spirit would guide me to my dream guy, but it never did. Finally, I stopped searching and settled for yet another control freak—this one a small businessman with an obsession with his unisex boutique and an unusual addiction to lipstick lesbians.

Michael Jordan is his name, and no, not the basketball player, though I did meet him on one of my flights and turned down his advances, *stupid stupid*. I'm speaking of a man slightly vertically challenged in comparison but just as charismatic.

I've been trying to get this man involved in our relationship by asking him to take another trip to spice things up. I'm getting bored with the simplicity of his courting style, which mainly consists of three lovely parts: Phase one—the part of our relationship where we enjoy company at his house; Phase two—phase one again only we assemble at my loft; Phase three—bowling-golf-pool hall. One of these activities, not all three.

I'm so mad at Nina for not supporting my relationship with Michael that I may skip the next GNO. At our last meeting, Nina expressed to me how she feels phase one should have been, and she felt it was appropriate to run her big mouth off that night and tell all of my business to the other girls. She even got my other friend, Sheila, in on the Michael-bashing bandwagon.

"Miniature golf?" she said. "You don't even like real golf, Gypsy. You said it was like watching grass grow. And don't get me started on the bowling outings with the renting of shoes and the germ-infested bowling ball holes. You're germaphobic, for God's sake." Sheila's Spanish accent always gets heavier as her anger rises.

"Gypsy, I didn't know you had a phobia," my former neighbor Miyuki said.

"Oh, yes she does. Look in her bag, and I guarantee you will find a bottle of antibacterial hand sanitizer in it."

"Okay, Sheila, you need to put as much energy into your own dysfunctional relationship as you do mine and leave me alone."

"Gyps, if you don't want our suggestions then I suggest you stop introducing your concerns during the girls night out gab sessions."

Humph, I wasn't even the one bringing my business to the gab session on that night. It was Nina's instigating that started it all, and then she sat back looking pleased, watching me squirm while the girls verbally assaulted me. And how can Sheila propose that I stop taking advice? That's the sole purpose of GNO. My friends feel I suppress my desires and only do what Michael likes for entertainment. What they don't understand is that Michael doesn't have a lot of free time and I prefer doing things I know he will enjoy.

The three phases occurred in one year, and yet we only managed to squeeze in one measly vacation, which was a memorable weeklong trip to beautiful Maui at a fabulous resort with an astonishing view of the ocean. My body was in superstar shape that year, and I was having the most amazing good hair week ever. I could not have scripted a better visual. The trip was especially unforgettable because Michael preferred to post up in the hotel room and watch the view from inside our suite the entire seven days. I guess because Maui didn't have grimy, smoky bowling alleys or boring grass-growing golfing events, and zero stupid pool tables for Michael to take pleasure in, I was made to suffer. Humph.

So here I am today unexpectedly at my trendy, well-groomed, reclusive non-boyfriend's boutique (we never formally made a commitment). I normally help out at his boutique, Mod, on the weekends, but because Nina is being such a bitch today, I decided to skip my Friday dinner with her and come help Michael close the store.

As Michael and I are closing the boutique, in walks one of the local lesbians named Simone, a boyish-looking female with a buzz hair cut, shopping for an outfit to wear to Club Passion's Fashionista Friday. She approaches Michael, who is standing next to me.

"Hello Mike. Are you coming to Passion tonight? 'Cause we missed you last weekend." The boy-girl looks straight past me and waits for Michael to answer.

"Gypsy and I had a prior engagement, but we will definitely be there tonight." Finally, some acknowledgement. Wait . . . did he just say definitely?

"Good, I'll make sure we save a dance for you."

Simone puts her hands in the front pockets of her baggy pants and walks to the men's section where the new arrivals are being displayed. She settles on a pair of slouchy khakis and swaggers to the counter, avoiding the women's dressing room on her way over to pay for her pants. I watch her the whole time, trying to figure out what her deal is.

"What is she talking about, Michael? I thought we were going to watch the Discovery Channel's *Extreme Engineering* marathon tonight?" I didn't really care to sit at home again watching a television show but . . .

"Gypsy, we never go dancing. And besides, we can catch the encore presentation they're having next weekend," Michael insists.

"They have encore presentations? It's not like we're talking about *Project Runway*. Oh, never mind."

"That *Project Runway* marathon comes on next month."

"I said never mind." He has got to be fucking kidding. Like I would really choose to watch contractors put together a tunnel under a river presumably to connect a city or two over a night of dancing.

"We need to get the store closed early so we can go home and get dressed for the evening."

"Will I have time to stop by the loft to pick up something to wear?"

"Nope, we don't have time. Matter of fact, get your things together and prepare to set the alarm and I'll grab the keys."

"Well, I can choose a quick outfit from the boutique."

"No time. You'll want to try it on, twirl around in it, and end up changing your mind."

"I pose, I do not twirl!"

"You twirl, Gypsy. Let's get going please."

As I wait to set the store alarm system, I wonder if my desire to get out of the house and explore has turned into desperation. I am actually willing to go to an alternative dance club. Dang. I walk out of the boutique ahead of Michael and wait while he locks the doors.

"I'll drive." Michael's voice barges into my thoughts. Why must he keep saying that? He always drives, and he always announces the fact that he will do so.

"Hey, where's my sexy white Versace dress?" I ask myself out loud.

"What Versace dress?" Michael answers from the bathroom of his master bedroom.

"The Marilyn Monroe dress that blows in the slightest breeze, the one you said you love to see me in. Oh, never mind, I was talking to myself anyway." I know I picked it up with the rest of the dry cleaning and hung all the pieces on my side of the walk-in closet:

- Marciano jeans . . . here

- Goldsign jeans . . . here

- Juicy jeans . . . yep

- Two Chanel blouses (one pink, one white) … double check

- Escada black dress . . . here

No sexy white Marilyn Monroe dress. I guess I'll have to wear the Escada instead. All of my other cute dresses are at the loft in my own closet. Humph, maybe that's where the Monroe dress is too. Maybe my little sister, or shall I say my roommate, snuck into my wardrobe again. Kat feels like she lives alone because I'm always over at Michael's place. I get the feeling she loves our relatively new living situation and having the whole loft to herself.

One time I let her spend the night with me when I first moved in with Ali. I had to leave early the next morning to run some errands, so I crept past Kat sleeping on the living room sofa and quietly closed the door behind me. When I came home later that day, I caught her playing dress-up and dancing around the apartment to Madonna's "Material Girl" wearing my mother's vintage flapper dress that was given to me after she died. I instantly blew up and threatened to send her back to G-ma's house if she didn't take it off immediately. I was so angry, but that was years ago and I later apologized. Now that I'm with Michael, I'm much calmer. He's good for my soul. I'll give Kat the benefit of the doubt since she has gotten much better about asking to borrow my things instead of just taking them and trying to return them to my closet without my knowledge. I'll assume that she didn't get a chance to ask me if she could borrow the Marilyn Monroe dress.

"Hey Michael, did I bring my Pam Anderson shoes over here?"

"Gypsy, I don't keep up with your ever-changing trendy fashion collection. Are you ready to go?"

"Almost. Give me a few more minutes."

"We need to get going. I have people waiting on me."

"You're not even ready."

"Yes, I am."

Michael steps out of the bathroom looking like he just walked off the cover of a *GQ* magazine in his Ralph Lauren Black Label three-piece suit, a custom-fitted Borelli white dress shirt with silver cuff links, and a pair of black Cole Haan loafers. I guess my little black dress will be perfect after all.

We arrive at Passion in Michael's Mercedes S550 sedan, his baby. He is so protective of it that I don't even ask to park the damn car, much less drive it. Michael drops me off at the entrance of the club where I wait for him and watch as he searches the lot for the perfect door-ding-free spot. After driving around the lot twice, Michael decides to valet park. I continue watching as he slips the attendant a $20 bill and instructs him to park the car away from others.

We enter through a set of large mahogany doors into this contemporary new concept dance club. Club Passion has a take-control chrome stripper pole stabilized in the middle of the flooring, rouge carpeting covering the staged area, velvet burgundy drapes pulled across the back wall of the dais, crystal chandeliers hanging from the vaulted ceiling, and nine-foot windows dressed in the same luxurious printed fabric as the raised platform area. The spacious refurbished warehouse has several modern penthouse sofas sitting on top of dark Italian wood floors, and it even has the nerve to have a loft upstairs for VIP seating only, with separate bathroom facilities. I wish I was sitting up there with those glamour girls in that VIP section, holding a fancy martini glass and flicking my long curls over my shoulder. I watch with admiration as the fashion show of stilettos strike across the wood flooring and secretly wonder if those glamour girls are looking down on the patrons because of their vantage point, or are they *really* looking down on us?

"Hey, Mike." Simone the boy-girl is back.

"Hello, Simone. Have you met Gypsy?" Michael forces her attention on me this time around and points in my direction so there will be no mistakes as to which female he is referring to.

"Hi, Gypsy. Do you mind if we steal him? He owes us a dance." Simone is speaking at me the same way a blind person would, but clearly her attention and her eyes are fixated elsewhere.

"I guess." I respond with a nod and wonder as they walk away, who are *we* and *us*. No sooner than my last thought is complete, I look over by the stripper pole and see a group of girls surrounding Michael as he is dancing . . . like Prince . . . the Purple One. Oh. My. God. It's like a re-make of the *Purple Rain* movie with a fake Sheila E. and everything.

I slowly walk closer and watch in amazement as he imitates Prince's dance moves. Michael spins around and dips into a Chinese split. Ouch.

Oh my God! He has on my Pam Anderson platforms! This man is performing in my heels better than a Vegas showgirl. What is really going on? These women all seem to know and love Michael and his silly ways. This is so funny; "1999" is starting to play over the sound system, and Michael grabs the mic that one of his lipstick lesbian lovers is handing him and begins singing each word in perfect tune. The crowd is cheering his goofy ass on, and I'm wondering when did he have time to perfect his routine and where was I during those rehearsals?

Strumming an air guitar, Michael decides to get a running start and drops to his knees, gliding across the dance floor in his Ralph Lauren trousers, jerking his head violently back and forth as if he's having an exorcism performed on him. He halts right in front of the boy-girl's feet. Simone herself can't stop laughing as she helps Michael to his feet. "Little Red Corvette" comes on next, and that's when Michael and Simone begin doing some little rehearsed-looking skit where Prince aka Michael is driving an imaginary Corvette and the girl he is after in the song speeds away just as he gets within reach. Unbelievable. Look at what I have been missing out on.

Wait . . . now when did Michael have time to practice that with her? Maybe on a Thursday night when I was at GNO. Michael knows that girl's night out is an all-night affair, and I always go home to my loft to sleep after hanging with the girls. That would have given them ample time and a good opportunity to execute their moves.

He's rounding out his performance as "Delirious" blares through the speakers, and it's about time too, because now I'm worked up with plenty of questions. Simone and her lovers surround Michael and dance in a seductive come-hither way. I know Michael isn't enthused by the butch girls' attention, seeing that he prefers the lipstick ones better. He hands the mic off to an eager Michael Jackson look-alike who immediately begins to moon walk across the floor. The crowd applauds as Michael attempts to escape the overcrowded dance floor and walks in my direction.

Now nothing makes sense to me, especially the high heels. What I thought was an addiction to lesbians and an acceptance of a lifestyle is turning out to be some weird real-life *Rocky Horror Picture Show*. How could I have been so blind that I didn't see these women, who pretty much fund his lifestyle, also supplying him with endless entertainment? They not only frequent his business but also visit him at his unlisted home address. I understand that without them Mod boutique would not have flourished and there would be no Ralph suits to imitate Prince in, no Mercedes S550 that I'm not allowed to drive, nor would there be a fabulous bi-level museum suburban home on the west side of town to feel trapped in. But why must his life be so intertwined in theirs?

I want to trust Michael, but I can't silence the little nagging voice inside of my head. Maybe it's my own guilt stemming from my failed marriage that makes me have such misgivings about Michael. I thought I was somewhat satisfied with our relationship, and I love to see my handsome guy's free spirit, but this kind of activity is suspicious, confusing even.

"Gypsy, are you ready to go? We can still catch the last hour of *Extreme Engineering*," Michael excitedly says.

"Ah. No . . . where are my shoes?"

"You noticed, huh? Simone put them in the car for me. Are you ready to go?"

"No, what's up with the . . ." I'm holding my left fist up to my mouth in the form of a microphone.

"I just do it to relax and to relieve stress. You do know its karaoke night, right?"

"Oh, yeah I know." My bad I didn't know.

In the background, I hear the deejay shifting the music from Michael Jackson to trance, a faster paced beat that began in Detroit in the early eighties. The city comes alive whenever techno music is introduced to a party, which is why I decide to stay a little longer and give the club another chance. I kind of feel bad about judging Michael too, so I'll give him another chance as well.

"Let's dance, Sir Purple One."

"Okay, but don't get mad if I outshine you with my new moves. You saw what I'm capable of."

"And don't you get upset when I trade you in for Simone. I'm sure she understands what moves women desire."

"That would be very interesting to see."

"Okay, stop. I am not going to feed into those fantasies, mister."

The night proves to be very refreshing, and I fall in love with Michael all over again, despite his odd behavior. And my shoes better be in the same condition he found them in.

Most of my weeknights are spent at Michael's ultra-sweet bi-level house on the Westside. Sometimes when I'm at his place, I start to feel trapped in his immaculate museum home. I don't want to touch anything for fear I might break an irreplaceable statue or I'm not willing to eat snacks with him in his entertainment room because I feel I may stain his Roche-Bobois sofa. Instead, I sit next to him, motionless with my stomach growling, pretending to be interested in the History Channel. Well, I shouldn't say trapped because I am free to leave, but these are the only moments we get to spend alone time together, and I feel I have to keep an eye on the lipstick lesbians who not only visit him at his store but also pop up at his home, unannounced.

The next morning when we awake, before going to the boutique, I bring up the subject to Michael about a second vacation at the Bellagio casino and resort hotel in Las Vegas. "This could be my graduation present," I say convincingly. "We will only stay for four days because I know you can't keep the store closed during the weekend." That's the busiest and most profitable part of the week, plus all of his regulars come to visit him Thursday through Saturday, the true reason I believe why he insists on returning before the end of the week. I persuade Michael into believing that some time away together would do wonders for our sex life. Those last two words were all I really needed to say.

I am so psyched that Michael agreed to a second vacation, but he insists on going sooner rather than later. He's only giving me two days to plan our getaway. I'll need to coordinate the trip ASAP, plan our excursions, and submit to Michael the itinerary. He wants to know the specifics of the vacation, insisting that he needs the itinerary to determine if he should take inventory of his stock and order new shipment for the fall season now, or if it can wait until his return. Either way, he needs to prepare the store for his employees during our absence. That's what he says. I believe he wants to control whatever aspect of the trip he can and he's also trying to make sure we will return in time so that he won't miss his lesbians on Thursday. And speaking of inventory, I need to re-inventory my closet at Michael's house. I still don't know where my Marilyn Monroe dress is.

It is 110 degrees in Vegas when we arrive and blazing hot. We check into our room and the air conditioner is on freezer mode. It feels like winter in here. I consider going back outside on the Strip, but it's too hot out there. There's just no median. The room doesn't even have an extra bed, like I requested, for my luggage. The conniving taxi driver took the longest route around the Strip to the hotel. I can't seem to locate my much-needed sleeping pills, and Michael is preoccupied with gay girls on the pay-per-view channels. This fucking vacation is supposed to be relaxing, but I'm worked up, so worked up I could vaporize. I need to remove myself from all of this negative thinking and complaining and try to tune into a positive frequency.

I glance over at the open marble shower, and it looks like a lovely place for me to begin my non-hostile retreat. Little jets are positioned in every crevice, ready to massage my tensed body. Naughty thoughts run through my mind as I eye the deliciously gigantic showerhead that is placed strategically in the middle of the stall, as though it's ready to target my sensual unreachable areas, places Michael hasn't yet managed to reach.

"Hey Michael, I think I'm going to take a shower, baby. You go ahead and try to nap before we have to attend the 7:30 *Zumanity* performance."

"I'll wait for you to take a nap with me, honey."

"No don't, I'm going to . . . uh, exfoliate, yeah, so it will be awhile."

"You sure? I don't mind waiting."

"No, sleepyhead. Get some rest. We have a long night ahead of us."

"Come and lie with me when you're done. I want to hold you in my arms like I used to do."

"Okay, and can you order a bottle of champagne? I feel like having Mimosas. Oh, guess what I found?"

"What honey?"

"I found my sexy white Marilyn Monroe dress. I found it in Kat's closet last night when I was looking for my blue-jean jacket with the mother-of-pearl buttons to wear on this trip. I told her if she takes my clothes one more time without asking, I'm going to send her back to G-ma's house and I meant it."

"Sure you did. She knows as well as I do that you're just trying to scare her."

"No, I'm for real this time."

"Alright, honey. Enjoy your shower."

When I come out of the bathroom after my long, exhilarating shower to get dressed, I notice Michael has fallen asleep with a half empty glass of Dom P. balancing in his hand and he is beginning to snore. I am restless and eager to explore Las Vegas, and I don't want to disturb his sleep, so I remove the glass from his hold and polish it off myself. I grab my leather Coach bag and sneak out of the room to do a little gambling and lots of shopping, and later maybe pick up our show tickets from New York, New York's box office.

On the second evening of our trip we attend a boxing match at MGM Grand. I don't care for boxing, but Michael said it will be fun to get dressed up for the fight. Our seats are in the first few rows, near the television cameras. I thought about how this could be my chance to get discovered on national TV and launch my acting career, so I had Michael run out and purchase me this silk Roberto Cavalli dress to wear, the one that scoops low in the front. I saw it downstairs in the store window when Michael was getting us checked into our room. Michael knows how badly I want to act, but that doesn't stop him from laughing at me as I'm getting dressed for the evening. He says that it's silly to wear such an extravagant gown and that no one watching the fight will be interested in my attire. That comment alone puts him on sex restriction for the night. In any event, I pre-ordered the tickets before leaving Detroit to surprise him because he loves the violence these boxing matches supply. I can't stand the inhumane way the contenders treat one another, but tonight is his night. I even heard one of the girls talking when I went to the bathroom, saying that once a well-known boxer bit the ear of another. What kind of human does that? This will be the last time I put Michael's needs before my own if any of these types of shenanigans happen tonight.

The next morning while we are having breakfast in our king-size bed, Michael gets down on one knee.

"Gypsy."

"Yes, Michael."

"Will you marry me?"

"Marry you? Michael, get up."

"Marry me, please. I'm serious. Be my wife."

"Now? In Vegas?"

"Yes. In Vegas."

"I can't. I'm still kind of married." I give a questionable half-smile.

"What do you mean you're still kind of married?"

"Michael, we talked about this before. I explained it to you, remember?"

"You told me you started the paperwork for your divorce over a year ago!" Michael gets up from the bed and snatches the smile from my face with his furrowed brow and transfixing eyes.

"Umm, well."

"Umm hell, answer me."

"Umm, I thought . . ." All I can do is gaze at the micro-sprays of his forced words traveling from his salivating mouth through the air and crashing onto my eyelashes, making me blink.

"ANSWER ME!" Michael yells at me for the second time in our one-year history together.

"I'm sorry. I thought you understood the process." I wipe as much spit juice off my face as I can without his noticing. "It takes longer sometimes … it's very time consuming . . ." My eyes are filled with tears, and my face is glistening with saliva.

"Gypsy, I'm leaving. You don't even have the decency to tell me the truth."

"Wait, Michael, give me a chance to explain." I get up and race to my purse so I can present the unsigned divorce papers I have been carrying around.

"I'm out of here!"

"Wait, I have proof I filed."

"You had a year to explain. You had a year to show me proof, and you had a whole entire year to get the damn divorce!" Michael is throwing his clothes into his suitcase as we argue.

"Michael, wait. Calm down."

"Do NOT tell me to calm down." Michael begins marching to the door. "And don't follow me."

"Wait. Please don't go."

The door slams shut. Michael is a ghost. Dang.

I sit on the edge of the bed crying until I can cry no more. I unpack my toiletry bag and locate my precious sleeping pills hidden behind a cardboard panel in the zipper pocket. If there is ever a reason for swallowing a handful of orange pills, this would be it. I stare at the little killers and decide to take only one.

The next morning is our original departure date. I check out of the Bellagio at 11:00 a.m. and grab a taxi to the airport and cry quietly during the plane ride home. I know Michael is a man of reason and he makes his own decisions, but I feel I need to convince him to reconsider our relationship. Of course he will determine if he wants to be with me without my input on his own accord. Still, I want him to answer his phone and allow some manipulation on my part.

My plane lands in Detroit in the early afternoon, and Kat is there in her Mustang waiting to pick me up at arrivals.

"Hey, sad face. Are you feeling any better today?"

"No," I respond in a cracked voice.

"Well, I have a surprise for you waiting at home." She smiles at me as we pull off.

"I don't want any surprises."

"You'll want to see this one."

"No, I won't."

"Yes, you will."

"No. I won't."

"Yes. You will. Stop arguing with me."

"I'm going to throw it away, whatever it is."

"Read it first, and if you decide to throw it away after that, I won't say another word."

"Promise?"

"I promise."

"Deal."

"So, have you heard from Michael today?"

"No, and please don't say his name anymore."

"You must really be hurting."

"Let's make another deal. No talking."

We arrive at our loft forty minutes later to an opened letter sitting on the granite counter waiting for its rightful owner to read it. Kat has once again opened my mail without permission.

I had applied to Dubai Airlines in Dubai, the second largest state of the United Arab Emirates, for a position as a flight attendant early last year. My future ex-husband moved to Dubai and started a successful business after he was honorably discharged from the military, and he encouraged me to seek employment with the highly recognized airline's American division. Ali always knew I wanted to travel and experience the world. I have been using his corporate account to fly with Michael whenever he traveled to Europe to shop the warehouses, and I flew with him when he attended the merchandise shows in search of the latest fashion trends for the boutique. Come to think of it, I fly more often using Ali's account than I ever did when I was with Islander Air. There has to be some secret type of ploy on Ali's behalf for him to be so accommodating and allowing me to travel on his passes unconditionally.

I'm getting spoiled and becoming totally dependent on him, like I was when we first got married. I'm starting to let my guard down. If I'm not careful, Ali may be able to swoop down and gain control over me once again. He is the one who talked me into this whole Dubai situation in the first place. Now all he has to do is get me to reside in the Middle East, and then all he has to do is use his influence at the Embassy to get my passport revoked so that I will never be allowed to leave the country. That has to be the reason he's being nice.

"Kat, this letter is congratulating me on passing the interview process and the medical exam." Dubai Airlines is offering me an invitation to training. Nina is going to freak.

"It says here that I was on the alternate list."

"What's an alternate list?"

"It's a back-up list of desirable candidates. Hey Kat, I only have a couple of days to decide. Someone must have turned down the position, and I was next in line to be offered the job."

"I know. I already read it. What are you going to do?"

"How could you know, and you don't even know what an alternate is, smarty?"

"So, I know what 'congratulations you got the job' means."

"Such a smart ass."

I want to share the news with Michael and get his take on what to do, but he isn't taking my calls. Ultimately, the decision will be mine to make alone. Kat said she can handle the rent on her own now that she has a steady income from that modeling contract she landed with the auto show. All I need to do is arrange my personal business and make some calls to the university to have my name removed from the graduation lineup. I hate missing my ceremony, but I have no other choice. I also need to have the post office put my mail on hold. Other than that, I am good to go. I hope Michael calls before I leave for the Middle East so we can reconcile. It would be nice to hear his voice and get some input from him on my decision to relocate. I wonder if he will try to talk me out of going.

The airplane lands safely in Dubai, and it is a warm welcome to hear everyone speaking English, the language of the state. My future ex, Ali, picks me up from the airport and drives me to the banks of the Dubai Creek, a high-end exotic destination for Europeans and Americans, which translates to great shopping excursions. Dubai Airlines has established pre-arranged apartments for the new trainees' comfort. However, my first order of business is to get the divorce papers I have been carrying around for months signed by Ali. I gather my luggage from baggage claim and proceed out the sliding glass doors.

"Gypsy Moon! You still go by your maiden name, right?"

"Hey stranger." I always call Ali stranger, that or the jerk who cheated.

"You look great!" Ali offers a hug. "How is my favorite wife?"

"I'm fine. How's what's her name?"

This remark would have angered me a year ago, but over the past few months we have managed to become friends and I have manned up.

When we married, we had little in common, which may be the true reason our union only lasted eleven months—that or the fact that I wouldn't carry his last name. Or convert to his religion. Or cook. Or was it the knowledge of a second wife? Ding. Ding. Ding. Ding.

"Her name is Makah. Are you hungry?"

"Pretty name. I have the divorce papers you said you would sign."

"Yeah, yeah. You may want to reconsider since you're going to be here for a year. Why not use the perks that come with being my wife?" Ali continues to keep his vow and provide for my needs. "Are you hungry, Gypsy?"

"No, that's what got me into the situation I'm in now. When we first separated, you said the same thing." I look Ali straight in his eyes.

"You enjoyed the medical and dental package, and you especially enjoyed the travel benefits." Ali made his point clear. "And the new cars. Now, do you want to get something to eat?"

"Um hum, I lost a good man trying to enjoy those benefits, too!"

"He lost a good woman. Take it from me. Did you explain our financial arrangement?" Ali questions.

"No, he wouldn't hear me out."

"Did he really believe you could afford all of your expensive possessions on Islander Air's salary?"

"What? I dunno. I should have told him."

"You think he would allow you to be taken care of by another man?"

"Allow? See, that's why I should have gotten a divorce from you sooner."

"Okay, lady, calm down. After I buy you a drink and put some food in your stomach, I'll let you try to convince me to sign the divorce papers."

"Don't tell me to calm down." I snicker at my words. I see how Michael felt when I told him to calm down. "And what do you mean by convince?"

"You'll figure it out."

"Don't play with me, Ali."

"I'm not playing. You're still my wife, and I have certain privileges to you."

"Try acting on those privileges and *Makah*, your other wife, will be disappointed when you're unable to perform in the bedroom for the next six months."

"Ouch, such harsh language, Gyps."

Ali is not an orthodox Muslim. He applies the rules when they work for him. He agrees to endorse the documents over lunch after I remind him of the falsified papers kept in the safe at our home about the handling of the sudden honorable discharge from the Air Force, and the other confidential files he left behind in his rush to flee to the Middle East. And then, and this is the best part, I have him stop at this gigantic indoor shopping universe on our way to the training center and make him take me shopping at all of the high-end boutiques before dropping me off at my new temporary home.

Ali promises to continue to provide for me just as he has in the past, though this time he did it on his own, without the bribery tactics I used before. I turn down the offer though. When he signs the papers, I hand him the incriminating evidence I've been holding over his head during our separation and wish him good luck. I want to start my new life here in Dubai on a positive note and leave all the foolishness behind, no more trickery. I need to gain my independence from Ali and begin fresh by supporting myself with the generous alimony payments Ali and I agreed on during lunch. Hopefully, in the near future a marriage proposal will come back around for me, and hopefully it will be from Michael. If he decides to respond to my emails or answer any of my calls, I swear I will never give him another reason not to trust me ever again.

Looking out the window of my new apartment, I consider what the future holds for me, and it is a lot to take in, like does the post office forward U.S. mail out of the country for individuals? I need my fashion catalogs if I'm going to be spending months on end in the desert. I look at some of these women walking around in that garb, and I swear I'm not going to wear any clothing covering my body from head to toe. Not me. Before that happens, I'll go back to the States and start a new life selling insurance or something. I know how to close a chapter and begin a new one. I closed that Ali chapter today, and it only took just over a year.

CHAPTER 6

Glamorous Stewardess

I finally made it to major airline status in the states. When I saw the ad in the paper that Encompass was hiring I quit Dubai Airline and jumped right on it. I had completed Dubai's vigorous training; I mastered their strict serving practices, fine-tuned the art of persuasion, and sharpened my verbal communication skills. I knew exactly what to say to get the job at Encompass. And it worked. I'm working the first-class cabin as the lead flight attendant on Encompass Airline flight #2112 delayed from Detroit to Denver. My ears are plugged on this three-day trip because it was colder than expected in Atlanta and last night's party clothes (jeans and a sapphire halter top) did not fully protect me from the damp air that whipped across my bare back and raised the tiny bumps on my skin.

The entire crew is on board, and we are growing bored waiting for the mechanics to fix the plane.

"What did you do on your layover, Gypsy?" Debra asks as she begins straightening the first-class seat belts.

"I'll tell you during the flight. It was a long night," I say, tugging at my skirt.

"Come to the back when you're ready. I saved us a row of seats." Debra works her way to the back section of the airplane, straightening more seat belts along the way.

"Oh, good. I love it when we get to sit down during the flight," I answer, looking down at my lopsided name bar.

"Gypsy." The captain comes out of the flight deck wearing his standard navy suit jacket with four gold stripes on the sleeve. "I'll let the gate agent know it's okay to begin boarding."

"Don't worry about it. I see the passengers coming down the jet way now. Here we go again. . ."

"Welcome aboard sir . . . Hi . . . Hello . . . Welcome aboard . . . Hi there . . . Hello ma'am . . ."

"They need to install pre-recorded welcome announcements because this is redundant," I whisper to the pilot who is standing next to me at the boarding door. I notice that his pants are a tad long and are in need of a little tailoring. "Welcome aboard . . . Hi . . . Hello . . . Oh, here comes the agent now."

The gate agent is racing down the jet way with paperwork in hand, ready to close the flight, unaware that we have a tanned, pony-tailed mechanic in the flight deck with a puzzled look on his face.

"Slow down," Captain Ray tells the agent. "The mechanic has informed us that there is a slight problem. An indicator light has illuminated on the enunciator panel."

"How long?"

"We are looking at a forty-minute delay in departure."

"I'm sure this is going to go over well with the passengers," I say with a huge smile as I accept the passenger list from the agent. "My ears are plugged and nothing I've tried, including chewing gum, holding my nose, and gently blowing, is working. Nothing at all."

"Did you try putting Styrofoam cups stuffed with hot steamy towels up to your ears?" Ray asked.

"No, that's to relieve pressure, not to unplug ears," I answer with an upward inflection. "What I need is a decongestant, something to dry my sinuses. I must be coming down with a cold. Dang it, I hate flying with a cold. This is so messed up."

The mechanic summons Ray into the cockpit to discuss the problem. He seems truly concerned about the airplane's bleed valve situation. That's his problem and I have trust in his abilities to find a solution to his problem. Meanwhile, I have my own problems, plugged ears! Why me? Why not one of the pilots? I eye the captain walking back into the cockpit.

I am so ready to depart and get to my layover . . .

What the hell, why is 1C staring at me? Strange, jittery man. Now I feel obligated to approach him and ad lib an interview to make sure he's not a terrorist. Last thing I need is for the plane to be hijacked and taken to Vancouver, Canada. Not that there is anything is wrong with Vancouver, it's just the farthest destination we would reach before running out of fuel. Actually, if he is a terrorist, I'm going to request a warm destination, say south Florida, the Keys. I can imagine the company later requesting a de-briefing with the crew after the hijacking and asking me why I cooperated with the terrorist. I'll pretend to have Stockholm syndrome, you know, the having-sympathy-for-your-kidnapper disorder, that way I can keep my job. I wonder if I will still want to fly after I have been kidnapped. Can large jets even land in the Florida Keys?

I confront the stranger after carefully planning my strategy and turns out that he's a doctor, and he is kind enough to offer me some meds. Perfection. Drugs, just what I need. I thank Dr. Mitchell and reward him with a mileage certificate. I should go and interview my other first-class passengers to see what else I can score. On second thought, I better not. How would I explain to the company why so many of my passengers have free miles added to their accounts? I can't very well tell them I bartered with the business-class passengers.

"Gypsy, the passengers in the main cabin are getting feisty and I asked the captain to make an announcement and inform them of the problem," Debra, the hyper flight attendant working in the back, says.

What's up with her uniform? Her pants are all droopy and unflattering to her figure. I shake my head in agreement as I try to refocus on the predicament, straining a bit to understand the announcement being made. After hearing the pilot pause his way through a lengthy speech as if he wasn't sure the problem was fixable, a few people want to get off and take another airline, which is fine. I express to one nervous lady that if flying this plane was truly dangerous, neither I nor the captain would be willing to take off, not to mention the company doesn't want to take chances with a $40 million jet. She looks at me and thinks for a moment, then goes back to her main cabin seat. I may be a total stranger to this lady, but she trusts my logic and assumes the crew doesn't have any death wishes.

Thirty minutes have since passed, and the mechanic's puzzled look appears pieced together, and it's good because that valve controls the pressurization in the cabin, which could have an effect on my plugged ears. In any event, we are ready to push back and taxi to runway 2-1 right. I pop the decongestants that the doctor gave me, and I'm ready to soar into the friendly skies. Flight time is three hours and thirty-eight minutes. Three hours and thirty-eight minutes too long if you ask me.

On this leg, the passengers will choose between a chicken pasta salad and a turkey with Swiss cheese sandwich. Each meal is accompanied with a slice of German chocolate cake. I'm hoping someone will turn down the pasta salad so I can devour it along with that tasty cake. I passed out the menus earlier to the first-class passengers so they will be prepared to make their selections when I get to their rows. I tend to get snippy with ill-prepared passengers.

The lunch service is going smoothly until I reach row four, a homely woman seated near the window with a psychedelic pillow supporting her back. She's managing a collection of colorful pills on her tray table and appears a bit bemused.

"What the heck are you doing, ma'am?" Yes, I said heck.

"I am taking a form of Valium that I purchased overseas, thank you very much." She proceeds to crush the white ones into a fine powder.

"Ma'am, you're not allowed to use illegal drugs on an aircraft."

"I'll have you know, I bought them legally in India, lady." She begins rolling up a dollar bill.

"They are not legal in the United States without a prescription, ma'am."

"Listen, I will ingest whatever, however I please. If I want to use them as a suppository, I will do just that!" She leans over the tray table, looks up at me, and dismisses me with her eyes.

"Oh, alrighty then, hold that thought." I turn to walk away. We didn't study this in flight-attendant class. I suppose if we had to cover every nonsensical behavior imaginable, there would be no time left for the grooming portion of training, and that would just be wrong.

I use the interphone to contact the cockpit and inform them of my dilemma. The first officer looks through the peephole and opens the door for me to enter. As I step into the cockpit, I observe the captain reading a learn-how-to-fly book, which I don't find funny. Ignoring Ray's attempt at humor, I close his book and guide his attention to the dilemma at hand. I try not to get too distracted by the breathtaking panoramic view as we fly over the clouds, observing that nothing beneath us for as far as the eye can see. I look to the left, the port side of the aircraft, and to the right, the starboard and see magnificent celestial bodies. There are no borders, only miles and miles of blue sky, no limitations above either, just the heavens with the moon situated in the center of the sky. Posing. Pristine. The sun has begun to set and is coloring the clouds a sherbet orange.

I give the pilots an account of the goings on just so they are aware in case we need to have the authorities meet the plane, or worse, have an emergency landing. Hesitatingly, after filling the guys in, I leave the cockpit to approach the sniffer with a card in hand, which spells out in no uncertain terms her fate if she insists on continuing with these antics.

My attempt to defuse the situation is easier than I expect. In her haze, the sniffer agrees and puts her pharmacy away, reclines her seat back, and sleeps the remainder of the flight. Or maybe she passes out, thank goodness for whatever the reason! Now I can go sit in that saved row and tell Debra the story about my layover in Atlanta.

"Okay," I say to Debra. "Let me finish telling you about the party last night . . .

"My girlfriend named Summer, we met while in flight attendant training at Islander Air and worked our first commercial flight together to Cancun, Mexico. You heard of that slogan, 'What happens in Vegas, stays in Vegas,' right? Well, turns out that that slogan started in Cancun at Big Daddy's nightclub on the same foam-covered dance floor that Summer and I danced around on. Groups of drunken frat boys were known to customarily chant at midnight, 'What happens in Cancun stays in Cancun,' and then they would sound a bell that represented the bewitching hour had begun. Summer and I know firsthand that this is true because we witnessed the tawdry acts at Big Daddy's and participated in a few ourselves. I definitely understand why that saying was created. We bonded on that layover and swore never to drink tequila or party with frat boys again, and we have been friends ever since. Anyway, she now flies for Southern Airlines and she hosted a jeans and stilettos party this weekend, so after we landed and 134 bah-byes, I gathered my belongings, switched my cell phone from airplane mode to transmit, and charged up the jet bridge toward the entryway to Hot-lanta. The crew had left me, remember? It was okay because I told you guys to go ahead, and I caught the tram to the main terminal by myself. Did you see that scary-looking van driver waiting at the shuttle bus pick-up area? Man, I wanted to tell him I was going to catch a taxi instead. Okay, so twenty terror minutes later I arrived safely at our hotel downtown, and that's when my cell phone started purring . . ."

"Hey girl, it's party time. When will you be ready?" Summer gave a slight girl chuckle. "All I need to shop for is a pair of stilettos and a blouse," she informed me.

"Summer, have you forgotten the extreme need to nap? I have been flying around from coast to coast for nearly eight hours," exasperated, I continue. "I am so incredibly tired."

"Sorry, it did slip my mind. I haven't flown in four days," she giggled again.

"I just need to rest for a couple of hours. I'll call you when I wake up." I hung up the phone and swallowed half of a sleeping pill.

Two hours and fifteen minutes later, my nap was over. My body was recharged, and I was ready to explore. I jumped into the shower with my Lush products from Amsterdam in hand, dried off, lotioned with Potion (more Lush stuff), squeezed into my Seven stretch skinny jeans, put on my Hot Topics fairy shirt, and slid into my new red Laundry strappy stilettos that make my outfit rock! After winking at my reflection in the mirror, I called Summer to have her meet me at the Westin Hotel in the Sundial restaurant. There, we met up with a friend and got a great view of the city from the revolving rooftop.

"Hey girl, it's party time!" Summer screeched as I approached the restaurant.

"Do you even know my name?" I giggled. This always happened when I was around Summer.

"Come on. Blake is waiting for us. We'll have one drink with him before hitting the mall." Summer tossed her hair back.

"Okay, one drink only. Otherwise I'll be too buzzed to shop, and this time I did bring my Black Card with me." I tossed my hair back. I kept adopting her habits.

"You have a Black Card?" she questioned.

"Summer, no, Ali has me on a fixed income now, remember?" I twisted my lips at her. "I have Michael's."

"What I remember is Michael breaking your heart."

"Well yeah, but since I have returned home from Dubai we've been working on our relationship."

"He missed you a lot, huh?"

"Yeah, he finally called when he heard that I was back in the States."

"He'll take you for granted again. You just watch."

"Okay Summer, this conversation is over. Didn't you say Blake was waiting?"

"There you go again, running away from the truth. Come on, you Gypsy you."

We entered the lounge and found Blake, a 6' 3" 280-pound, full-of-solid-muscle ex-football player, waiting for us at a booth near the window.

I met Blake five or so years ago when he got injured and retired from the NFL, but who the hell is that with him? Is that? That's not Adam, is it? Damn, it is conman Adam. Despite the fact that he is tall and slender with curly hair and could easily double for an older Justin Timberlake, he's a pain in the ass. He and Blake are fraternity brothers, but Adam knows that Blake is by far our favorite. I can't say the same for Adam. He was with Summer and me on that unmentionable night in Cancun. He conned his way into a friendship with us, and now we are stuck with his slimy ass. We have to let him tag along from time to time. It's all we can do to keep his mouth shut about Cancun.

I stiffened at the sight of Adam.

"Come on, girl. We can't let his presence ruin our evening." Summer grabbed my hand and pulled me in the direction of the stained-glass window where the guys were seated.

Summer, Blake, and Adam each ordered a variety of martinis. I ordered a Guinness Draught. Yum. I remember one time Encompass lost me in Dublin, Ireland. That's where I learned to drink Guinness beer. I did as the natives and drank stout all night. I didn't bother calling crew scheduling to inform them of my whereabouts (they should not have misplaced me to begin with). I figured what was the rush; plus, I was still on the clock and earning per diem. The company finally located me five days later and flew me back to base.

Anyway, two beers later I was ready to head to Lenox

Square Mall. Blake was cool, but I was not as forgiving as Summer. I would much rather be shopping than hanging out with double-crossing Adam, and it was getting late. I still needed a sexy halter top to wear tonight to the stiletto party. Summer had already given me a limit on mall time, which meant I must power shop, and lucky for her I had plenty of practice with this power-shopping phenomenon due to the short layovers in Beijing, China, and Bussan, South Korea, running from one vendor to the next trying to get the best knock-offs available in the shortest amount of time. Otherwise, I would have insisted on taking my time and enjoying the moment.

We said our good-byes to the boys and proceeded past the elevators into the lobby and out the door to valet. As Summer's black 300C pulled up, I could hear her Aerosmith CD playing. I jumped into the passenger seat and pushed eject before Summer even had a chance to hop into the driver's seat. We pulled out of valet listening to the Usher CD that I slid in the player, and we merged into Atlanta's traffic, traffic that would test my nerves and road-rage control levels if I were driving, but since I wasn't, I sat back, relaxed, and enjoyed the flight—I mean ride—to Buckhead.

We prowled the mall faster than hell, too fast; I didn't even have time to look at the new collection in the Vera Bradley store. And now we were headed to the Cascades where Summer's two-story Victorian-style home was sitting pretty, like a model on a runway, only the brick houses in her neighborhood were on a cul-de-sac. Inside, the home was romantic and dressed up with unspoken areas set for lounging in the great room, dancing in the dining room, watching the fight in the family room (located off of the kitchen), and having dessert and drinks in the kitchen. Although Summer is partial to neatness and has control issues, and although the party atmosphere is pre-set, I'm sure the festivities will be boundless and exuberant.

At 21:00 hours, or 9:00 pm, the first of the guests, a group of ballplayers with their accessories of Crayola women, began to roll in. The players gravitated toward the desserts and drinks room to indulge in the chocolate-covered strawberries and champagne with their aphrodisiacal women following close behind. One of the players looked familiar and not because I've seen him on TV. I think he was on one of my flights.

"How do I look?" Summer was ever so conscious of her physical appearance.

"You look like me!" I responded.

"Well then, you are absolutely beautiful." More giggles escaped from Summer's glossy lips.

"Hey, is that Wyse Jones?" I squinted.

"Um hum, he plays for the Denver Nuggets now. You want me to introduce you to him?" She tossed her hair back and began walking in his direction.

"No wait, my cell is purring. I'll be right back." I looked at the name on the screen and walked away to find a private area to bicker.

It was Michael, my non-boyfriend boyfriend whom I decided to send straight to voicemail, not the time for the who-what-where drama-laced conversation.

He hates Summer because she has been married four times, and he feels she's unstable and a bad influence on me.

So no, instead it's time to commit to one of the four predetermined mood areas. I pushed ignore on my cell and began my night in the lounging room. I found a spot on the sofa to squeeze into next to my stylish friend, whose long, brown hair with blond highlights covered part of her very friendly smile. Summer had on dark True Religion jeans that looked like a size four with a backless silk chiffon halter-top and my black Jimmy Choo stilettos. I needed to borrow those pants from her and the top, too. I was sure I could fit into everything she had on, and I wanted my shoes back.

We were surrounded by a group of inquisitive individuals with an abnormally high interest in our careers; questions about layovers, favorite places, usual routes, near misses, and questions about having a man in every city were coming from every direction.

Summer and I love to talk about flying if only to point out

the fact that we do not have a man in every city, nor do we have usual routes (they change monthly), no near misses with other aircraft that we are aware of (we prefer the pilots not clue us in on those details), and my favorite place to travel is the islands—an island that doesn't fall below eighty degrees and has an all-inclusive resort with white sand beaches, beautiful multi-shaded blue-hued water to dip in, Lava Flow smoothies to drink with an extra shot of coconut rum, pulsating rhythmic reggae beats coming from the live band, sun-bathing, and a quiet spot where I can watch as my skin color deepens in contrast to my silver-infused white string bikini. However, Summer and I never mention the Cancun layover, not even to each other.

Yells, hoops, and hollers from the other room disrupted my daydreaming and brought me back to reality. I got up to view the boxing event in the fight room and found a cozy corner to stand and watch as two heavyweight contenders entered the ring. I decided to make small talk with a handsome South African pilot standing next to me.

"Hi. Are you enjoying the party?" I asked.

"Yees ido enjoi de pote," he replied.

"Good." Realizing that this conversation would take too much energy because I could not understand a word that was coming out of his mouth, I smiled and quickly ended our chat. "Good day."

I shuffled off into the dance room to get my groove on. All of the ladies were on the dance floor pivoting, rocking, and gyrating to the music while the men were standing around holding up the wall, admiring the women on display. I swayed to the center of the floor and grabbed my friend Sandy's hand (she flies for Islander Air and knows Michael), and we started ballroom dancing. I think Sandy is bi-sexual because she always plays in my hair and she knows that my soon-to-be-ex, with his addiction to the rainbow society, loves lesbians. She is a great lead though. I was following most of her steps until the DJ so rudely and abruptly switched songs so the old heads could do the Hustle and the Electric Slide, at which point everyone swarmed the dance floor, even the men on the wall.

"Gypsy, girl, I've been looking all over for you. Wyse wants to meet you."

"It's 1:00 in the morning now, and I have to fly to Denver in less than twelve hours. I really don't have the time. I asked Adam and Blake if I could finagle a ride back to my hotel on their way to the loft party downtown, and I think they're ready to leave."

"Don't you want to meet Wyse? He's rich!" Giggles, giggles, giggles.

"No, you know I'm still ending my relationship with Michael. I'll call you tomorrow." I kissed Summer's cheek. "This party is one of your best."

Blake pulled up to the hotel, and Adam, being the swindler that he is, walked me to the elevator and posed the question of his spending the night with me. I gave him the evil look and strode into the elevator, letting the doors close behind me. When the doors opened on the eleventh floor, I headed directly to my room alone. I heaved off my smoke-filled halter top, stepped out of my aching heels, peeled down my jeans, washed the makeup off, turned on the tube, pulled down the sheets, and dove into bed. Too fatigued to put my pjs on, I fell fast asleep.

"And that was it. What did you do?" I ask Debra.

"Nothing nearly as exciting. I went to McDonald's and brought my food back to my hotel room to watch pay-per-view all night. What is the big pact you and Summer have with that creepy Adam?" she responds with a quizzical look.

"Oh my God, Adam. We met that fool one evening at Big Daddy's night club. He was playing drinking games with the guest bartender Joey and invited Summer and me to join in. Big mistake, Big Daddy's had $2 tequila shots that night. The entire bar was on tequila. Several severe shots later, I was on the dance floor with everyone else and we all had on our swimsuits. Tuesday night was known for its bikini bash. I dragged Adam onto the foam-covered dance floor and left Summer at the bar with Joey throwing back those $2 shots. The club was engaging with sparkling white bubbles rising to a height of at least four feet. All I could see were shoulders and tops of heads bobbing around. Ladies outnumbered the men three to one, but that didn't appear to matter because everyone had a dance partner no matter if it was boy/girl or girl/girl or girl/boy/girl. No one was left unattended.

A shirtless Adam commenced his fraternity games and started pulling the strings on my triangle top, exposing my bosom beneath the popping bubbles, and he urged all the other men to follow suit and yank at bikini tops. I was so out of it and into the music that I wasn't aware my nipples were on display and giving salutation to the onlookers. It was not until I saw Summer dancing next to me topless that I realized the radical conduct happening around me. Adam was dancing in between Summer and me, and I felt his stiffness brush against my bikinied bottom. I knew without a doubt that Adam was now butt naked. The massive amounts of foam being forced out of the bubble maker mixed with the shots of Patron made the flight of the imagination acceptable, no rationalizing or inductive reasoning to be had. I'd given into the bliss!

Needless to say, Summer and I could not stagger quietly down the few blocks along Cancun's peaceful strip of resorts and manicured lawns alone. We needed an escort to make sure we made it back to our room without mishap, and we chose Adam as our guarantor.

"Flight attendants, prepare for landing."

The captain's voice scratches the exterior of the conversation, allowing me to regroup just in time before freeing my mischievous fairies onto the likes of Debra, a well-known gossipmonger. Seventy-five miles outside of Denver, we begin our approach.

When we land in Denver, it is sixty-five degrees. I'm going to get sick if I continue to fluctuate between extremes in temperatures. More bah-byes ensue, and the passengers flee to make their connections. Outside of the airport, Debra and the other main cabin flight attendant rush to get a quick smoke in before the hotel van comes. I wait and watch in amusement as a family of four from our flight struggles with their ski equipment, dog kennel, and car seat–stroller combination. I would have left the dog and the kids at home if I were vacationing in Vail, the husband too for that matter.

I see the van arriving, and I can't wait to go to bed. I'm still tired from the Atlanta layover, and plus my ears are plugged. I kind of wish I had some of the sniffer's Valium. After the hotel's front-desk lady checks us all in on the seventh floor, the crew plans to meet downstairs at the bar in fifteen minutes. Screw the plan, I'm going to bed.

On my way to my room #703, I run into Angela, a Honolulu-based flight attendant. I have not flown with her in over two years when we had a forty-four-hour layover in Lafayette, Louisiana. I fondly remember that layover. The NHL chartered our airplane, and we flew the hockey team into Lafayette to play an exhibition game. The Dallas Cowboys cheerleaders were also in town that same weekend. At the airport when we first arrived, some of the vendors asked if we were going to cheer for the Minnesota Wild at the hockey game, and I said yes, thinking they meant shout approval for, not professionally root for the team. Then, at the hot spot where all the locals gathered, everyone there thought we were the Dallas Cowboys cheerleaders, too, and welcomed us into the club. Guys sent drinks over; girls asked for autographs, and pictures were being snapped. Good thing we had a long layover with enough time to recuperate because that night we reaped all of the benefits of being the most famous cheerleaders in the country.

"Gypsy, oh my God. I missed you."

"Hey Angie." I put on my most cheerful smile, the smile I save for the senior citizen men who like to flirt.

"My crew is meeting downstairs in the lounge for a few drinks. You have to join us."

"Oh I . . ."

"Don't give me that fake smile, missy. Bring your ass downstairs. Your attendance is mandatory."

Ten minutes later, I'm at the bar singing karaoke with the captain. I'm Tenille, and, of course, he's the captain. Angie and I reminisce about our deceitful night in Lafayette, and before you know it, it's 1:00 a.m. Again I'm back on the elevator going up to my room on the seventh floor. I strip my clothes off, too tired to get my pjs out of the luggage. I pull back the sheets and lie down, out like a light, except the lights were still on the next morning when I am awakened by a call from the front desk at 11:00 a.m. Shit.

I didn't get my scheduled wake-up call, so I am literally running downstairs where the crew is waiting in the van for me with astonished expressions on their faces, revealing positively that they are unaccustomed to seeing me in such a rumpled manner. My hair is a complete mess. My uniform is looking offhand, and my shoes are all scruffy. The van driver exceeds the speed limit on the way to the airport and we make it curb-side one hour before departure, and with only five minutes left before boarding time. I head straight to the ladies' room, refusing to roam about the terminal raggedy-looking any longer. I'm determined to vamp up my clothing a bit and straighten out my hair, second stop the coffee house. The crew decided to meet me on the plane instead of waiting for me while I stopped for my caffeine fix. I take another glimpse at my compact mirror (no lipstick on teeth) and finish my coffee, and now I'm fully fueled, ready to meet and greet the guests for today's flight. We have two more legs to go before the termination of this three-day trip, thank God.

It is 1:00 p.m. and flight #333 is ready for departure. I'm not feeling my normal bubbly self today, either because of the adult beverages from last night or the lack of sleep. I only managed eight hours instead of my usual ten, so I just don't feel like smiling. Mr. Blue Suit, please find your seat, sir, and stop worrying about my visage.

The doors are closed, the passengers and flight attendants are seated, and we are rolling down the runway at 150 miles per hour, climbing up to an altitude of thirty-five-thousand feet, and gliding above the clouds in our attempt to expose the hiding sun and the secrets of the sky. The pilots turn on the green light, and I make my PA announcement before unbuckling my seatbelt and harness to begin my beverage service and deliver drinks to the fifteen first-class passengers. I open a bottle of Merlot and a bottle of Chardonnay, push the brew button on the coffee maker, pull out my half-cart, and set it up with napkins, lemons, limes, a bucket of ice, and tidbits. Ready, set, go.

Rolling my beverage cart down the aisle, I begin at seats 1A and 1B. There sits a retired couple going to visit the grandkids. The old man with a wide denture grin orders tomato juice, and he says the wife will have the same. Seats 1C and 1D, two twenty-something girls who look as tired as I feel and I'm jealous because they are sound asleep. I want so badly to crawl back into bed and rest. On to seats 2A and 2B, I find a friendly, talkative woman on her way home from Europe. She's excited because this is her first time sitting in first class, and she informs me that she always wanted to be a flight attendant but never had the opportunity to pursue it. Her trip to Europe is also a first, but sitting in first class seems to have overshadowed Europe. She orders a hot tea with sugar. In seats 2C and 2D sit Mr. Blue Suit and a small-framed woman, one beer, one H_2O. Seated in 3B is an upset passenger complaining about the bumps, nothing for him.

Seats 3C and 3D. There is a young, happy couple with their own popcorn and diet soda watching *The Thomas Crown Affair* on a portable DVD player. I take a short recess and invite myself to view the next part. I elbow her tolerant guy who is seated on the aisle, and he moves over a little so I can squat down and rest half of my butt cheek on the armrest. This is the best scene coming up where he flies her in his glider on a impromptu trip to a villa on an island. Once inside, she visits the closet and finds it full of clothes all her size! I love that movie. The couple saw the movie over a dozen times before, too. Matter of fact, the girl states that her guy surprised her in a similar way. She says he had chartered a small jet instead of a glider, the island was actually Antigua, and they went shopping as opposed to the closet already being filled, but everything else was the same. I rise up from the armrest to complete my service at seats 4ABC and D, the party section, a group of college kids ready to drink. I asked for IDs, and they produce them. The sorority orders two vodka tonics, one gin and soda, and one screwdriver with a splash of cranberry juice.

"What's the special occasion?" I ask the young adults.

"Spring break!" they reply in unison.

"Oh, you're traveling through Memphis to the Caribbean. How could I forget?"

"Do you fly this route all the time?" the young girl asks.

"No, my schedule changes monthly."

"Do you have boyfriends all over?" the other young girl asks.

"Pfft. Hardly, I can barely manage the one I do have. Men tend to be insecure when their girlfriends fly for a living. Would you guys like anything else?"

"No, thanks." Again in unison.

"Okay, enjoy the flight." I smile, happy to be going away from the party section.

I try to fly as little as possible during spring break, and this month I'm flying to locations that do not cater to spring breakers, no Florida trips and no Mexicos, which was specified in my bid when I submitted my request for this month's flying. I rush to finish my service so I can prepare for my favorite phase of flight, descent. Landing is what flying is about, and on this trip, we will soon be landing in Memphis, home of the King of Rock and Roll. I make the welcome to Memphis pre-landing announcement, and I put my cart away, close up the galley, check the passengers' seatbelts for compliance, stow luggage, and am seated for landing before touchdown. Only one more leg to go.

Once the passengers deplane, the crew gets off to take care of personal business. We separate and will meet back on the plane in twenty-five minutes for our next flight to Detroit that's scheduled to board in thirty minutes. I need to go to the cash machine, buy a new magazine, hit the coffee house for my second dose of caffeine, and call Kat to make sure she can pick me up from work.

Strolling through the B concourse and pulling my black flight bag behind me, I stop and beam at Patrick as I withdraw $40 from the ATM located next to his shoeshine stand.

"Hello."

"Hi Gypsy, do you need a shoe shine today?"

"No, but I'll come in next week for a mega-shine."

Cruising through the terminal wearing my custom-fitted navy skirt, flesh-tone thigh-highs, and a pair of black patent leather Nine West pumps, I breeze by my favorite bookstore to check for the latest arrivals.

"Hi Miss Lady, did you get the new *Fitness Rx* mag in yet?" I keep forgetting this lady's name at the magazine stand.

"Our shipment is late today. I'll put one to the side especially for you when it arrives," she replies.

"Thanks. Have a good day." What is her name?

My hair is pulled back into a neat ponytail. My red-painted lips and nail tips shine as I manage to dial my sister's number left-handed using my pink paisley print BlackBerry pearl mobile with the jeweled cell phone charms from Japan dangling.

"Hey Kat, I get in at six. Is that a good time for you?" My voice explodes through the receiver thanks to the large coffee I got from the Beanery.

"Yes Gyps, I will be at the airport at six," Kat replies in her agitated, sleepy voice.

"Okey dokey, go back to sleep."

"Yeah, and you try to calm yourself."

"It's the coffee. I'm on my second cup."

"Yeah, I can tell. Bye."

"Bye Kat. Love you."

I hang up the phone and begin walking back to my gate. All eyes on me. People love to watch flight crews. It's like we have our own watered-down fan club, so at all times I make sure I'm looking fierce! My pace is on autopilot and quickens as it is getting close to boarding time. After presenting my company badge to the gate agent and getting access to the plane, I hoof it through the entrance of the boarding door where I find Debra seated on the aisle with her crossed legs positioned away from Captain Ray and holding the latest issue of *Encompass Newswire*. Ray is in the window seat reading over Debra's shoulder and smiling broadly. From my vantage point, I can see the company's logo and boldly printed words *profit sharing*. Maybe today will be a good day after all. Hey, my ears just popped!

And it was a good day. Now I'm at home in my loft. It has been five days since I've flown, and I am ready to go back to work. If you think about it, nowadays flying is not that glamorous as one may be led to believe, but it is definitely interesting, and I can't wait to see what new adventures lay ahead.

I begin dressing for my six-day Asia trip, but this time I'm going to wear my A-line herringbone dress. I pin my wings on my right lapel and my name bar on the left. I slip on my thigh-highs, strap on my wedge heels, grab the navy sweater the company provided, and take one last look at my reflection in the wardrobe mirror.

I walk to the parking garage, pulling my roller bag behind me to the trunk of the convertible Mustang that I so generously gave to Kat. She lets me park her car at the airport when I fly and I let her drive the Lexus. I would hate to come home to my car all dinged up, I inherited this pattern of baby-ing my car from Michael. Anyway, I think Kat has the better end of the deal in this situation. On the ride to the airport, I look for my treasured mood-setting Usher CD and remember that I left it in Summer's CD changer, so I am forced to drive in silence, contemplating what position I want to work, be it lead flight attendant working in first class or a main cabin attendant where you have less work to do but more people to do less work for.

Downstairs at the airport, I check in for my flight and converse with many of my colleagues. Some I have not seen in weeks and others in years. I empty my mailbox that was full of company correspondence and find a note from Debra, that flight attendant from my last flight:

Gypsy, I was determined to get the goods on the Adam story just before our descent, I can't wait to hear what happened. We fly together again next week. Let's finish talking over a cold beer. Until then, Debra.

Absolutely not! The ending I gave her was good enough. She doesn't need to know the details of that insufferable night. I tear up the note into teeny-tiny pieces and proceed to the Century Room to change my next week's schedule so I won't have to fly with Debra again, and I'm hoping to catch one of the senior flight attendants (the dinosaurs) on the computer who may be trying to get rid of their superior Rome, Italy, trip—or even a Frankfurt, Germany, trip will do.

I take the elevator to the main level of the terminal and surround myself in all the divine sunshine. It is such a beautiful day for air travel, and I have come to realize that flying is truly about the journey, the encounters, and the ride . . . not just the landings. I love traveling and meeting new people. I love my job!

"Flight attendant Gypsy Moon, please report to gate A11 for immediate boarding," a loud voice calls over the public announcement system. Okay, so sometimes I hate that they depend on us the way they do. Good lord.

CHAPTER 7

Uniform Love

*A*s I walk along the riverfront in downtown Detroit touring the Techno Festival at Hart Plaza during this hot, humid, and hypnotic summer weekend with two of my closest friends, Sheila and Nina, I take notice of the sun beginning to set as we wait for the free concert to start.

"We still have thirty minutes before the performance," I announce. "I'm going to go get an elephant ear topped with cinnamon and powdered sugar. You guys want one?"

Sheila and Nina both make gasping noises as if I am stealing their breathable air.

"Eww, no thanks, we'll go on ahead to look for good seats near the front of the concert hall and meet you there," Sheila says.

"Okay, I'll be back."

They proceed without hesitation directly to the concert hall to people watch, and through the festive noise I can hear Nina's distinctive snicker in the distance teasing the lady wearing shorts with Ugg boots. I turn on my heels thinking how just yesterday I returned from my weeklong vacation in the Dominican Republic where I received the deepest tan I have ever had. My halter top is showing off my bikini lines, and my long shorts are exposing my newly acquired toned calves that I got from running on the soft sand beaches of Punta Cana.

I had just broken up with my boyfriend James and needed to go on holiday to clear my head and maybe find Dexter St. Jock, Eddie Murphy's character from his Raw concert. What was I thinking anyway, committing myself to a guy who was only committed to his metrosexual stylist career? I was so over James's prima-donna ways that I craved for a rugged man with calloused hands to touch my body, and a weeklong rest in paradise is where my search began. I didn't find Dexter. Instead there was Miguel, and he treated me so well during my stay that I returned home with an evolved spirit, mended heart, and refreshed sense of being.

Anyway, the free concert at Hart Plaza is about to begin, so I take a bite of my elephant ear and sashay toward the concert hall intentionally walking in the opposite direction I had come from to avoid the fudge stand. On the way back, I notice a handsome police officer standing at his post, watching me. Poised in my two-inch heels, I continue toward the concert hall, which happens to be in the direct line of the officer. To get a good look at him, I slow my pace and pretend to rearrange my Chanel belt. Close up, I see that the man has gorgeous greenish-gray eyes and an awesome athletic build. He's so handsome that I find myself fidgeting too long, and I look extremely obvious.

"Ma'am, do you need assistance?" the police officer asks.

"Yes, can you show me to the concert hall please?" I purposely look in the wrong direction.

"My pleasure," he grins and offers me his elbow for guidance. "May I ask you what your name is?"

"It's Gypsy, sir."

"Gypsy, that's different."

"Everybody says that."

"Are you here by yourself?"

"No, my friends and I wanted to get out of the house and enjoy a night of music and take advantage of this good weather."

"It's a beautiful night isn't it?"

"Yes it is."

"Where are your friends?"

"Near the front, that's where they said they would be."

"I'll help you down the ramp, it looks slippery from all of the soda spills."

The police officer escorts me another twenty feet to the concert, and during our stroll I learn that his name is Kyle and that he likes lunching in the park during the weekday. His partner is watching as we exchange telephone numbers and gives Kyle a corny thumbs-up motion. I flash a fake smile at his partner and write down my cell number. After thanking the police officer for his guidance, I race over to where Sheila and Nina are and settle into my saved seat and I start boasting about my new uniformed man. I begin describing how cute he is to them and how his pretty eyes almost put me in a trance. I went on and on about his strong arm muscles and the grip I had on him as we walked through the festival. As I speak, I can see the excitement in Sheila's face.

"Remember what your mom said, Gyps: 'Nothing is random.'"

"I know, right?" I agree.

"And remember you need to have ample 'me' time in between relationships. Your last boyfriend was a rebounder, you know."

"I know, right?" Not sure if I agree with her on Michael being a rebound boyfriend. It was more so a "for the time being" kind of relationship. Or is she talking about James?

I had a hard time dealing with my break-up from horrible James, during which time Sheila became my personal cheerleader. Reciting quotes from my mother is one of her famous strategies to pep me up, and I admire her that much more for being so concerned about my mental status. Nina used to do that for me but has since stopped. Now all she does is show envy whenever I talk about my men, like Miguel, my recent adventure in Punta Cana. Nina shows no interest in my stories, probably because she hasn't had a steady boyfriend in over a year, let alone a hot date, and look at me snagging a new candidate.

The next morning, the sun shines on my checks through the opening of the blinds and gently wakes me with its warming touch. I welcome the rays of sunshine into my home and begin my day dressing in its yellow glow. Mornings are the best time for me to hit the gym, and normally I work out alone, but last night Sheila asked me to call her and wake her up so she could join me. For some reason, I feel like wonder woman today, like anything is possible, even wearing a cape to the gym seems realistic.

"Hola, usted ha alcanzado a Sheila. Please leave a message."

"Hey Sheila, take that Spanish shit off of your answering machine." I give a little giggle. "It's leg day, and our routine is going to include sets of squats, lunges, step-ups, and dead lifts. Make sure you put something in your stomach before coming to the gym because after we push weights we'll do forty-five minutes of intense cardio." I'm talking to her answering machine because I know her lazy ass is screening her calls.

"You know how tough I like to work the legs, and I just downloaded the new Ultimate Hype CD onto my iPod for you. It's guaranteed to motivate you through the cardio session. Oh, and no ab exercises today, okay? I hate doing abs. Pick up the phone . . . Okay, just meet me at the gym, fatty."

Sheila is totally skinny, but that last comment is necessary to force an active response out of her. She'll show up for sure even if it's just to do some cardio. I hang up the phone and walk out the door ecstatic because it's leg day.

Nearly two hours later, my super workout is complete. I hop down several stairs to the locker room of the YMCA. I can hear my reminder tone on my cell phone alerting me that I have messages. I rush to check it and find that I have two voice messages and one text. The text is from Sheila trying to see if I had left for the gym. She knows I'm serious about my workouts and if she is not there at the specified time I'll start without her. The first call is from Kyle, the protector of the city. He wants to go to the park on Wednesday at 1:00 p.m. I'm so excited to hear from him so soon, and I'm impressed that he's making all of the arrangements. All I have to

do is show up. The second call is from horrible James, the loser ex-
boyfriend, saying that he misses me and would like it if we could
spend some quality time together this weekend.

Note to self: Delete that last message. I'll never go back to
James after that time he told me about a designer hiring him to assist with styling some of the models at New York's Fashion Week. I
was so excited for James getting recognized in the fashion industry,
and with my being the fashionista that I am, I begged him to let me
come too. After much pleading on my part, James gave in but he
insisted that I come only if I promised to stay out of the way and not
get mad if one of his clients needed a lot of attention.

Simply blissful, I, of course, agreed. My need to see all of the
upcoming fashions being presented far outweighed my concern
about the amount of time James and I wouldn't be spending together. I gathered all my high-end clothes and dumped them into
my trunk with the rollerblade wheels and immediately booked myself on the next flight to JFK airport. Upon arrival, I caught a taxi
to the Drake Hotel where James had a reserved luxury suite and a
key with my name attached was waiting at the front desk. In the
atrium of the room, sitting on the sofa table, was a note from James
welcoming me to NYC along with a ticket for me to attend the Miss
Sixty show that evening. I tipped the waiting bellman who stood
next to my wardrobe trunk and watched as he escorted himself out
through the French doors.

I followed behind and locked the doors, took a long, hot shower, and got dressed so that I could catch a cab over to Fifth Street
where the event was being held. I arrived early to get a sneak peek
at the behind-the-scenes setup. James was backstage arguing with
a tall modelesque figure wearing black Miss Sixty jeans with gold
zippers at the ankles and a gold metallic tank top. She was waving
some black knit material in James's face. I avoided the scene and
took a seat a few rows from the front alongside the wall. When the
show started, that same girl James had been arguing with modeled
an off-the-shoulder top with those black ankle-zip jeans I saw her in
earlier. James must have given into her demands and allowed her to
showcase what she felt was more appealing. Some assistant stylist he

was. I would have told her that I was the professional and that she needed to listen to me.

After the show had ended, I went backstage to look for James to congratulate him on getting such a prestigious show. I approached the backstage area slowly, and I heard Modelesque's voice and saw that she was back in James's face and giving praises of her own. Out of respect for the venue and not wanting to cause a scene, I paused and waited for my turn to speak to James.

"Thank you so much for choosing the knit over the tank top, James. I love how you listen to what the model wants. I'll show you how much I appreciate you tonight in my hotel room. We can take another bubble bath together."

"We certainly can, and you can tell me more of what you want then. And have housekeeping bring a fresh new robe for me; the one from last night is still damp from our Jacuzzi experiment."

I couldn't believe what I was hearing. I stomped across the end of the runway and cried out. "James!" I yelled. "You fucking liar! You fucking liar! Do not in any way ever try to contact me again. There's no way you can explain this one; you fucking liar! Fuck you!"

I didn't skip a beat and stormed down the catwalk in my new chocolate pumps. Those were the last words I verbalized to James.

After showering, I arrange to meet Sheila for lunch at Somerset Mall. We always have great conversations over lunch, and she often asks for my advice about going back to college to get her master's degree. She's growing tired of the legal assistant thing. Sometimes she'll ask for my opinion concerning her decision to move in with her boyfriend Brandon, the love of her life. She's been dating him since we graduated from college years ago, but she still can't find it in her to shack up with him. I told her a long time ago to follow her heart, even if it does lead them to live in sin.

Once the pesky task of giving our bodies nutrients has been accomplished, we will be able to concentrate on more fun and wished-for things, like going directly into shopping mode.

"Okay Gyps, we haven't had Mexican food in over a month."

"Yeah, I know you're into your culture and everything, but being that it's my turn to pay for lunch, and seeing that I'm into my culture too, we're having gourmet cheeseburgers for lunch."

"So your perpetuating the fat American?"

"I'm not fat."

"Not now, but if you keep eating burgers all the time you will be."

"Like Mexican food can't be fattening."

"Not as fattening as American food is."

"Whatever, Sheila, when it's your turn to pay then you can choose Mexican. Today it's cheeseburgers."

"At least it will be quick. I can't wait to see what's on sale."

We are eager to check out Nine West's summer sale, so after a quick lunch I leave the check along with the money and a tip on the table for our waitress. The sooner we can get out the door and into the mall, the faster I can enjoy the unique smell of leather and that wonderful scent of new clothes filling the atmosphere.

As our four-inch heels click on the ceramic tile of the mall, we acknowledge one another with a simple gesture, a good-bye wave, our signal that it is time to separate. We have different tastes in clothing and can never agree on the same stores. I like very trendy styles, and Sheila, well let's just say Sheila has a tastefully odd sense of style. She likes to mix reds with pinks, checkered with stripes, chunky gold jewelry with thin silver chains, that sort of thing, so she shops boutiques like Betsy Johnson. We do agree, however, on meeting up after each clothing store to compare our new purchases, and we also agree to do our shoe shopping together. We know to save the best for last, like dessert.

Before exiting the mall, Sheila suggests I call Kyle to confirm our rendezvous and to also ask if he would like for me to bring anything special. I listen to her advice and punch in the number on my cell phone. The phone rings twice before a husky voice answers, and I suddenly get really nervous.

"Hello."

"Hi Kyle, this is Gypsy." My voice even sounds nervous. "I got your message. Wednesday at Metro Beach sounds great," I awkwardly say.

"Good, I've been thinking about you ever since we met at Hart Plaza. I'm looking forward to seeing you again."

"Me too, I'll see you later then." I pause. He sounds nervous, too. "Would you like to bring me something? I mean would you like me to bring anything?"

"Just yourself, the boat is fully stocked with everything we'll need."

"Okay great, I'm looking forward to it." How dorky I must sound.

"I am too, and I'm glad you called."

"Okay then, talk to you later."

"Later."

"Okay, bye Kyle."

I hang up and elbow Sheila to inform her that he has a boat docked at Metro Beach. Sheila smiles and suggests that we stay at the mall to shop for new bikinis. She's full of suggestions.

"Okay, let's have a glass of wine at the Steakhouse. I need a buzz before trying on bathing suits," I say.

"Why is that? Not that I need a reason to drink."

"If I'm a little tipsy before going into the dressing room, I will be more daring in my selection. I want a sexy 'can't keep your eyes off me' suit."

"How about I get you drunk? Do you think you will be daring enough to let me pick out a swimsuit for you?"

"Sheila, for that to happen, I would have to be passed out and you would have to physically maneuver my body into one of your get-ups."

"Gyps, that's mean."

"Sorry, I like the way you dress, Sheila. I just don't like it for me, Ms. Sensitive."

"All right, Ms. Over-the-top," Sheila fires back.

"No, that's Nina. I'm more fabulous."

"Okay, Ms. Glamorous."

"I said fabulous."

"Ms. Fabulous. Now I really have a reason to drink."

After nearly four hours, we are finally leaving the mall and going our separate ways. I jump on I-75 toward downtown to meet with a few colleagues from Encompass for drinks before calling it a night, and Sheila turns off I-75 onto Route 696 in the direction of Southfield Township to spend a quiet evening with her man. The back seat of my Lexus is filled with shopping bags. I don't like putting my new clothes in the trunk because I don't want to be separated from them. I also like to be able to look through the rearview mirror when I'm on the freeway and smile at my new purchases.

Tomorrow is the big date. I already have my outfit planned, so today will be my pampering day. I even made a list:

1. Fairlane Mall
2. Mani/Pedi
3. Mustache Wax
4. Bikini Wax
5. Body Scrub
6. Massage
7. Shoe Shop

My list will take about three hours to complete. Afterward, I'll need something to take the stress off of shopping in heels whilst shopping for stilettos. Happy hour seems to be calling my name.

I called Nina to invite her to join me at the Friday's restaurant across from the mall. Nina's a buyer for the women's clothing at Hudson's department store. She orders fashion for the full-figured women, but she hopes to transfer to the junior's division by the fall. Anyway, we are going to meet around 5:00 p.m., and she better come alone.

I arrive early to get a wooden stool around the bar area near one of the many flat-screen televisions. I have on my Daisy Duke shorts today, and I prefer not to have my thighs sticking to the leather stool tops. Along with my Daisy Duke shorts, I have on a *don't bother me* printed tee. Talk about sending mixed messages.

"Hey sexy!" I call out to Nina as she enters Friday's wearing her gold silk Gucci mini-dress and matching heels.

"Hey girl, you look cute. Who did your eyebrows?" Nina always notices small changes. She's a girly girl, too. I like that about her.

"I got them done at that new Vietnamese shop in the mall."

"How much? I want to get mine arched like yours."

"I'm not sure. Here's my receipt. I indulged in every luxury they had to offer, including a head massage."

"You got a head massage? Your hair looks great!"

"It was a mess after my massage, that's why I had to stop by Strands salon before coming here."

"Who did your hair? Chris? I mean Christopher?"

"You know Christopher did, and all the new gossip came free of charge."

"Ooh, what's the latest?"

We sit talking about my day at the spa, and a gentleman to Nina's left invites himself into our conversation. He informs us that he is a massage therapist and suggests that we come to his place of business one day for a complimentary massage. I think to myself, "What kind of lame line is that?" but obviously Nina doesn't feel the same. She swings her bar stool around away from me to face the intruder and begins giggling at his every word. This irks me. We are supposed to be spending time together, not her and lame-o. I'm frustrated with Nina once again, so I turn my back to them and continue to sip on my chocolate martini. Why does she always choose men over our friendship? I down the rest of my drink and mentally fade to black, escaping the company seated next to me.

Despite being abandoned by Nina last night I woke up early and had a really good day at the gym this morning. I blasted 500 kcal in my kickboxing class, then ran two miles and walked home to take a long, hot shower before getting ready for my date with Kyle. He said he would pick me up around noon, which gives me plenty of time to primp and make certain my outfit fits my current happy mood. If my mood changes, I will have to rethink the whole what-am-I-going-to-wear process. I turn on my Bob Marley CD to keep my spirits mellow. I learned this trick from Alfred in the Bahamas.

I choose for my boating date an innocent little pale yellow sundress with green and red printed flowers and hang it fashionably over the wardrobe mirror that I got from Pottery Barn. On the chaise next to the mirror is a green pair of freshly picked espadrilles, still in the box they came in, waiting patiently. Underneath my dress, I will wear my new red Brazilian cut string bikini, which matches my new Brazilian bikini wax, also in red.

Kyle picks me up early in the afternoon like he promised and we arrive at Metro Beach and find a cozy little spot for our date. I watch as Kyle does his picnic setting-up thing. He spreads out a queen-size black duvet cover over the grass under an evergreen tree and places a huge wicker basket at one end. At the other end of the duvet, he sits a stereo system, and I can hear soft jazz resonating from the speakers. Kyle reaches for the gourmet spinach wraps he prepared this morning with fresh ingredients and places them on China plates. He then pulls two tall glasses out of the basket and fills them with ginger lemon iced tea. As he continues setting up, I take in our surroundings. We are situated near a stream by a wooded area away from the main strip but with direct access to the beach. The beach is a bit muddy, but it's still a beach. Kyle finishes setting up, and he offers a toast.

"To our first date out of many."

"To us." I blush at his confidence and take a sip of my delicious tea.

Kyle raises his glass to his mouth and draws my attention to his inviting set of lips. I'm attracted to the movement and the flutter of his tongue, and I zone out. I hear only murmurs. I can't say for sure what words are being spoken, but I can say for sure that I love his lips and I want him to continue talking just so I have a reason to stare. I wonder if he kisses as well as Michael.

I eventually tune back in to our conversation and figure out that we are discussing his upbringing in Bermuda and how much of a cultural difference it is living on an island versus in the city. I am relieved to know that he's from Bermuda and not the Bahamas. My favorite islander lives in the Bahamas, and I wouldn't want the two to meet. Alfred would be able to describe every inch of my body to Kyle if he were to ask.

"Kyle, I need to be home by eight tonight, if you don't mind. I have a flight in the morning. I have an exciting three-week trip I would hate to miss."

"Who do you work for?"

"Encompass Airlines."

"Where are you flying to?"

"My mini world trip begins in North America, obviously. Then I fly to Europe, then over to the Asia, and we finally end in Africa."

"So you're going to need plenty of rest. I can't talk you into staying longer?"

"We still have all afternoon, Kyle," I say with my hands fisted on my hips.

"I know. I'm being greedy. It was worth a try."

Kyle changes the CD on the stereo from jazz to salsa music and opens a bottle of Perrier Jouet champagne. We continue discussing our childhoods and the differences between the two, and I seem to be falling in love with Kyle with each glass of champagne. I notice Kyle is doing the same, falling for me too, as he examines the strings of my bikini poking out from under my sundress.

"Ready to take the boat out?"

"Sure, if you're ready." I really want to say, "Hell yeah, that's why I have on my new swimsuit," but I don't.

We begin packing up the duvet, the stereo, and the basket, and walk hand-in-hand to the harbor where his boat *Bermuda Dream* is docked.

"Oooh, nice boat, Kyle."

"Thanks. You can change while I untie us."

"Where is the bathroom?"

"Down below. Take a look around, and make yourself comfortable."

"Okay, I'll be right back."

I carefully step down below to the cabin area. There is a small lounge and a tiny kitchen area and a bathroom with a showerhead over the toilet. All I need to do is pull my dress off, re-apply my Mac lip gloss, and adjust the strings on my swimsuit to make sure my girls are secure in my triangle bikini top, oh and pee before returning to the salon where Kyle is positioned at the helm ready to navigate.

As we cruise St. Claire Shore's calm waters under the blue skies, the breezy air cools our hot skin. Kyle is very talkative and manages to pry information out of me that I wasn't yet ready to divulge on the first meeting, like how I love men in uniform, my favorite number is three, and that if I had a super power I wouldn't use it to save the world, instead I'd use it to walk on water because I never learned how to swim. Kyle is fun and interesting and punctual, too. He respects the fact that I have a long flight ahead of me tomorrow, so on his own he ends the cruise and guides us back to the dock without my asking. I am at home in time to get my required ten hours of beauty rest.

The season is getting listless. The long, hot days are gradually getting shorter and it seems as though summer is quite ready and willing to hand over the reins to the fall season. Three weeks have passed since I left for my world trip, and I'm back in the United States of America. It is now late August and cooler than normal, and though I miss everybody, my YMCA family, Sheila, and Nina (I miss my sisters Kat and Melody as well), I'd rather be on a warm, sunny island trying to recapture the summer. I kind of miss Kyle, too, who happens to be the first person I call upon landing.

"Hello honey, welcome home." Kyle's voice sounds happy over the phone.

"Hi handsome, what did I miss while I was roaming around three continents?"

"The question is who did you miss. Did you miss me?"

"Yes, I did miss hearing your voice. What's going on?"

"How about after you get situated, come over and have a drink with me? I'm having a barbeque."

"Absolutely. Can I bring a couple of friends?"

"Only if they are female friends. There are enough men here already."

"Okay, I gotta go. Here comes the bus."

"Call me back when you get to your car."

"Okay, I have to go. Bye."

It is 4:00 in the afternoon, but I need to nap. Kyle said the party will continue past midnight and that his other invited guests will occupy him until I got there. I immediately call Sheila to invite her and ask her to contact Nina, who I haven't heard from since that night at Friday's. The employee bus is pulling up to my stop at the terminal, so I put away my cell phone to free my hands in order to lift my heavy luggage onto the back of the bus.

On the way home from the airport, I want to finish talking to Kyle even though I don't have my Bluetooth with me for the drive. I search for my cell phone in the side pocket of my purse to call Kyle and notice that I have several messages that I received while I was gone. Three of the calls are from horrible James taking up my voice mail space that I'm tempted to erase because I don't wish to hear his voice, but I press the retrieve messages button to listen to each message anyway, ignoring my right mind. The last message that James left said it is important that he speak to me soon. Delete. Delete. Delete.

Sheila and Nina pull up to the barbeque at the very same time as I arrive and we walk into the backyard together arm in arm. Kyle's yard is full of unfamiliar faces and loud music, the smell of ribs, hot dogs, hamburgers, and sausages from the grill is saturating the evening's air. People are dancing and having a fabulous time, and like the boat, the bar is fully stocked. Kyle is bartending and stops when he spots me in my stretch denim jeans, a trendy *total airhead* printed tee with a picture of a blow dryer, and my Nine West sandals. He walks toward me as he shouts from the bar area over the loud music.

"Hey Gypsy, I'm so glad you made it. I thought I was going to have to come looking for you."

"You really missed me, huh? I'm glad because I feel a magnetic pull between us," I say as I pull him closer. He guides me back to the makeshift bar, and I pull away to introduce my friends. "Kyle, this is Sheila . . . " Sheila is wearing her spinning shoes and an odd little *take it easy* tee with a picture of a Weeping Willow tree. " . . . And Nina." Over-the-top Nina has on kitten heels and a printed tee that says *it's all about me* featuring Veronica from the Archie's comics.

"Pleased to meet you, ladies. What would you like to drink?"

I don't know what style Kyle is expressing. I'll have to go with him to the mall to chaperone next time he goes shopping.

"Both of my girls would like cosmopolitans," I proudly announce.

"Two cosmos coming up." Kyle begins mixing and shaking.

"Now that you can read minds, Gypsy, I'm sure it won't be hard to figure out what my next move will be."

Nina, in an apparent huff, spews forth her edgy words and saunters off to the grill. She's been stand-offish every since I left her at Friday's with that guy.

"I'm guessing she's mad about something, but I'm not in the mood to figure out what exactly," I say.

"She's so moody. I'll take her drink to her, Gyps," Sheila offers.

Sheila takes the two cosmos and blends into the crowd of people. Kyle grabs me in his arms and gives me a long, tight hug and kisses my full lips. I look into his deep green eyes and melt away. When we first met, his eyes were more gray than green. Now they're just beautiful. I can't take my eyes off of him, and he has a perfect set of white teeth. I hear his sexy low voice seep into my thoughts.

"Gypsy, I said how was your trip?"

"Oh great, I took lots of pictures. I'll email you the cute diva shots when I get home."

"Sweet. This is my song. Come on diva; we have got to dance to this."

He motions for his cousin Travis, who is also from Bermuda, to come and take over bartending while we go dance.

During the barbeque, Nina manages to affect Travis in the

same way that a nerdy school-age boy would be affected if the head cheerleader had kissed him on the cheek. She has him following her around like a puppy dog, which works perfectly in Nina's world; they seem to be getting well acquainted. Kyle and I, on the other hand, are so busy kissing that I don't notice how truly taken Travis has become by Nina. He asks me at one point if I think Nina is interested in him. He said he is trying to figure out if she is put off a bit because he never asked her to dance. Travis has been bartending for Kyle most of the night and never got a chance to hit the dance floor with her. Travis said Nina kept watching me and Kyle dancing and it seemed like she wanted to be out on the floor, too.

Travis is mentioning this to me now that the crowd has dwindled down and only four couples, including me and Kyle and Nina and Travis, remain. We gather into an intimate setting on the back screened-in porch with candles as our only source of light. The two other couples mingle with each other against the rear of the porch. Travis sits by Kyle on the sofa, and Nina and I stand close by, whispering about the guys. I think Sheila left a while ago when I was on the dance floor with Kyle. She said something about work and getting home because Brandon was coming over to spend the night.

"Sit down, ladies," Kyle politely orders.

"Don't mind if I do," Nina responds.

Taking the lead, Nina sits on not Travis' lap but Kyle's lap. Surprised by her actions, Kyle quickly moves her to the side and stands up to excuse himself.

"Girl, what's wrong with you!" My tone is firm. "Why would you do that?"

"Sorry." Nina's tone is unapologetic.

"Yeah, you are sorry Nina."

I follow Kyle off of the porch and into the yard where he is leaning against the car.

"Gypsy, you want to go to Bermuda with me?"

"Hell yeah!" This time I say the words out loud.

"What's up with your girl?" Kyle looks hopeless. "My cousin really liked her."

"I don't know what her problem is," I respond. "But I need to get home to my loft. I'm jet-lagged from the trip and don't have the energy to deal with her drama."

"Okay honey, call me and let me know you made it home safely." Kyle kisses me good-bye. "What about your girlfriend?"

"What about her?"

Kyle and I have been dating for a month, and now that his vacation is coming up soon, I am excited and thrilled to be the one invited. Knowing that he only wants to spend his precious vacation with me, I'm not threatened one bit by Nina's moody ass. I unlock my door, hop in the car, and leave her at the party. I can't wait to I get home to my bed. Tonight I will sleep for twelve hours straight. My body will probably take over a week to get back on Eastern Daylight Time.

In exactly one week, I will be in Bermuda, and thankfully I have the rest of the month off. I worked that Europe/Asia/Africa world trip so I have a lot of work hours already in. I have been pre-shopping, washing clothes, house cleaning, getting groomed, and post-shopping for this getaway for over two weeks. I am fully prepared to go to Fantasy Island and stay for a month if I have to. I'm so excited, soon I will be spending seven wonderful days in a deserted house with my new boyfriend. Kyle said we will stay on his family's property while they're away for the summer. This is going to be such a fantastic trip, having my own personal tour guide to show me all of the nooks and crannies the average tourist wouldn't get to see. I can't wait to leave for Bermuda, but first I need to call Sheila and have her meet me at the mall. I desperately need island clothes and a new black bikini to showcase my superstar shape. I've been hitting the gym extra hard lately, and I'm starting to see a hint of a four pack. Sweet.

My phone is purring, and I look at the caller ID. It's horrible James calling again, and I'm going to answer it this time so he can stop bugging me.

"Hello."

"Hey baby, I really miss you."

"Hey baby?"

"I'm sorry for what happened during Fashion Week in NYC. I didn't know Natalie was modeling the Miss Sixty line."

"Natalie?"

"Yeah Natalie, I didn't know she would be there."

"Oh please, you know who's modeling what before the fashion show is even announced. I don't want to hear that fiction anymore horri . . . um, James. Dang, what's the point of this call?" I cannot tolerate anymore of his lame excuses.

"Baby, it was all innocent. She asked me to come to her room. She couldn't get the Jacuzzi to operate properly."

"Well Nat-ta-lie could have called maintenance if she was having plumbing problems, James. I'm hanging up."

"Wait. I wanted to tell about your friend Nina. She called shortly after our breakup while you were in Haiti."

"Pfft. Dominican Republic. I'm listening."

"She told me that she had always found me interesting and wanted to know how I felt about her." He finally informs me. "The girl was way out of line."

WTF? The one thing about James is that he never liked Nina and only tolerated her because she was my friend. Or so I thought.

"Not to worry," horrible continues, "I told Nina to go to hell."

"Well good for you, James, but you should have also used that phrase on Natalie. I'll credit that to your 'concern for Gypsy' account anyway. You've earned it." I hang up the phone on James. I so didn't need to know modelesque's name. Natalie, great.

Though I'm not surprised by Nina's actions, I am hurt by the information. Nina seems to view me as competition. I know how she is, and subconsciously I have always kept her at a safe distance. Even back in the day when we would ride around on our Huffy bikes, I always knew she would turn out to be just like her mother, a home wrecker, and I don't expect her to change her ways.

When we were growing up, Melody and I had to sneak off on our bikes to other neighborhoods for adventure. We knew not to ask our parents because they would never allow us to go, but Nina's mother always gave Nina permission to come along. Her mom, Ms. Walters, would wait until we left for our bike ride, and then when she knew my dad was home alone she'd change into her shortest skirt and high-heeled shoes just to walk down the street to our house, supposedly to notify Dad out of concern for us about our whereabouts. She wanted to make sure she had total access to Dad. My dad was loyal to Mom, and he told her each time this happened with Nina's mother, and Mom, being the daughter of the universe, simply stated, "What goes around comes around." She was never threatened by that woman.

Man, this Bermuda trip can't come around soon enough. I need a break from this James/Nina calamity.

On the eve of our vacation, I'm staying at Kyle's house so we can spend our first overnight together. We decide to go to bed early and try to get used to each other's sleep habits. I need to know if this man snores, has night terrors, or is possibly a spooner. Oh, please let him be a spooner. I love when a man holds me in his arms all night long and protects me from the evil spirits of the night.

Come early Sunday, I am awakened by the sound of birds and the next-door neighbor mowing his lawn at 6:30. Who gets up this early to cut grass? I don't even get up this early to go to the mall, but only because the malls aren't open yet. Kyle is already up preparing breakfast. I informed Kyle last night that I'm usually a little cranky before my morning coffee, and I told him that I don't like talking first thing in the morning. I gave him a clear warning, and he still insists on greeting me this morning, wearing his tighty whities, with a pleasant smile and a "good morning honey" pre-conversation starter, holding a hot cup of Joe with two sugars and lots of cream. He's even bringing me the *USA Today* to read while he cooks breakfast.

"I'm making banana pancakes and eggs with turkey sausage. You're having breakfast in bed today, honey." He pauses for a response before walking out.

I manage a faint smile to acknowledge his efforts, but I don't say a word to him. Kyle will eventually get used to my early morning lack of social skills or concede to cooking breakfast every morning only to receive a plastered-on smile. I'm not as evil this morning, and how could I be when he's being so accommodating.

After breakfast, I check the digital clock on the bedroom wall. Our flight leaves in three hours, and slow-poke Kyle still hasn't washed his clothes. I get up to start cleaning the kitchen and tell Kyle to go ahead and put a load in the washer and start packing. I have ulterior motives for getting Kyle out of view. Once he's in the basement, it will give me the opportunity to learn more about my guy and his housekeeping secrets. It won't be a full-on investigation just yet. I'll start by looking around and exploring his medicine cabinet first to make sure there are no empty Valtrex or Penicillin prescription bottles lurking about, and then sneak in his closet to see if any of his exes left clothing behind that needs to be thrown out. Maybe I'll even check his file cabinet for credit reports to see if he has ever filed for bankruptcy. Bad credit can't be overlooked. If we were ever to marry and look for a new home, all of the financial responsibility would fall on me.

The morning is advancing along quickly, and we need to leave the house to arrive at Metro Airport one hour prior to departure as advised by the airlines. Duty-free shopping is also a must because everything in Bermuda is expensive, and if we get there early enough, we can stop in and purchase some liquor for the trip and get new reading material and snacks for our flight.

Inside the airport, I hear the Encompass agents paging us to our gate over the public announcement system. We have only been browsing the shops for twenty-something minutes and already we're being forced to board the plane. What is the deal with international flights? I did express to Kyle this morning how important it was for me to have extra time to shop, but apparently I didn't manage to make my point clear. Angry about the mis-management of time, I gather my one magazine, and we frantically run to board the plane. The flight attendant checks our boarding passes, and Kyle and I settle into our coach cabin seats. I'm seated by the window, and Kyle is on the aisle, and there is an empty seat between us. I made sure to grab a pillow and blanket because I'm so tired and as soon as we depart I'm going to recline my seat and go back to sleep, six miles up, away from the birds and lawn mowers.

After three hours of flying, in which I sleep through two of them, we land in Bermuda to sunny skies and ninety-five degrees of pure bliss. Travis meets us at the passenger pickup area, and he pulls up in his four-door Jeep. He is looking as though he has just left the beach, wearing loose Bermuda shorts, a beater tank top, and plastic thong sandals, jellies. He had flown home soon after the backyard barbecue and has since settled back into island living.

"Welcome back, cuz." Travis man-hugs Kyle and gives me a gentle squeeze. "Good to see you again, beautiful lady."

"Man, it feels good coming home. I need to schedule more days off to keep my sanity." Kyle jokes with his cousin while I volunteer to ride in the backseat.

"It may be too late for that, cuz. How is Nina doing, Gypsy?"

The boys start laughing, and I make a mental note to remember to ask Kyle what is so funny about that comment. I get the feeling that Nina must have done something more to embarrass herself that night at the barbeque after I left.

We drive along the ocean side toward the family home and up the winding road on the opposite side of the street. Travis' driving doesn't scare me, but I keep looking in the other direction for traffic anyhow. This driving on the wrong side of the street is going to take some getting used to. We pull up to a two-story peach home with an attached guesthouse, and I assume that this guesthouse will be our temporary living quarters during our stay. Kyle gives a sigh of relief and opens the Jeep door to gather our luggage from the trunk and carry it into the home.

"Make yourself at home, Gypsy. The bar should be stocked," Kyle says as he places the luggage on the marble floor.

"Why do you keep saying that, 'the bar is stocked'? Do you think I'm an alcoholic or something? You're constantly telling me 'the bar is stocked, Gypsy.'"

"That's my first time saying it. Do you have a guilty conscience?"

"No, that's the second time." I think for a minute. "Yeah, twice you've done that."

"Here, drink this. It should help you relax." Kyle hands me a bottle of Guinness from the refrigerator.

"Thanks."

I smile and happily take the beer from him and begin to sip the contents and unpack my bags in search of my two-piece bathing suit to change into. Kyle shakes his head and steps out back to assist Travis, who is firing up the grill and listening to reggae music.

Inside of the guesthouse, I am captivated by the glass sliding doors surrounding the living area. The kitchen is open and faces the living room/bedroom, and off to the right is a full bathroom with a walk-in shower. This setting is flawless, and it's romantic enough for our first anticipated love-making session to begin. Heck, it's romantic enough for a honeymoon.

As night falls, the stars fill the sky and dance with wondrous charm. Kyle and I watch with fondness as we caress and explore each other with the love sickness of newlyweds. I can feel Kyle's breath on my neck as he speaks in his ultra-masculine voice, instructing me to follow him to the outdoor hot tub.

Kyle strips off his swim trunks, and his manfulness extends as he submerges into the humid Jacuzzi where he sits and waits for me, the weaker vessel, to follow. I descend into the water and graze Kyle's thickness as I lower myself onto his lap, facing him. I look into his green eyes that are full of eroticism and allow my tenderness to meet his firmness, separated only by the fabric of my bikini. Kyle pulls the string on my triangle top to expose my full breasts that are waiting for his affection. He sucks and licks my nipples with the appetite of a hungry tiger, and I give him my undivided attention. The sensation I receive from Kyle's experienced tongue is delightful. My breathing increases as he moves my bikini bottom to the side and slides inside of me with manly vigor. His tongue continues to titillate my protruding hard nipples while his thrusts push deeper into my soft, sensuous inner being. I am completely sexed and in a state of aphrodisiac. I whisper in his ear to announce my devotion to him and detonate with what seems like the force of a tsunami. Kyle holds me tightly as we sit, spasmatic, clutched in each other's arms.

The following morning, I'm awakened by the smell of coffee brewing, and as my eyes focus, I see my satisfied man standing over me in a superman stance with his tighty whities on.

"Today is a happy day," Kyle recites in an announcer's voice, "fresh fruit and toast with peanut butter is waiting for you at the table out on the deck."

"What are we going to do today?"

"You will have to wait and see, honey," Kyle answers while maintaining his character.

"Oh, please give me a hint," I plead in a kindergarten way.

"Come with me, dear. You will not be disappointed."

"Aren't you going to put some clothes on first?"

"No, we are all alone. No worries honey."

"Naked breakfast, I'm in."

Kyle and I watch the news over breakfast, and he tells me a little bit about our day ahead, and once again he has everything planned. We will hop on the motorbike and ride alongside the pink sand beaches into town to tour an old cave, and then ride to the highest point of the island to have an intimate lunch on the hill. Later we plan on meeting up with a few of his childhood friends for drinks, and after that we get to come back home to pick up where we left off last night, only this time it will be raining outside and I anticipate the warm gentle drops accentuating our yearning desire and adding extra lubricant to our love making. I hope the time passes away swiftly.

On this third day of our vacation, I find Kyle contemplating deeply and staring off into space during the early morning hours. He has been complaining about his job a lot lately and how difficult it is for him to go to work with a positive attitude. Kyle drives the patrol car in the poorest section of the city, and each time he's called to a scene, it is always a negative experience. On this particular morning, I crawl to the edge of the bed where Kyle is seated hunched over and try to get him to talk about his feelings. I probe until he gives in.

"Sometimes I feel suicidal," Kyle hypnotically speaks. "Sometimes I would like to be the villain and terrorize instead of being the savior." He's looking into my eyes, but he doesn't seem to see me. "Sometimes the idea of intimidating and threatening others pleases some deep parts of my soul."

Oh my God, what? I look back into his dark, smoky gray eyes in search for the caring, gentle Kyle, but I don't see him. "Sometimes people should seek professional help," my mind whispers in response to Kyle's crazy talk.

This man clearly needs to take the police department up on its offer for free counseling. He has experienced too much tragedy during his career, and I am concerned about his mental health. I'm going to take the liberty and suggest that he consider the department's help. Well, after his eyes lighten back up, I'll suggest that he seek help. His behavior is too odd and unpredictable for me to bring it up now.

Kyle's dramatic mood swings continue sporadically for the rest of our vacation, which makes for intense days and extremely passionate nights, and though the airplane ride home is quiet, our connection remains strong. I keep a watchful eye on Kyle while he sleeps, and I have come to the conclusion that his fragile reasoning struggles with his strong rationale in an attempt to find balance. I studied these types of behavior problems in my psych class at Madonna University, and I will continue to analyze Kyle during the remainder of the plane ride home, taking notes. Maybe I'll be able to get him to expand his consciousness and help him evolve into a better person spiritually.

Back home the weather is starting to shift as we begin to embrace the fall season. Things are almost back to normal, and Kyle seems to have gained some benefit from the Bermuda trip and from my amateur counseling. He comes home from work every day in a bad mood, but I always manage to cheer him up. I'm feeling confident enough to leave and take that two-week trip to China that had become available while I was in Bermuda. Scheduling called me and left a message to call back if I was interested in accepting the trip. I'm one of the few flight attendants who have a Chinese visa, and they saved a space for me hoping I accept as I always have in the past.

I try talking to Kyle about going to China, but he doesn't believe it's a good idea for me to leave for such a long time. In fact, he is having a fit. I have become his refuge, and he feels that he may falter if I'm not around to console him after he has had a brutal workday. I'm so good at this psychotherapy thing. I was able to assure Kyle that he will be just fine while I'm gone. Matter of fact, it was so easy to persuade Kyle that I should consider changing my name to Dr. Sike, the psychiatrist. I say whatever needs to be said to get away from this new clingy Kyle that has surfaced since Bermuda, in order to go to the mall and do a little shopping for my trip before the stores close. I have to be aggressive and deter Kyle's whimpering. I don't have much time to prepare for the China trip, but I know anything I do forget to buy in the States, I can purchase there in Asia where they have authentic "made in China" items.

My two-week China trip ends earlier than expected because the wealthy businessman who reserved our aircraft for fourteen days finished his business in just ten days and wanted to return to the States. This is good news to me because we still are paid the full contract amount, not that I can count on seeing any of the money I made from working in my next paycheck. They had so many great deals in Beijing that I felt like I was a buyer for a big chain department store buying up all the goods in China and shipping them to the U.S., and not only do we get home early with more days off, I also get to sleep in my own bed tonight. Yay!

I call Kyle as soon as we land on American soil to surprise him. When he answers the phone, he seems a bit unnerved and he asks if I can come right over before going home so we can talk. I finally have him to the point where he's asking to talk instead of my forcing him to share his feelings. I must be doing a great job psychoanalyzing him. When I get to Kyle's house, I find him sitting on the porch in his tighty whities. He appears frightened as he sits me down on the step to explain.

"What's wrong, Kyle?"

"I was reported to Internal Affairs while you were working in China. I had an, uhh, a misunderstanding with a few young adult males during a raid at an apartment complex on the east side of town."

His eyes are dark again, and I don't want anyone to overhear what it is he may say.

"It's a little chilly out here, Kyle. Mind if we go inside?" I coax Kyle into the house, and he continues his interpretation of the events.

"My partner and I were called to the scene where three men tried to flee but we—uhh—managed to uhh—apprehend and take them to the precinct—uhh—hours later to be processed."

"What do you mean 'hours later'? You know what, never mind."

His ambiguous translation makes me want to probe for clarity, but I decide not to after the flashback I have from that early morning in Bermuda.

"Uhh, my partner Mike wanted to uhh . . ."

Kyle's long-winded explanation has my mind drifting off and looking around the family room. On the sofa table, I notice a book titled *The Faces of Death*. As I sit listening to Kyle, I find myself interested about the book's contents. I refrain from reaching for it because I need to focus on Kyle and hear him out, let him vent before I tell him that I desperately need to sleep. He gets so upset when he thinks I don't care about his situations. It's getting hard for me to keep my eyes open. I have been flying for sixteen hours non-stop, and it's having a negative effect on my alertness, or lack of. I let Kyle rant for a few more minutes, and when he is finished and his eyes are slightly lighter, I subtly remove the book from the table and have him follow me upstairs.

Kyle and his partner Mike may get a week of suspension with pay for not following regulation, but other than that their jobs are protected. He's stressing over nothing, really.

I take off my blouse and skirt and lay them across the chair and toss *The Faces of Death* under the bed before climbing onto Kyle's king-size mattress. All is well.

Umm, I love his scent. When I first walked into the room, I could smell his cologne, but lying on his sheets and resting my head on his pillow I can smell his natural aroma, a clean manly musk. Peacefully, I doze off, engulfed in Kyleness, and dream of our days spent in Bermuda.

Mid-nap I am awakened by the sound of a loud lawnmower and the eerie presence of my man standing over me in that same Bermuda superman stance, though this time is different. A storm is brewing, and Kyle is in the midst of it. His eyes are smoky gray and full of intense darkness. The evil exuding from his core is coloring his aura a deep purple.

"Get up and leave!" Kyle demands.

"What? Pfft. Okay."

I am shocked, but I don't have questions. Instead, I quiet my mind like how I do on my layovers, or how in the early mornings when I wake up I'm silent. I'm just reacting to his words right now, not saying a word. I look over at the La-Z-Boy chair where I laid my clothes and follow his orders. I reach for my skirt and blouse and attempt to put them on so that I may leave without anymore confrontation.

"No, leave the clothes behind and walk out the door!" Kyle grabs my arm as his voice intensifies.

"What's wrong with you?"

I snatch my arm away and stare at his contoured face and decide that now is not the time for talking. I grab a shirt of his off of the floor and descend the stairs to escape.

"Leave without any clothing, now!" he commands and snatches the shirt away, too.

I cross my arms to cover my breasts and back down the last of the stairs, refusing to say a word. I reach the landing and grab my keys from the kitchen counter and exit the side door, slamming it shut behind me.

"Crazy fool!" I yell after jumping naked into the sanctity of my Lexus GS350 parked on the side of the house and backing out of the driveway. I drive a couple of blocks before pulling over to get my luggage from the China trip out of the backseat, no telling what this bi-polar cop may be thinking. He may feel suicidal again and decide to race behind my car in his gay tighty whities. If he runs and jumps on the hood to attack me, that would scare the hell out of me, like the movie *The Shining* did.

I make sure I am far enough away from his house before stopping to put on some clothing. I know you're not supposed to call a crazy person *crazy* to their face, but there are no other words for his behavior. Well, *manic* will suit him, but that's why I kept my mouth shut. *Manic-depressed crazy fool* would have been the next words to come out of my mouth, and that probably would have enraged him even more. My mind is all over the place. We didn't explore the manic-depressed crazy fool chapter in psych class thoroughly enough. What the hell do I do now? I put the car in gear and reach for my purse in the backseat to take out my cell phone. It's illegal to talk on a cell phone and drive in Michigan, and I forgot my ear piece at home, but who's going to catch and ticket me? Kyle? I don't think so. I call Sheila, and she suggests I go directly to police headquarters to make a report.

It is nearly 10:00 p.m. when I pull up to the police station. I park my car on Clinton Street and use the main entrance. Inside of the station is nice and peaceful. A young rookie seated near the front desk gets up and asks if he can help me. He is tall with curly hair and light eyes, just like Kyle. Instead, I bypass him and approach the female officer who is standing behind the front desk.

"I need to file an incident report, please." I make eye contact with the middle-aged woman. "It's against a police officer."

"Just one moment, ma'am. I need to consult with the sergeant." The officer appears caught off guard and unsure of what to do. I watch as she disappears through a set of stainless steel doors, leaving me alone with the rookie. I don't dare take my eyes off those silver doors because I can feel him staring at me and giving me the stink eye. The nerve I must have for reporting one of his fellow officers, or maybe he's thinking of how sexy I look in my new white linen pant suit that I got from China. Of course he doesn't know it came from China, but if he is looking at my outfit, he has a good fashion sense. He's wondering about something because my ears are burning. Or is that when someone is speaking badly of you?

Just as I raise my head to see what his expression tells me, the female officer propels through the stainless steel doors and hands me a stack of papers.

"Here ma'am. You can fill these out, but you will need to take them over to Park Street in the morning when Internal Affairs is open."

"Thank you, thank you very much." I grab the papers and turn around quickly without making any further eye contact.

The next morning after my one-hour workout, I make plans with Sheila to accompany me to Internal Affairs. I'm not sure of what to report, but I know I must inform them of the bomb they have in the department set to explode. I arrive at IA with Sheila by my side. I sign in at the front desk and sit patiently in the lobby waiting for someone to come and interview me and take my statement. Sheila uses this opportunity to plead Nina's case.

"I know you're angry with her, but you two need to talk. She is really sorry, Gypsy." Sheila wipes a silky curl from her forehead and places it behind her ear.

"I know she's sorry!" I reply sarcastically. "I'll call when I'm ready to deal with another one of her performances."

"Gypsy, she's always been dramatic. Remember the time . . ."

"Hello ladies, I'm Lieutenant Booth. Which one of you is Ms. Moon?" The gentleman walks up from behind and is a welcome interruption.

"Hi sir, I'm Gypsy Moon." I rise from my seat and look down at Sheila. "We'll have to continue this conversation later."

Damn, a cutie with authority in a suit, and his eyes seem pleased as I stand up wearing my ultra-feminine soft pink Guilty Pleasures dress that I got from Century 21 in New York. I was going to buy the blue one but pink is my favorite.

"Follow me, ma'am." He turns to Sheila. "The process will

take about a half-hour to forty minutes. You can relax in the cafeteria on the lower level, and try the coffee. It's good."

A man in control, I like that. I follow behind Lieutenant Booth down a long dull orange carpeted hallway, and we enter a white conference room with an old lacquered formal dining table and six mis-matched chairs. I smooth out the invisible wrinkles of my dress and sit down on the edge of my seat to begin giving the detailed answers to Lieutenant Booth's questions about last night's tragedy.

The process flies by too fast as I was beginning to enjoy watching the lieutenant's muscles shift around in his tailored jacket and loose-fitting slacks. He moves around the cold room with deserving arrogance as he interrogates me, warming my senses with the smell of his freshly showered body. Lieutenant Booth wraps up our meeting without so much as a hint of interest in me and walks me back down the hallway, guiding me by the waist toward the cafeteria where I am reunited with Sheila.

"I just got off the phone with Nina, and she wants to be there for you, Gypsy. Please talk to her."

"Okay, girl, dang. Call her back and tell her to meet us downtown at Seldom Blues in the GM Building and tell her not to bring the drama."

"Thank you, Gypsy. I'll call and reserve a table near the window so we can take in the beautiful view of the river and have a few martinis."

"You need to remind her not to revisit that night at Kyle's barbeque."

"Okay, I'll tell her not to bring it up."

"Good, also tell her that I will try to reason with her unreasonable ass later, not now. Now I just want to not think."

"Noted. So did he hit on you?"

"Who, the lieutenant? No, can you believe it, and I have on my shiny new dress."

"Oh well, you didn't need another cop in your life anyhow."

"Yeah, right."

Over the next couple of weeks, Nina and I smooth out our

----

friendship, and now that we are back on track, Sheila, Nina, and I resume our rollerblading adventures at Metro Beach. I haven't been back to Metro Beach since Kyle took me on that first-date boat ride. I feel somewhat nervous about visiting the park, but I am ready to face this final stage of letting go and completely moving on. It has been six and a half months since that incident with Kyle, and in my attempts to get over him, I have changed my mailing address to a P.O. box, I changed my phone number to an unpublished one, and even I changed my hair color—I have blond highlights now. I still work for the airlines though. I can't change every aspect of my life, right?

The park is calm. Most of the people are at work this early in the day, and I feel we have to take advantage of this opportunity. The girls came to pick me up early before I had a chance to run over to the downtown YMCA for a quick workout, so rollerblading will have to be my cardio substitute for today, and later I'm going to demand that we go swimming (with a life vest on, of course, if that's possible) for an extra calorie burn. I need to boost my metabolism a little.

We strap our rollerblades on tight. I plug my ears with my iPod, and we blast off to rollerblade the length of the five-mile trail. I'm leading in my new Nike dry-fit bike shorts, the one that's featured on the cover of this month's *Shape* magazine, and my lazy girlfriends are trying to keep up. Sheila has on her non-descript direct-to-the-clearance rack biking outfit, and Nina is a head turner in her hot pink bikini with matching sarong. They are talking of course and leisurely skating, but not me. I have work to do, many calories to burn. I'm ahead of them by far and heading toward the beach to prepare for the swim portion of this bi-athelon.

Sheila and Nina are finally making their way to the end of the trail in no apparent rush. I watch them as they begin to change out of their blades and into flip-flops in order to walk through the sand. I wait at the edge of the walkway, tapping my right foot on the asphalt and keeping a stern face. On the way to the beach, I point out to Sheila where Kyle's boat, *Bermuda Dream*, is normally docked, but the well is now empty. We continue walking to the beach area, and Nina mentions something about wanting to catch some rays and check out the scenery instead of going swimming. Lazy ass Nina, I knew she was going to try and switch our plans around. She always manages to change our plans.

We begin to set up our towels on the beach chairs when I look up and spot Kyle walking in a security uniform in the parking lot.

"Oh, damn," I say, wearing a shocked expression.

"What?" Nina asks.

"Nothing, I thought I left my purse."

I figure Nina's only concern is that I don't forget my sunscreen. She has eczema, and I usually provide the sunscreen, so I quickly change gears and regain my relaxed facial expression. I'm in pursuit of a getaway and decide to make up a little white lie to assist in my retreat.

"You guys, I have to use the restroom. Do you want anything back from the snack stand?"

"Yes, bring me back a hot dog, please." Sheila peeks over her sunglasses.

"Nina, anything for you?"

"No thanks, I know you're just going because you saw Kyle in the lot."

I told you, Nina always notices small changes. Anyway, I am still vexed after nearly seven months, so I walk away from our lounge chairs and prance over to Kyle in hopes of gaining true closure.

"Hey Gypsy, is that you? You cut your hair."

"Yeah, I got new highlights too. Can we talk, Kyle?" I scratch my head.

"I'm so glad to see you."

"You too. There are benches over there."

"You look really good. Still working out?"

"Yes, it's a lifestyle for me. You know that."

"It shows."

As though nothing ever happened, the gentle Kyle I once knew has resurfaced. We sit on a park bench near the snack stand and talk about that dreaded evening.

"What's going on with you these days? Other than . . ." I point at his uniform.

"You mean after we broke up?"

"Well yeah. If you want to call it that."

"I was feeling lost. I was drowning, and getting fired was the life raft that saved me. You saved me, Gypsy."

"Glad to be of help."

"I couldn't handle the pressures of police work, but I didn't want to disappoint my dad. You know, he retired from the police force."

"Yeah, I remember."

"This job is only part-time. I have a full-time job as a chef at the Westin in Southfield."

"So, how are you . . . mentally?" I hesitate a bit with the wording.

"I took an anger management course to learn how to deal with a few issues."

"Anger management? They didn't put you on any mind altering medication or drugs of any kind?"

"What are you trying to suggest?" He chuckles.

"Not suggesting, I'm thinking the episode I was watching went way beyond anger."

"Well, thank you for taking such a forceful step and reporting the incident to Internal Affairs. It saved my life."

"You're welcome. No drugs, huh?" I fake smile.

"No drugs." Kyle reaches for a hug.

I hesitate again before embracing him. "Well, I'm glad you're better."

"Can I call you sometime?"

"Sure, you have my number." I stand up and wave good-bye before walking away.

I return to the beach area with a chocolate/vanilla swirl ice-cream cone, a pleasant disposition, and a hot dog for Sheila who is putting her hair in a ponytail. She looks up at me from her chair and notices a difference immediately.

"Don't ask. I will fill you in later. Right now it's girl time!" I flop down, reclaiming my position on the middle chair. Sheila and I lie back and begin people watching and cracking jokes. Nina is lying on her stomach getting some sun and periodically looking up to see the characters we are talking about as they pass by our lounging chairs. We stay at the beach past dusk making plans for a girls-only island vacation and deciding on where to stay. This will be a fun-filled GNO trip, no boyfriend issues, no girlfriend drama, and no mood swings allowed!

CHAPTER 8

Wisdom in the NBA

I absolutely love basketball, which is one of the reasons why I continue to fly for Encompass Airlines, that and all of the other high-profile clients Encompass has contracts with who rent our planes and fly to remote locations. I'm hoping I'll even find an agent on one of my flights to represent me and offer me a lucrative contract. I do aspire to be a soap opera diva one day like Susan Lucci from *All My Children*. She has a fab-paying job with just the right amount of celebrity. I want to be able to shop without interference from the paparazzi trying to snap my picture while I'm trying on clothes. Until any of my magical thinking comes to life, I need to keep my current paying job; that's why I'm rushing to gate A36 to meet with the three other charter girls (flight attendants) waiting for me to board the flight.

I'm rarely ever late to the airport, but I had to make an emergency stop at Electric Ladyland to see if my extensible stretch denim jeans I ordered last week had been delivered to the store. Well, actually, I stopped by the Internet cafe on Telegraph and visited Electric

Ladyland's website after receiving a text message on my cell from the sales lady. These *must-have* jeans are of extreme importance. I need them in case I get invited to another one of Summer's marvelous stiletto parties in Atlanta on my layover. The store is located all the way in Arizona, which means I will have to jump on a Delta flight to Scottsdale, pick up my jeans from the denim bar, and get back to Atlanta in time to participate in the bizarre drama that seems to unfold at the hottest nightclubs in Georgia. The jeans are *so* worth my making the trip.

I'm running behind schedule, and these high-profile people are going to have a hissy fit. They feel the flight has to depart on time. The pro teams are so superstitious, like if the flight is delayed the plane will mysteriously drop out of the sky, such scaredy cats. The most dangerous parts of the flight are take-off and landing, not the cruising stage, except for the danger of a mid-air collision, but that hasn't happened in years.

Okay, so I'm fifteen minutes late, and to my surprise the crew doesn't seem angry, but why should they be? We are the chosen non-fraternizing few who get to travel the U.S. flying dozens of young millionaires around from one game to the next. Such fun. I wouldn't get mad if a crew member was late to the aircraft either, especially if that crew member was wearing the new Mark Jacobs pumps like I'm wearing.

I do enjoy meeting the players during the season, *and* I have managed to keep a reasonable distance from them, except for this one time when I fell victim to Wisdom "Wyse" Jones, a 6' 3" point guard for the Denver Nuggets. Wyse has been pursuing me for months, trying his player's game on me. I have never given into his smooth talk until now.

Okay, so I'm scheduled to work flight #313 departing out of Detroit en route to Atlanta at 4:00 p.m. This trip is so cool, mostly because the Nuggets are one of my favorite teams. Well no, mostly because they give their tickets away, which makes them my favorite team, and when I get a seat on the floor, I call Kat to have her record the game so I can see myself on TV. I know I'll get discovered one day when the cameraman pans the stands and zooms in on me like how it happened for Pamela Anderson. Oooh and maybe I, too, will get my own private detective show. The only problem is I don't have a sexy tee advertising some brand of beer printed across the chest in my luggage. Humph, should always keep one of those packed.

Our pilots inform us that the Nuggets have won the game, beating the Pistons 89 to 84, and the starters are finishing up their interview with Channel 7 news and are now headed for the locker room to shower. The captain said the bus should be leaving the arena for the airport in thirty minutes. I'm glad I made it here before the players' arrival because the four of us charter girls need to prepare the airplane and set up the club seating tables with all the special amenities requested by the team for the trip to the Atlanta. It's easy enough to score tickets to the game from the guys if they lose, but when they are winning and in a good mood they give up the all-access passes, too. I once saw Steven Spielberg backstage, but this was before I decided I wanted to act. Talk about missed opportunities.

"Gypsy, I need a fruit tray in the coaches' section!" Becky, a tall, thin, and attractive blonde, yells from the middle of the aircraft.

"I'll bring it to you after I finish setting up the buffet in the players' section!" I yell back.

"Gyps, can you please speed it up? I'm going to need extra time to do my makeup and change out of this regulation uniform skirt suit and into my shorter, tailored uniform dress." Becky hikes up her skirt and poses.

"Well, then I suggest you get it yourself, Ms. Sassy." It's easier to yell than to actually pick up the interphone, wait for a flight attendant to answer, and then speak your request. Plus it's faster.

The specially configured airplane has three sections:

1. The players' section is located in the front of the aircraft. The rows are five feet apart with lots of room for the players to stretch out their freakishly long legs. One would surmise the players would love the extra space, but a couple of guys use it for bag stowage. (Hey guys, luggage must be stowed in the overhead bins!)

2. The coaches' section is designed with a flat-screen TV monitor and is equipped with a DVD player for the coaches to replay the game or study the style of the players for the upcoming game. We once witnessed a player putting a porn tape into the video system. When the coach went to press play and a close-up of genitals came in view, the coaching staff got an eyeful and that poor actress in the movie got a mouthful. Yuck!

3. The media section is in the back and includes the most demanding people on the sixty-seat airplane.

Encompass supplies the team with a huge buffet loaded with tons of snacks, chips, candy bars, licorice, chocolate ice cream, and various beverages, just a few carbs to satisfy the players until we take off. I stuff a few candy bars into my flight bag before the players get on because I know I'm going to wake up in the middle of the night hungry, craving chocolate and salt. Normally I'd take a sleeping pill, but I ran out of them yesterday and I'll need something to munch on when my eyes pop open from the lack of a sleep aide in my system. After we get in the air, we will be able to offer the players hot meals to fill their bellies. Most of them eat before coming to the airport and refuse our crappy entree. It seems no one wants to eat airplane food anymore, even if it is an upgraded meal selection.

"Hey Becky, have you seen the flexible straws?" I have a hint of sarcasm in my voice.

"Julie put them on the players' table, next to the Fiji water. Oh, and Gyps, make sure she placed the *Fiji* and not the Evian water there." More sarcasm, except Becky smiles when she's being a smart ass, kind of like diet sarcasm.

"Okay, gather together. I have to make sure all of the flight attendants are onboard," the heavy-set pilot abruptly chimes in, "Julie, Gypsy, Becky, and Rita. Correct?" The pilot concludes as he eyes my curvy figure.

"Right," I manage to reply without his detecting my extreme annoyance.

"The team's bus is on airport property. They should be here any minute now," heavy-set informs us.

Becky and I will work the A and B sections of the aircraft (players and coaches) while Rita and Julie will serve the media section (the misfits).

"Becky, did you bring your Cool Water perfume? I left mine at home." Wyse Jones loves the smell of Cool Water for Women. He said it smells better on me than anyone else, and I enjoy the detailed attention he showers me with.

"No, I only have my Paris Hilton." Becky avoids eye contact and hands me the pink bottle. She expects that I have a "what the hell made you buy Paris Hilton cologne?" look on my face.

"Umm, this smells really good." I am surprised. "Okay, it's show time! Smile girls. Smile."

Wyse is the first to enplane, always eager to get some alone time with me before the other players board, slipping me little notes, asking me to listen to some new R&B music on his video iPod, showing me pictures of his big-boy toys, and smelling me. He walks into the galley behind me and hovers as I remove the dry ice from the Dove ice-cream bars. I smell his Cool Water for Men, my fave, so I don't need to turn around to identify him. Plus I am afraid that if I do, I would look into those lovely brown eyes and get swallowed into his web. I don't know what it is on this day out of the many I've flown with this team, but I pay special attention to him. The inflection in his voice captures my curiosity, and without looking up, I feel myself drifting and getting caught in his net.

"Damn, you smell delicious. What do you have on?"

"Soap and water." Wyse likes the sweet smell, but I'm not telling, not yet anyway.

"Hey Wyse, can I get your tickets to tomorrow's Hawks game?" The players have good seats, but the coaches have the best seats.

"Yeah, come to my hotel room and pick them up. I want to figure out what kind of soap you are using."

"Boy no!" I believe he is sincere about giving me the tickets, but there is something in his tone that sounds off balance, other than the actual words.

"Girl, I'm not trying to run game on you. I need your opinion on something. I can't ask the guys 'cause they would never let me live it down. Come and go out with me tonight, and you can decide later if you trust me enough to come to my room."

"Out where?"

"My boy's new club. I promised him I'd make an appearance."

"Okay, but don't play. This means I can have your tickets, right?" I still have my doubts about Wyse, but I am intrigued and want to go out tonight. Wyse laughs and hands me another small piece of paper.

The media misfits' section has boarded, and the misfits are eating everything in sight, especially the ESPN and the Fox Sports guys; they are the greediest. The rest of the misfits follow the same script. Not one of them seems to own a decent pair of slacks or a stainless tie. I'm glad I'm not working in the back. I can't handle this fashion slander.

The players' section does not have all twelve players boarded yet. As usual, a couple of starters are taking their sweet time while the whole team and crew wait for them to drag their lanky bodies onboard. One of them is Flexible Straw (Austin), and the other is Fiji Water (Greg), always last and always making an entrance. The coaches' section has also boarded, but instead of eating, the coaches are going through some old footage of a Hawks game. I made sure to check the DVD player before Coach Chip presses the on button, wouldn't want a triple X reoccurrence to ruin the night. Coach Chip looks at his wrist to check the time on his Rolex. Displeased with the result, he bolts from the middle of the plane to the boarding door.

"Greg, Austin! Next time you're late, you're going to take a commercial flight at your own expense!"

Coach Chip stares the two players down for several seconds, straightens his sports coat, and walks at a tortoise's pace through the players' section, eyeing each player as he passes. The rookies hold their heads down and snicker as soon as the coach is out of ear shot.

"Greg, would you like for me to take your jacket?" Becky appears ready to please.

"Man, get on the damn plane and sit y'all asses down." Wyse is ready to begin the traditional card game of tunk.

"Greg, are you ready for your Pepsi now or would you prefer to wait?"

"No, he don't have time for a Pepsi. I'm ready to get this game started and take some more of his loot."

"You want to wait, Greg?" Becky insists.

"Baby, look, when I'm done with him he won't be of any interest to you. Between me winning his money and coach making him pay to fly, he'll be broke." Becky, embarrassed by Wyse's words, scampers off to the rear of the plane.

As soon as the doors are closed, it seems like the pilot thrashes the yolk forward to accelerate the plane to ascend into the air. I don't believe he even bothered using much of the runway for take-off, which is fine by me. The faster we get into the air, the better. I really need to arrive in Atlanta early so I can catch that flight to Phoenix and purchase my new jeans. I hope the pilots are doing at least 500 mph!

Oh boy, here comes Wyse again. He must have tunked-out because why is he now in the galley with me?

"Gypsy, you coming for sure?"

"Yes, Wyse. I said I will meet you at the club. Now go back to your seat and sit down. You're going to make everybody suspicious!"

"You have a clean rep. What are you worried about?"

"It's not me I'm worried about. It's your reputation for being a playboy that concerns me." I smile and shoo Wyse out of the galley, and I pick up the interphone to call Rita and Julie in the back. Rita answers.

"You guys need anything? The service in my section is complete. The players have finished eating, and I have a bunch of leftovers if you want to give them to the media misfits."

"Desperately. Bring all the extra chicken and rice you have. They won't stop eating!"

"I'm on my way." I giggle and hang up the phone. Becky and I *hate* working in the back. The misfits are *sooo* incredibly needy.

Flexible Straw stops me on my way to the dungeon to ask how much time is left in the flight. He has a bantering look on his face and is seated next to Wyse.

"The captain just made an announcement stating our arrival time. Weren't you listening?" I look over at Wyse with a grim expression.

"Naw, what he say?"

"Forty-five minutes of flight time left to go, Austin."

"Cool, you coming back this way?"

"Yeah, why?"

"I want a Pepsi."

"Becky's right over there. Ask her." I roll my eyes and wonder what Wyse has told him. The company does not tolerate the flight attendants fraternizing with the players, so any communication I have with Wyse must be kept on the down-low. Not the gay down-low, I'm talking hush-hush.

Anyway, on my way to the back, I pass through the coaches' section, and Coach Chip stops me to inquire about the players' drinking conditions. I tell him there has been no consumption of alcohol on tonight's flight. He then goes on and makes a query about Wyse's drinking. I respond with an emphatic "no, no one is drinking, sir." I wonder why he singled out Wyse. If Coach Chip knows about us, then everyone must know. His gaze from me to Wyse and back to me burns with disbelief, and I quickly continue to the rear of the plane.

"Here you go, Rita. I have five chicken-and-rice dishes remaining."

"Great, I only need three. On your way up to the front, can you stop and give this tray to the Fox Sports guy?"

"No, I cannot stop." I'm tired of stopping, but I shouldn't be upset with Rita. She doesn't know anything about me and Wyse. "Anyway, I thought you had a crush on him?" I question her motives.

"I did until I found out he's married. The jerk doesn't wear his wedding band on road trips!"

"How do you know he's married?"

"Julie overheard him talking to the ESPN guy about his wife before take-off."

"Oh. Dang. Okay, I'll take it to him for you." I regain my composure and carry the meal to the ring-less sportscaster.

The one-hour-and-thirty-minute flight is uneventful with the exception of Flexible Straw needing attention, which is nothing out of the ordinary. The guys are all in an upbeat mood now that they have won a game against the former world champions. If they keep this momentum up, they may have a good chance at ousting them from the conference. The guys are looking forward to playing the projected NBA champs, the Hawks, in Atlanta, and Wyse is particularly excited. He keeps staring at me whenever I walk by his row. He better learn to control his eyes and put that beer down before Coach Chip catches him and asks how or where he got it. I swear if Wyse implicates me, I'm going to deny everything. I'll go so far as to say I wasn't aware of his drinking any beverages this season. Not even a pop.

The airplane empties, and it's our turn to deplane. The crew limo is waiting on the tarmac ready to take us to the downtown Hilton. Tonight Becky and I are going to meet Wyse and a friend of his from Atlanta who owns a jazz club. Becky has agreed to come with me. I had to beg her to come along because I'm not sure what Wyse's true motives are, and I told her if his friend looks like throwup or she doesn't identify with his essence, we would leave, no questions asked. We pull up in valet (the hotel has a courtesy car for crew use during layovers) and ask if our names are on the list.

"Yes, Ms. Moon and Ms. Haynes. You are both on the list, and your valet has already been taken care of." The valet's searching blue eyes are trying to figure out which one of us is here to see Wyse. I can tell because he paused just long enough before opening my door, as if we were going to blurt out that kind of information to a complete stranger. We didn't even tell the rest of the crew about tonight.

Inside of the ultra-lounge by the piano are Wyse and his friend

Jackson. Jackson is kind of short for a man, about the same height as Becky, and has a slim, muscular body like a hockey player. He's small but very cute with thick eyebrows framing his dark, mysterious eyes and a strong jaw line. Becky chews on her bottom lip unconsciously as she sizes him up, which signals to me that she's pleased with the arrangements.

I am looking like a superstar in my one-piece, front-zip denim jumper. It's not fully zipped, and it's positioned so that Wyse can get a sneak peek at my cleavage. My hair is pulled back into an I-Dream-of-Jeannie ponytail, stretching down to my mid-back, and I have on my super high five-inch Rupert Sanderson pumps. Oh, *and* I have the new Pollini bag. I'm positive Wyse won't notice, but the ladies in the club all know it's the hottest purse carried by all the celebrities.

"Hey, Wyse." I sound more excited than I had planned to.

"Ms. Gypsy, you look sexy as hell. I didn't know all this was hiding under that blue uniform."

"You lie. What are you drinking?" I point to his glass.

"Gin and tonic, but order whatever you want." He hands me the martini menu.

"You have a game tomorrow. Should you be drinking?"

"What?" Wyse scrunches up his face. "Excuse me, miss."

Wyse summons a barely dressed, barely legal–looking thing to come and take my drink order.

"What are you going to have, Gypsy?"

"A girltini, please."

I wait until the little girl leaves and I have Wyse's full attention. "I thought you guys had a rule about not drinking before a game."

Wyse stares blankly at me and then lowers his eyes to my breasts.

"Nothing. Forget it." I wave my hand in front of my face from side to side, imitating a Japanese woman when she is declining what is being offered.

Becky and Jackson are cozied up across from us on the plush sofa in the VIP section. Wyse is sitting next to me with his arm across

----

the back of the loveseat, and I'm positioned with my legs crossed, facing him, feeling euphoric from my girltini. The club is dark inside, and all of the furnishings are in colors with shades that range from violet to deep plum, almost black. Very sexy atmosphere. Very sexy man sitting next to me. Wisdom. Very sexy indeed.

"What are you thinking about, Gypsy?"

"Nothing. What's up with the tickets, Wyse?"

"Nothing, huh? Come to the Four Seasons tonight and pick them up. I told you I needed to talk to you about something. How 'bout I ride with you and Jackson can drop Becky off?"

"What?" I look at him with disbelief.

"He's trustworthy. Believe me. He has too much to lose just like I do." Wyse speaks matter-of-factly and points to Becky and Jackson.

I get up and walk to where Becky is seated to offer the suggestion to her, and as Wyse figures she is cool with it—a little too cool if you ask me. Becky wants to live the good life like her mom lives, and I can see through all the Revlon on her face that she has chosen Jackson as her newest quest.

"What are you drinking, Rebecca?"

"Please don't call me 'Rebecca.' Mom calls me that. I'm drinking what I always drink, and I know how to handle my liquor. One shot at a time." She laughs and sways to the music, but her mannerisms remain intact. Bubbly Becky. "I'll stay here with Jackson. You go and have fun."

"All right. Call me when you get back to the Hilton. You know my room number?"

"Yes girl. Now go." Becky is having a good time with Jackson, and Jackson seems pleased to be sporting my sassy friend. He has his arms around her waist in a possessive manner, and Becky loves it. In a couple of shots, she'll be sitting on the man's lap, I'm sure.

Twenty minutes later, Wyse and I are opening the door to his hotel suite.

"Okay Wyse, what is your dilemma, your secret that needs my attention?"

Wyse unbuttons his shirt and shows me a burgundy bruise on his neck near his collarbone. The bruise is about an inch round and looks like a hickey. I take a closer look because I know this fool is not really showing me a hickey. Right?

"Look here, Gypsy. I'm going to need to cover this up."

"How did it happen?" I ask innocently.

"Me and my boys played a game of pick-up. My boy Marvin came down on my collarbone with his elbow. See, that's why I don't like playing ball with street guys. He always got to prove something."

"I know. You have too much to lose," I say sarcastically. I can't help it.

"We need to go to the mall tomorrow and get some foundation or something to cover this up before my game tomorrow night."

"So what, you expect me to stay here tonight?" This man is on crack.

"Girl, I can't go to the mall asking for cosmetics. 'Wyse Jones in Lenox Mall shopping for makeup.' Do you want to see that in *People* magazine next week?"

"Okay, now you're over-exaggerating. Basketball players aren't in *People* magazine, well not since Kobe Bryant, anyway. They're just not that into you."

"Please, Gypsy, I promise to be on my best behavior. Stay the night with me." He gives me the most adorable puppy dog eyes, and such beautiful eyes they are.

"Nope, I'm out. You don't really expect me to believe that story, do you?" I begin putting my wrap over my shoulders.

"No, wait. How do I know I can trust you?"

"Trust me?"

"I mean, how much can I trust you?"

"Trust me with what?"

"Okay, let's say I want to believe I can trust you." He's making small circles with his hands as if to say, "Keep going, keep going."

"But I need a positive connection, something about you. I hope I'm making the right decision here."

"Wyse what, just what is it?"

"Gypsy, please stay here with me tonight. I need to feel connected first before I confide in you."

"If I decide to stay, I'll need one of your T-shirts because I won't be sleeping naked, and if I stay I would expect, during our sleepover, something more out of you other than those Italian hand-waving gestures, maybe a conversation about why I'm here." Humph, maybe I'm the one on crack.

Wyse is a true sweetheart. He rubs my feet and speaks to me in Italian. He plays with my hair and passionately kisses me throughout the night (he's an excellent kisser), but not once does he mention his dilemma. Grrr. So irritating. Nor does he try seducing me—I must admit I am a little miffed about that.

When I wake up the next morning, Wyse is lying behind me holding me in his arms, inhaling my aroma.

"You feel good in my arms, Gypsy. Why you make me chase you for so long?"

"You like the chase; I can tell," I respond. "Okay Wyse. What's going on?"

"Back to that, huh? Well . . . Coach put me on probation."

"He put you on probation for what?"

"I was in a car accident a couple of weeks ago. Nobody knows this, especially none of the players. Coach said I had to tighten up my act before the end of the season if I intended to stay on the team."

"So what does this have to do with probation or that bruise . . . or me?"

"It was a DUI."

"Oh." I'm looking at the bruise a little closer now.

"And a hit and run. The bruise came from the accident."

"Humph." Maybe a hickey would have been better. Damn.

"Coach managed to keep it out of the media and I've been paying the for family's expenses. I promised him that I can control my drinking."

"Have you been able to?"

"Yeah, I have to, I had an earlier court date, but coach made some kind of deal to get it pushed back until after the playoffs."

"Intense. I need something to eat, and then . . . I don't know, maybe I'll be able to digest this . . ." I get up and walk to the other side of the bed. "Why are you confiding in me?"

"We have been flying together all season, and I like your style. I watch how you interact with everybody on the plane, and I'm digging you." Wyse's face looks sad as he speaks. "You remind me of a next-door neighbor I grew up with in Texas. She died seven years ago of cancer."

"I'm sorry, Wyse."

"Thanks. She was the last female I vibed with, until now."

"Cool. The vibe part, I mean. I like that."

We order breakfast in bed, shower (separately), and get dressed for our hunt to find the perfect shade of concealer. Now that I know Wyse's secret and he trusts me, I'm willing to help make his life less stressful—at the mall, mind you.

"Lil' Baby, you can look for an outfit to wear for today if you want. I can tell by the way you accessorize your uniform that you're not used to sporting the same outfit two days in a row."

"Okay, we can go to Nordstrom to get some cover-up for your bruise and I can get those new KLS jeans I saw in the designer's collection, um, I forgot the brand."

"Kimora Lee Simmons," Wyse fills in effortlessly.

"Right. Kimora jeans." He pays attention to details. He better not be gay!

I try to wrap up my shopping hurriedly. It only takes us forty-five minutes to shop the mall. I know you're not supposed to profile but Wyse proves to be the typical male, not much of a shopper. Though he is patient and hasn't rushed me, I know he'd prefer to be in an electronics store versus the women's accessory and handbag department. Or maybe not. Wyse did know the name of those jeans, and he probably takes girls shopping all of the time, so why am I feeling exclusive in his life? He only shared one random intimate evening with me as I'm sure he has done with many other women before.

On our way out of the mall, Wyse stops at Sunglass Hut and buys me a pair of Ray-Ban sunglasses without any influence from me whatsoever. I must have glared at them a bit too long as we were passing by. I should have glared at a pair of VVS1 diamond stud earrings too seeing as he's in a giving mood, but anyway, I'm ready to get back to the room and see if Wyse is willing to tell me more about that hit and run.

After shopping, we return to Wyse's hotel and he begins getting ready to go to practice. I finish applying the concealer to his bruise and prepare to go back to my own hotel room.

"What are you doing?" Wyse inquires.

"Going back to the Hilton."

"No, Gypsy, stay here. I will only be gone for a couple of hours. Order a movie and room service. I want you here when I get back. There's something I didn't include about the DUI and I have to tell you before the game tonight." Wyse speaks with slight desperation in his voice.

"Seriously, Wyse, if you don't tell me when you get back . . ."

"I will, I will. I promise."

"You mind if I call Becky over to watch a movie with me?"

"No, if it means you will stay. I'll get the tickets to the game and bring them with me when I get back."

"See, I told you not to play. I knew the tickets should have been at will call."

"You sound like you know the drill."

"I do know the drill. The coaches sometimes offer us tickets, but we always pick them up at will call." I look down at the stationery sitting on the desk next to his iPhone. "Not at the Four Seasons Hotel."

While Wyse is at practice, Becky and I watch *Original Sin*, starring Angelina Jolie, and have a delicious seafood lunch with a bottle of White Star Champagne. Becky and I are fond of deceit movies. My favorite is *Unfaithful* with Richard Gere and Jessica Lange. Becky prefers *Cruel Intentions*–type movies. I have a feeling that someday I will be watching Becky's real-life tragedy unfold before me. She enjoys participating in the deceit rather than watching the action on a DVD player. The way that Becky likes to keep things stirred up, I imagine she will no doubt end up being the main character on some trashy talk show in the very near future.

Before Wyse is due to return with our tickets, I talk Becky into hacking into his laptop. She's a wizard when it comes to computer stuff. I like to call her my broken genius, and in seconds Becky has the Denim Bar's website pulled up on the screen. She packs up and leaves quickly, stating that she doesn't want to be around when Wyse gets back and sees that I have infiltrated his Apple. She overstresses sometimes. I have over twenty minutes of down time to recheck electriclady.com for an update on my fabulous jeans.

By the time Wyse comes back, I'm off of the Internet and we spend the next three hours in his room watching the craziness of *Jerry Springer* and satisfying my addiction to *Judge Judy*. I have to watch *Judge Judy* every day. We take turns with the remote control, but mostly we talk and laugh and play. When it is time for Wyse to get dressed and catch the team bus to the arena, I give him a deep, long kiss and send him off to play the Hawks, thinking to myself "go to work and play ball honey; I'll stay here and relax until you finish your game." That lasted all of five minutes before I realized again he failed to approach the subject of the DUI.

After tonight's game, we have to fly the team back home to Denver. I wait an extra twenty to twenty-five minutes before leaving Wyse's room because I don't want to run into any of the other players, even though I was sure the team had already packed up and checked out of the hotel. If someone were to report me to the company, Encompass would restrict me from flying all charters and I would die if I had to strictly fly commercial. I would absolutely die!

The Greyhound passengers we transport drive me nuts. They walk around the plane barefoot trying to hand me their baby's dirty diapers. *Ah, no.* Or the teenagers who travel alone to spring break and forget to remove their retainers from the dinner tray we just collected and want you to go through the nasty filthy used-meal carts in search of the missing $150 piece of plastic. *Eeww.* Or even the CEO who walks up to the first-class cabin and whines about not getting upgraded because it's already full of platinum passengers (he's only a gold yet still one of our precious metals) and has to return to his coach-class middle seat where he sits and stares at you, willing you to implode when he should have instructed his secretary to pay for a first-class ticket in the first place. This is a very popular business flight to O'Hare, Mr. Blue Suit. Be mad at your hired help, not me. Oh and don't forget the crazy man who stands in the middle of the aisle, removes all of his clothing, and proclaims to be Christ. Butt naked. The things we have to deal with, *Jesus.*

On the plane back to Denver, the mood is somber. The Nuggets lost to the Atlanta Hawks, and no one wants to eat except for the misfits. The coaches replay the tapes from tonight's game, and the players sleep, no card games, no grand entrances, no nothing. The flight departed on time. Flexible Straw usually walks up and down the aisles needing constant attention like a two-year-old child, but not tonight. Tonight he's seated in his assigned seat next to Wyse, who is sound asleep. Fiji Water has his headphones on and is in a trance mode. Coach Chip is watching me watch the players. What's up with him? He's like a warden, always investigating. I hope he doesn't ask if Wyse has been drinking on tonight's flight because he has. Wyse said it would help him sleep if I gave him a couple of beers, which I did. Everyone else is in a foul mood except for Sam, the rookie. He is neither upset nor sleepy. He probably feels that since he didn't get to play in tonight's game that he is not at fault for the team's loss. In fact, he is so bored he helped me finish my crossword puzzle, Sudoku, actually, but still. Even the misfits are maintained. Sure, they gathered all their nuts beforehand, but they seem to be hibernating now. Good.

We arrive in Denver at 2:00 a.m., and the plane empties out quickly. Everyone is tired and disappointed about losing to the Hawks and wants to get back to their lovers, their sweet little girlfriends, their happy homes where their wonderful wives wait, back to the disciplining of the children or pets. They just want to get back to their normal, comforting lives and lick their wounds. If this had been a victory, the players would surely have been flirtier, but instead they have their tails between their legs.

"Hey sleepyhead, I'll call you later," I whisper into Wyse's ear.

"Naw come over tonight. I'll wait for you in the parking lot."

"No, I already stayed one night with you and we never got around to discussing your DUI. What promise will you make now that you have your cosmetics? I know how you players are," I say jokingly.

"Don't stereotype me. I know how flight attendants are." He takes offense. "If something does happen, know that we are both grown. No pressure, Lil' Baby. I just like kicking it with you." His tone softens. "Promise, confessions will commence tonight if you come with me."

"I need to fly back to Detroit tomorrow night. I'm expecting a UPS package from my favorite online store. Are you going to be able to take me to the airport at 7:00?"

"Yeah, I'll drop you off. So, what you want to do tonight? Play Chutes and Ladders?"

"Hilarious. I want you to tell me what's going on."

"I will, scout's honor."

Humph. I'm supposed to be the sarcastic one, not him. Anyway, Wyse is there waiting for me in his silver Range Rover in the private parking lot adjacent to the corporate terminal. We drive to his complex and take the private elevator up to his penthouse apartment. On the way up, he mentions that he resides in Dallas during the off-season in a five-bedroom house, and I ask him why he needs five bedrooms if he lives alone. He says, "'Cause."

Wyse's place is a typical bachelors pad. He has dark wood furniture, stainless steel appliances, a big-screen TV, an awesome sound system, and an Xbox. Typical but with an expensive twist—Drexel Heritage furniture some female must have picked out for him, Sub-Zero and Viking appliances (ditto on the shopping help), and a Sony flat-screen TV hooked up to a Bose sound system, and an Xbox 360.

"Where is the game?" I ask Wyse.

"We play here in Denver for our next two games. A week at home sounds good right about now."

"I'm talking about the Chutes and Ladders game."

"Oh, you're funny. Come upstairs. I have all the *Jerry Springer* seasons on DVD."

"Really? All the seasons? Great."

Wyse energetically heads for the carpeted stairway leading to the upper level. He takes the stairs two at a time, and as soon as he gets to his bedroom, he turns on the television set. I enter the room unnoticed and strip down to my Vickies underwear and slide onto his platform bed under his checkered down comforter on top of the black silk sheets that smell of cologne and immediately begin to doze off while he entertains himself with Jerry's outrageous guests. Wyse looks over at me and smacks me on my butt.

"You goin' to sleep?"

"Ouch, yes I am. You slept during the flight here while I worked. Remember? Wake me up when you're ready to let the truth escape your lips."

"My bad." He kisses me on the forehead.

"Wyse, you're not going to finish telling me about the DUI?"

"In the morning. Get some sleep. You worked hard today."

As tired as I am, I still mentally note that smart comment.

The next morning, Wyse is looking through the kitchen for something to eat when I come downstairs.

"Would you like for me to make breakfast?"

"That's cool, but the only groceries I have are, let me see, eggs, biscuits, grits … no breakfast meat, only bologna … Frosted Flakes cereal, milk, and some frozen Hungry Man TV dinners."

"As long as everything is eatable and nothing has passed the expiration date, I can prepare a king's feast." I smile at Wyse. "What are we going to do tonight for food? We'll have to make it an early dinner because I want to be at the airport by 6."

"We can stay in and order carryout from this restaurant called Gourmet. Normally they don't accept carryout orders, but they make an exception for me, Wyse 'The King' Jones." He smiles his beautiful smile. "We can have that DUI conversation over dinner if you want."

"If I want. You're full of it, you know that, right?" I say, still smiling. I have acquired an emotional attachment to Wyse. It's like he needs me to keep him balanced.

Over breakfast, Wyse explains how he is very much recognized in Denver and whenever he goes out in public his fans ask him for an autograph or a picture. Sometimes they give unsolicited advice on the weakness of his game and offer suggestions on how to correct those weaknesses, which pisses him off. Some want to have physical contact like a handshake. He's germophobic too so that sucks, and some just want to converse with a celebrity. He says he loves and appreciates his fans and is more than willing to participate in these antics after a game, but on his personal time he likes to chill and not be so active with the fans.

I order dinner from that gourmet restaurant Wyse told me about, and he was telling the truth. They refuse to deliver our dinner until I put Wyse on the phone and he confirms it by giving them some sort of password. Must be nice.

Wyse is a bit hyperactive and for that reason he talks for hours on end, and forgets about my flight to Detroit that is in a couple of hours. Of course, I remind him and of course, he pleads for me to stay longer, just one more day he says. I sense that he gets lonely held up in this big apartment all by himself, and on the road and throughout the season. He must miss all of his friends and family in Texas. I bet it gets a little hard to deal with being all alone during basketball season. Wyse only goes to work and back home when he's in Denver. He doesn't venture out on his off days at all, not even to go skiing. Oh, there's probably no skiing allowed in his million dollar contract, huh? Well, just the same, he never goes anywhere.

Also, I detect some jealousy when Wyse refers to the unseasoned players being "unprofessional." He doesn't hang with any of the starters, who by the way are somewhat younger and more into partying. I guess it's normal to be a little envious as you get older and pushed out of the limelight like an aging supermodel, like how Kate Moss must feel. When are she and Naomi Campbell going to retire anyway?

"If you don't *have* to go back to work soon, why can't you stay a couple more days? That package will be there when you get home. I'll even get you courtside seats, and you can cheer for me at our game against the Pacers on Thursday."

"I didn't bring that many outfits with me on this trip. Can we go shopping again?"

"Player, I feel you. Okay, we can go and buy you a cheerleading outfit."

"That's not funny." It's really not.

"Yeah, we can go shopping."

"Yay!"

"I need to stop and get some more beer while we're out."

"Booo."

"What's wrong with you, girl?"

"You act like you need to have a buzz in order to be around me."

"You silly. Naw, it helps me relax. That's all, Lil' Baby."

"Okay, if that's all." Looks like my psychotherapy will be needed here as well.

I end up staying an entire week, well, six days. We have such a good time spending every moment together. Outside of Wyse playing basketball, we enjoy each other's company from the time we wake up until bedtime. Even when he goes to the barbershop, I tag along. When I need to go to the store for tampons, he comes with me. Wyse turns out to be very sweet though a bit insecure. He needs continual praise and reassurance, but he is attentive and very giving. I even find myself imagining us as a couple until I realize again that he never did get around to vocalizing his DUI details. Didn't utter a word about it the whole time I was there.

My cross-country flight back to Detroit was a couple of days ago, and now I'm sitting at full attention like a military person in my loft in the Motor City watching the Nuggets game against the Clippers. The Nuggets are losing again. They have lost the past six games in their attempt to secure the eighth position for the playoffs, and if they lose tonight's game, there will be no playoffs. The season will be over for the Nuggets, and for Wyse too. These are the final months left on his contract and soon he will be a free agent. I'm concerned about the team losing its spot, and I'm especially worried about Wyse because when he's disappointed he drinks more than the average person's usual nightcap. A lot more.

I know when I spoke to Wyse two days ago he was perturbed about advancing to the Western Conference Playoffs. It's not likely that Wyse will get picked up by another playoff-bound team seeing that he is one of the older players in the league, and if he does get picked up he knows he won't be able to command a high payroll as he once was able. This may be just enough to nudge him into being a full-fledged alcoholic.

The Nuggets are down in the fourth quarter 69–76, and the star player Flexible Straw has fouled out. Wyse has been on the bench for most of the quarter but is now playing with four minutes left. I'm sitting on edge as though I'm part of the team. Wyse promised if they make it to the playoffs we would celebrate at the end of the post-season or after the championship, if they make it that far, in Bora Bora, so yeah, I do have reason to cheer, go Nuggets! Two minutes left and the Nuggets are only down by four. I can't watch anymore so I get up and go into the kitchen, which is adjacent to the living room, to get the container of butter pecan ice cream out of the freezer.

"I'm going to kick her ass!" I yell and slam the freezer door shut. Kat has eaten nearly all of my ice cream. Damn. I throw my spoon at the television and turn up the volume up so high that my neighbors may be able to feel the vibration of the "de-fense" chant. I cover my eyes and peep through my fingers to check the score. Eighteen seconds left on the clock, and we are down by two. Wyse has the ball, and he's running down the clock in order to take the last shot of the game. I can't watch. The final buzzer rings, signifying the end of regulation. I remove my hands from my face and open my eyes to see the results. The Clippers have won the game, 82–80, and the eighth seed spot as well. The Clippers coaching staff and the bench players have begun to swarm the floor, and the Nuggets quickly leave as the streamers fall from the ceiling and the Clippers celebrate. Wyse was one of the first players to exit, holding his head down low as he passed through the tunnel.

Shit, my phone is purring. I check the caller ID and see that it's Wyse. I don't know what to say to him or what tone to use. How'd he get to the locker room so fast?

"Hey, Wyse." I choose perky.

"Lil' Baby, did you watch the game?"

"Yes, I'm sorry, Wyse. How are you feeling?"

"Fucked up. I'm leaving for Dallas as soon as I get to Denver and pack. Can you come spend some time in Dallas with me? We still need to talk."

"Yes, I have an LAX layover, but after that I'll be off for a few days. Can't you just tell me over the phone?"

"No, in person will be better, Lil' Baby. I should look for you around Thursday or Friday?"

"Let's do Friday. Wyse, are you going to be okay?"

"No, I'm fucked up. Seeing you will make it better, but I'm fucked up right now."

"Okay, see you on Friday. I miss you."

"Miss you too. Later."

I end my phone call with Wyse and start packing my bags for tomorrow's Los Angeles layover. My trip overnights in the city of stars and then I will work the flight back to Detroit. I plan to get my nails manicured and window shop on Rodeo Drive. Then later after the sun goes down, I'm going to go for a long run on the beach. Talking to Wyse has me feeling a little down like I, too, have been cut from the team. It will be good for him to see me again because I know he needs some attention and a few laughs, and I kind of miss watching *Jerry Springer*. I never liked the show before. I'm not sure if I like it now. I just enjoy observing and listening to Wyse's view on the guests, and he has gained some legal knowledge from examining my court TV shows. He called me one day talking about taking one of his fans to small claims court for stalking him. He's funny. I guess he hasn't learned that much from my show, but I enjoy his company nevertheless.

Dang, now I'm sad. Usually I look forward to my L.A. layovers, but this time I'm eager for it to be over so I can fly to Dallas and meet with Wyse. He's been avoiding this chat for some reason, and I suspect he has a really hard time communicating his feelings. I can help him with the psychological, psycho-therapy seeing how helpful I was when my ex Kyle had mental problems. I'm sure this will be a breeze if all he's dealing with is a little over-indulgence when drinking.

      The weather sucks in L.A. It's unseasonably cold and rainy, and I only brought my warm weather outfits—a short set, my new Electric Ladyland jeans that I was finally able to pick up in Scotts-dale, and a pair of pink thong sandals, oh and my workout clothes, but that's a given. I have two choices at this point. I can either stay in the hotel all day and veg or endure the sucky weather and shop at the small boutiques on Beverly Drive for some ready-to-wear that nobody in the Midwest will be wearing. Maybe even go to Jamba Juice for a healthy smoothie after I work out at a 24-hour fitness gym, and I can check out the local board-certified plastic surgeons to see what new fat-dissolving treatment is on the market. Oh I can get my eyebrows threaded, too! I'm getting excited now. I'll call my friend Shannon, another charter girl who lives in California. She prefers working the NFL charters and she's always getting invited to football players' parties. Anyway, I'll call her and see if she can recommend a good restaurant.

      My phone is purring again.

      "Hello."

      "Lil' Baby?"

      "Wyse? Where are you?" I can hear in his voice that he has been drinking again.

      "In Dallas. When are you flying down?"

      "I'm in L.A., silly. I'll be there tomorrow. My flight lands at 4:00."

      "You need to hurry, girl." Wyse pauses and I hear a swallow-ing sound. "The boy's condition has been downgraded and he is now in the intensive care unit."

      "What? Wyse, what boy?"

      "What time is your flight landing?"

      "At four, but not until tomorrow. Are you okay Wyse?"

"No. I'm still fucked up."

"You want to talk about it?"

"I'm sorry, Gypsy." More swallowing noises cut through the phone. "I'll call you back."

CLICK. He hung up. He hung up! Aggg. Whatever, I'll do my shopping and veg the rest of the day. Wyse just blew my happy buzz I had going.

Now finally, I'm on my way to Dallas. Thank God. That man rang my phone off the hook, calling continuously during my lay-over, spewing out bits of incoherence and rambling on about some fifteen-year-old high school ball player. We are scheduled to land in fifteen minutes so I excuse myself past the sumo-wrestler-looking man seated in the aisle seat. I rush to the lav to check my makeup and make sure my new outfit I purchased from that stylish boutique on Beverly Drive is flawless. When I hear the landing announce-ment being made, I dart back to my window seat and buckle my seatbelt. I am anxious to sit Wyse down and get to the bottom of this DUI. It couldn't possibly be as bad as the image I have created in my mind: *Wyse meets his illegitimate son for the first time after fifteen years in the hospital. The boy's family tries to extort sympathy money from Wyse and tells him that the accident is draining their finances and will cost hundreds of thousands of dollars in medical expenses. This forces Wyse to drink, and in that drunken state he drives frantically through the streets of Dallas to escape the truth. A state trooper spots Wyse's speeding SUV after it strikes a parked car and pulls him over. Wyse gets cited for driving under the influence and is forced to attend a driving responsibility class.*

The captain's rough landing brings me back to reality, though in my book any landing is a good landing. I gather my bags from the overhead bin and walk through the jet way into the terminal and out the doors into the hazy city, charged up and ready to ride in the black Mercedes Wyse told me he purchased a couple of months ago.

Where is he? I have yet to see a black Mercedes, and I have been standing here tapping my foot for almost twenty minutes. If he's caught in traffic, the least he could do is call and inform me.

How hard is it to be considerate and press ten digits? Not hard at all. Where's my cell?

"You have reached 555-1272. Please leave a message."

I call seven more times in the next forty-five minutes and still no answer. If he doesn't call within fifteen minutes, I'm going to jump on one of these hotel shuttle buses and get a room for the night. I wish I could turn around and fly back to Detroit, but the last flight has already departed.

Thirty minutes later . . .

"I would like a room for one night, please," I say to the girl behind the front desk at the Marriott.

"Would you like a king or two double beds, ma'am?"

"Two double beds please. I like to put my luggage on the extra bed."

"We have luggage racks in all the room closets, ma'am."

"No, no. I like to use the extra bed."

The teenager smiles and hands me my room key card along with my MasterCard and points in the direction of my home for the night.

"OH I AM SO MAD!" I yell at my reflection in the mirror. "Who in hell does he think he is? Michael Jordan? No, he couldn't think that because if he was MJ he wouldn't be worried about getting picked up by a good team!"

I need to let go of the anger somehow. It's not good for the spirit, so I go for a long run to clear my head without any music. I just run until I am too exhausted to contemplate. I run for an hour and a half and return to my room soaked with sweat, feeling good about my run but still pissed off at Wyse. I search my bags for a distraction and find those little orange pills I got on my layover in India. I use them when I can't fall asleep on my Asia layovers. Aahaa, my sleeping pills and only one left. I have to remember to get a new pack when I go back to Delhi, if I can hold a Delhi trip. Those international flights are usually awarded to the senior dinosaur flight attendants, the same flight attendants who probably flew for the Wright Brothers. I pop my little orange pill, down a tall glass of water, turn on the shower to the hottest temperature I can stand,

and begin to lather away my sweat. My thoughts were still lurking, unfortunately. After several minutes in the sauna, I begin feeling the effects of the drugs. Good. Nite-nite time. Not wanting to be a "lady collapses, found dead in bathroom" statistic, I step out of the shower and put on my undies and fall asleep with the remote in my hand.

My wake-up call was set for 6:00 a.m., and the lady at the front desk calls up to my room announcing that very fact. I don't feel like moving one bit; not even my pinkie toe wants to move. The inside of my head is pounding because I wasn't asleep long enough for the effects of the drugs to wear off. I need some caffeine, black this time, something to counteract the drowsiness, and this damn fancy coffee maker in my room is making the simple task of brewing coffee complicated and intensifying the pounding in my head. Man I want to cry.

I went to bed still mad at Wyse and left the TV on CNN.

Breaking news . . .

"Denver Nuggets point guard Wyse Jones has committed suicide at his home in Dallas, Texas. We will go live to our local correspondent on the scene in Dallas . . ." My head begins to pound harder, and I feel like I have fallen from Mount Rushmore.

"Thank you, Spencer. It appears Wyse Jones has overdosed on a lethal combination of alcohol and prescription drugs, including the anti-depressant Zoloft."

Wyse left a couple of messages on my voice mail asking if I could come to Dallas sooner, and one of the last messages he left said that he was sorry.

Was that his cry for help?

What if I had come sooner?

Could I have helped him in some way?

Stop, just stop. I am not to blame.

Was I the last person he spoke with?

Are the police going to scroll through his cell phone for answers?

Am I a suspect? No, they said suicide, not assisted suicide.

I don't know any of his family, but if I did I'm sure it wouldn't be of any comfort letting them know about our brief affair, like how Wyse would take me shopping when I'd agree to stay a couple more days so he wouldn't be all lonely by himself, or how he got me the coaches' seats when they were available just so I would stay extra days. I could tell them how generous he was when I did stay; that may make them feel comforted. Or tell them how he always kept his many promises. Except that promise he made to tell me about the DUI, and except for the promise to . . . or the promise to . . . Well, maybe he didn't make many promises, and the one he did make he didn't keep. This is useless thinking.

Wait. His promises. His promise to talk.

The DUI. What was Wyse really sorry for?

I tried calling Summer in Atlanta for her input, but her phone went straight to voice mail, which could only mean that she is currently flying and her electronic device has been turned off. Good girl. I can never remember to turn my phone off.

"Back to you, Spencer."

"Thank you, Diane. And this just in, Wyse Jones was supposed to appear in court on Monday for a hit-and-run accident involving a high school basketball student. Wyse Jones fled the scene and was reportedly intoxicated at the time of the crash. The student was traveling across the intersection with two other passengers from the high school's basketball team when Wyse Jones ran a red light and his SUV collided with the young teenager's vehicle. Now let's go to Sinai Hospital where the teenager is in ICU for more details . . ."

I need to turn off the TV and get dressed for my flight back to Detroit. I am overwhelmed by the injured kid news and can't take anymore of this alleged suicide headline. Wyse must have been tormented. I wish I could have helped. I saved my ex's life even though I got him fired from the police force. If only I could have persuaded Wyse to confer with me sooner.

I flip through the channels one last time before pressing the power button and halt at the sight of *Jerry Springer*. *Jerry Springer* is on, and I feel I have to watch it. Taking strange comfort, I settle back under the covers and watch his show. I'm fucked up, but *Jerry Springer* is actually helping me get through this early morning shock.

I can hear Wyse's uncontrollable laughter, and I feel close to him.

My flight leaves in two hours, but I haven't moved an inch from the bed. WJBK is airing back-to-back episodes of the *Springer* show. Wyse told me about these Springer marathons and how he loved to watch them. I thought he was joking, but clearly there must be an audience or the show would not have survived. I can't seem to tear myself away from the tube, maybe this is my therapy. Jerry Springer is my therapist. He used to be a mayor, you know. Wyse knew a bunch of useless information about the host, like how he had a crush on one of the Mowry twins from the show *Sister Sister.*

I quickly reach for the telephone and dial the airline's 800 number to reschedule my flight. I can always catch another flight later. As Wyse would say, "I'm fucked up right now."

CHAPTER 9

Encompass Airlines

*D*amn, the phone is ringing off the hook and I know Kat is sitting right next to it in the other room, but I get up anyway and stammer across the cold cement floor to answer it.

"Mmm, hel-lo."

"Yes, may I speak to Gypsy? This is Brenda in crew scheduling calling," sings a high-pitched, high-energy voice into the phone.

"Speaking."

"Yes, hello Gypsy. You're late for your check-in call. Will you be at the airport by 0700?"

Startled, I bang my pinkie toe into the front leg of the vanity table and flick on the light switch to look at the clock. 0600.

"Ouch, yes I will be there and I apologize for missing my check-in call."

I hop on one foot over to the master bathroom to brush my teeth and wash my face. My uniform from my last trip is hanging on the hook behind the door. I give it a sniff test and put it on. I call Rhonda in valet to request that my car be brought down and grab my flight bag. Man, I hate waking up to a crew scheduler's call. It puts a damper on the entire day. The only good thing going for me so far is that rush hour has not yet started, and that scheduler from Encompass Airlines didn't help matters. Yes, I know she needed to verify that I was indeed going to work my early morning flight. Flight attendants at Encompass are obligated to call in for work two hours before the beginning of a new trip to confirm their itinerary, which I think is silly. What other job requires you to phone in hours before you're actually scheduled to show up? And the scheduler called exactly at the cut-off time to tell me I'm late, not a minute sooner. I guess the company feels that it can't count on us to maintain its fudged first-place, on-time departure status. Some schedulers will not hesitate to replace you with a flight attendant on reserve, one who is waiting by the phone on call in case the company needs someone in a hurry to fly your long-awaited Paris trip, the one you gave up Easter holiday to fly. I'm still mad about that one.

I hope Brenda doesn't inform my manager of the missed check-in call. It's my third tardy in three months, and last month the manager of in-flight called me to threaten disciplinary action if another late incident occurred. I'm beginning to believe that all of the schedulers are snitches. They will be nice on the phone but rat on you as soon as you hang up. The company seems to have zero tolerance for illnesses and no patience for lateness, and committing a no-show or missing an entire trip will get you fired. They're shameless. Rhonda, the valet attendant, used to fly for Encompass. She had four undocumented sick calls in three months, and look what she's doing now for a living, fetching my car.

The morning rush hour is slowly beginning to creep its way onto the highway, but luckily it's early enough for me to weave my Lexus into the gaps between the cars on I-94. Even though the posted speed is seventy, I'm keeping a steady seventy-five miles per hour. If I can stay under the cops' radar for the next twenty miles, I will make it to the airport without delaying the flight. I wish I had had time to recheck the weather report today. I checked the forecast last night, and it was predicted to be clear and sunny, a direct contrast from today's actual weather: cloudy, rainy, and slippery. I would have no problem making it to the airport on time if the weatherman had honored his original forecast. I keep losing traction as I drive across the wet overpasses on the balding treads of my tires. I almost lose control and slide right in front of a mega eighteen-wheeler that is barreling through traffic as if the pavement is completely dry. The heavy-set Santa Claus man driving the big rig pumps his brakes to avoid smashing into my sedan and killing me. Luckily for him, I regain control of my disobedient vehicle and give a gentle wave of apology to Santa as he roars by, blowing his horn and flipping me off.

My thirty-minute mad dash to the airport almost ends in a fatal crash, but I arrive at the terminal intact and am allowed to check in for my flight without penalty. I'm so glad hateful Brenda didn't give my trip away before I got to the airport. Otherwise, I'd probably be spending the night in Minot, North Dakota. I steady my shaking hands, which are shaking from almost being late and not because I nearly lost my life during the commute. I accept my flight information list from the lady at in-flight services:

- Special assistance: wheelchairs 1

- Special meals: vegetarian 2 Kosher 1

- Unaccompanied minors: 2

- Aircraft write-ups: broken tray tables (deferred)

- Boarding time: 0800

- Passengers: 50

I take the elevator up to the third floor to catch the tram to my departure gate on the opposite end of Detroit metro's mile-long terminal. I can't fathom how a major corporation expects its employees to look fresh faced and well groomed, wear three-inch leather heels, *and* arrive at the gate early when it parks all of the larger aircraft haphazardly and spreads them around the entire terminal. The company should rethink this setup and park the jets near the center of the main terminal and put the little prop planes around the perimeter. Once you have reached major airline status such as I have, there should be no excessive walking. Only the commuter airline flight attendants should have to walk long distances to get to their next flight; it's only fair. They haven't paid any dues yet.

I make it to the gate five minutes before boarding time. On board the airplane sitting in the first-class seats waiting to introduce themselves are two flight attendants.

"Hi guys, sorry I'm late," I announce.

"Hi, I'm Amy," a thirty-something pregnant blonde with braces offers. Should she be dying her hair this late in her pregnancy?

"Hello, Amy. I'm Gypsy," I counter-offer. "And you, sir, are?"

"Hey girl. I'm Stacey. I just got called out on reserve for this damn trip, and I didn't have time to do my face!"

"Hi, Stacey. I guess I'll take the lead position. I believe I'm the most senior flight attendant today."

"Oh, girl, thank you. I was hoping I wouldn't get stuck working first class!"

I smile at the flamboyant lip-gloss wearing Hispanic male, thinking to myself that Brenda, the scheduler, must have given Stacey some other flight attendant's fantastic Scottsdale layover. Glad it wasn't mine.

The senior flight attendant on the crew gets to have first pick of where to work on the plane, so after I choose to work up front I begin stowing my luggage in the first-class overhead bin and look at Stacey kind of sideways. He said he didn't want to work up front, but his bags are stowed in my overhead spot. Humph. He doesn't seem much like a people person like most flight attendants are. He's not happy-go-lucky at all. I'm sure he will be better off working in the main cabin with his poor demeanor, or more appropriately in the back galley where he can keep out of sight during the majority of the flight. And poor Amy is way too pregnant to do much of anything except maybe cater to the homophobic pilots who were behind me coming down the jet bridge. I can't wait to see their reaction to the super shine of Stacey's lips. The balding one, with four gold stripes on his epaulets and holding his uniform jacket over his shoulder, finally steps onto the Boeing aircraft and speaks at us like he's our drill sergeant.

"Hello, I'm Captain Bob and the co-pilot's name is Rich. As soon as I get the flight time, I will pass it along to you. Standard security procedures apply, and no turbulence is expected. Are there any questions or concerns?"

"No, but just to let you know my name is Gypsy and I will be the lead flight attendant. This is Amy and Stacey."

The captain acknowledges Amy and Stacey with a nod and continues into the cockpit to put away his luggage and begin checking the many buttons on the instrument panel. I notice he has a bag tag with a picture of his stunning twenty-something-year-old son on it. I like looking at the crew's bag tags to get an idea of what the person's character is. The tags show secrets of your personality that you're not even aware are being broadcast. I have a graduation picture of my sister Kat on my bag tag. I'm so proud of her, and my luggage displays the pride.

The gate agent is signaling to me with a raised hand that she wants to begin boarding, which means she's ready to rush the cattle onto the plane and close the flight. Even though today is only Tuesday, it must pose as her Friday because she's eagerly waiting for my go ahead to send the passengers down, tapping her foot in anticipation of a thumbs-up from me. Sure, why not board fifty people extra early so they can stop bugging you and start pestering us. It's all about you, Ms. Gate Agent. Lucky for me, Ms. Gate Agent isn't a mind reader, or so I thought. What is that look she just gave me? Oh, she's sending them down anyway without my thumbs-up approval. Humph.

First to board are the wheelchairs (wchr) and two eager unaccompanied minors (um's). Everything is written in code at Encompass, and it's up to us to stay current on all these short forms. This is what my trip instructions looked like when I picked them up this morning:

4-06-2008	P362	ETD	ETA	APRT	ACRFT
EMP: 222555	Flt#250	0830	0740	DTW-MSP	B-757
	Flt#743	0836	0900	MSP-PHX	B-757

We had to learn each abbreviation in flight attendant training. My name is even in code. See it next to EMP? That's my numerical equivalent of my existence here at Encompass Airlines. Today our trip will leave Detroit Metro (DTW), make a stop in Minneapolis (MSP) where we will have one hour down time on the ground, and then depart from MSP and head to Phoenix (PHX) to begin our thirty-two-hour layover. Our estimated time of arrival (ETA) is 0900 local. I can't wait to see Edwin, my boyfriend of eight months. He always has a surprise for me when I come to visit him.

On our arrival into PHX, I turn on my cell phone. I'm expecting Edwin's call. He is a captain on a 747, which equates to huge ego, and he lives partially in Phoenix and partially in Holland. He always calls at the estimated time of arrival. Even though we often have delays, he persists on calling at the ETA. I bid these PHX layovers so we can spend more time together. I usually have two weeks off every month, and we take turns visiting each another. Mostly I come to him because I know to expect a gift. It's his way of bribery. The last time I flew to see him he bought me a pearl bracelet that he had picked up in Shanghai on his layover. Edwin hasn't been to Detroit in nearly two months due to his busy work schedule and my willingness to fly out west.

The passengers have all deplaned. The pilots have shut off the electricity to the airplane. Now it's the crew's chance to disembark. We pull our roller boards behind us up the jet way and across the threshold into the solar system of Phoenix, Arizona, at 112 degrees. It's so hot here that I'm surprised anything electronic works, but it does because my phone is purring, and I'm sure it's Edwin. Yep.

"Hi, baby."

"Hey, Gyps. Where are you?"

"Hi, Edwin. Where are you?"

"I'm waiting on the south side of the terminal."

"Okay, I'm on the escalator now. Give me thirty-eight seconds, and I'll be there."

"Didn't I hear an agent in the background ask you to close the door behind you?"

"Yes you did. Okay, so I'm not on the escalator."

"Gyps, the police are making people move their cars, I'm standing in a loading/unloading zone."

"Why didn't you wait in the cell phone lot for my call?"

"Your plane was scheduled to land at 0900. It's 0945 now."

"My God Edwin. Do you not work for Encompass? When are we ever on time?"

"Hurry up, Gyps, the police are having cars towed."

"I'll be there in thirty-eight seconds. I'm on the escalator."

"I'm on the south side."

"Okaaaay."

South. North, like I know. I think I'm on the west side of the terminal. This man is always on time, always exact, and always has a blueprint. That's one characteristic I find in many pilots that I like, the predictable and reliable beings who fly the planes through the friendly skies and get us to our destination as scheduled. My Edwin's perfect for me because sometimes I can be a bit dogmatic myself and he understands my need to cross-check, reiterate, or interrogate. Well, he doesn't appreciate the interrogation part, but he is such a handsome man and has this sensual Dutch accent that I can't help myself and sometimes I ask one too many questions.

"EDWIN!" I release my roller bag and run to the waiting figure standing outside of his Yukon truck. "I'm so ready to get away from the airport. How fast can you legally drive here?"

"Why Gyps, you ask strange questions."

"Because I'm tired of being around people *and* I have a desperate need to feel you inside of me. How's that?"

"That's perfect. Whatever the speed limit is, I'll make certain that we surpass it. Keep asking me those kinds of questions."

"Okay, where's my present?"

"That's not the kind of question I had in mind."

"Eddwinn. Tell me where you're hiding it."

"It's in the glove box, spoiled."

"You trained me to expect rewards for coming across the world to see you."

"Across the world? It's not like you come all the way to Europe, Gyps."

"Well, then across the country, but I would travel the world to see you, baby."

"You can stop now. I already told your where your present is."

"No, I mean it. I would follow you anywhere. But if you insist, I'll look in the glove compartment."

"You're going to love it. It's a Swarvoski crystal bracelet."

"Grr Edwin, why do you always have to spoil the surprise by telling me what the surprise is?"

"My bad, honey."

"I should have expected you would do that. Never fails."

We arrive at his condo in half the time it normally takes, and I must say, absence does make the heart grow fonder. It may be a cliché, but it fits and so does Edwin, perfectly. I met Edwin when I was working in the first class galley on a flight from Amsterdam (AMS) to DTW, and Edwin was traveling on company business as a passenger. I had my eye on the sexy Dutch treat sitting quietly studying his pilot books. I spoke to him when he first sat down and watched as he arranged his papers in piles on his tray table. Even though he acknowledged me, he was intensely preoccupied and not paying much attention to his surroundings, or anyone for that matter. Two hours into the flight, the Dutchman had fallen asleep. Our meal service was complete in first, and I wondered if or when I would ever get a chance to enchant him with my pleasantries. Three hours, four hours later, and sleepyhead still hadn't come to. It was almost time for the final service to begin, and he was still sound asleep. I asked the crew for their input on how to introduce myself to him. Should I wake him for the meal service and say, "Hi, my name is Gypsy. I will be serving you today"? Should I wait until we land and bum rush him at the door and hand him my business card, or lie and say the captain needs to speak with him in order to get him out of his seat and corner him in the galley? This is most likely the last time I would ever see him so I had to seize my one opportunity. What did I have to lose?

"I need to be more creative but subtle," I whispered to the purser (PQA).

"You want me to wake him? I'll tell him you are interested in meeting him."

"No, that's too obvious. I have a better idea. My purse is stored in the overhead compartment above him. I'll make sure to accidentally bump his arm as I try to retrieve my lipstick out of it. That should wake him."

I began walking toward mystery pilot's seat to carry out my plan.

"You go, girl!" the purser said.

"Don't say that. That's *sooo* corny," I shushed.

Before opening the bin, I gave him the once over, twice. I wanted to lie on top of him to feel his firm body and kiss his quiescent lips … how about that for an unforgettable introduction? I bet that would get his attention and make him want to put away his paper piles. I bumped his seat and made as much noise as I possibly could, but he didn't budge. I then decided to casually, by mistake of course, drop my petite-size water bottle onto his lap, and when that didn't work, I gave him a shove.

"Oops, excuse me. I am so sorry." Finally he was awake. He's a hard sleeper.

"No, I'm fine. I was a little thirsty but could not seem to wake myself up to get a drink and there you appeared."

"Anything else I can get you? Perhaps my phone number?"

Either that was European humor the Dutchman was displaying or he was flirting with me so I went with it. Whatever it was I blew it. What happened to my being subtle? His eyes had lightened up slightly as he sat staring at me with mild interest, not saying a word. I thought to myself, "Okay, if he doesn't say something soon, I'm going to burst from embarrassment into a huge orange and yellow flame." Then I remember thinking, "It must be my beauty that has stunned him in his sleepy haze and has him feeling shy. I'll be a tad more direct." Before I could control my mouth the words came rolling out . . .

"When you get to Detroit, I would like for you to call me. Here's my number."

I handed him my pink business card. Unable to face the humility of being rejected, I turned on my heels and jettisoned out of first class back into the galley. I didn't return to the first class cabin for the remainder of the flight.

Later on that night, he called me.

The next morning in Phoenix, Edwin has this hellacious idea to climb/hike Camel Back Mountain, and for the first time in my life I became insane and agreed to go with him.

"I'm nervous, Edwin."

"Why?"

"You know I'm afraid of heights, and I'm not sure we should do the difficult climb in this heat. Let's try the easy climb instead."

I am trying anything I can think of to escape from this God-awful climb. Why would anyone want to climb a mountain when all you end up doing is having to come right back down, no graduation party at the top, no celebratory banners waiting at the bottom? Useless.

"Gypsy, you're a flight attendant. How can you be afraid of heights? And you completed that spin instructor course in May. I trust your heart can handle the difficult climb."

"Okay, okay. Which way is the quickest route to the top?"

"Stop it, will you. Follow my lead and everything will work out fine as it always does."

Edwin hates when I lose my nerve. Now we're even because I hate when he has the nerve. Following him will make everything fine as it always does . . . the nerve.

It took us an hour and a half to reach the top. My competitive nature kicked in somewhere around the middle of the climb, and I successfully made it to the top of the mountain without Edwin's guidance. Edwin was right about my not having a heart attack, but he was wrong when he said I'd get used to the elevation. I'm feeling a little lightheaded up here in all this thin air.

"Oh my God, this is amazing. I can see all of Scottsdale from here. I even see the general aviation airport where you fly your Cessna Citation out of." I lift my sunglasses to get a better view. "Downtown is over there, oooh and Fashion Square Mall is that way. Let's see behind me is . . . Edwin?"

Puzzled, I look for him and spot his drenched shirt rising up from behind the final portion of the mountain, dragging his sweaty out-of-breath butt up that mole hill, smashed ego written all over his face.

"Show-off, you saw me limping, Gyps. You should have waited or at least slowed down."

"Oh boo-hoo, you made it, didn't you? Where's your limp now, sore loser?"

"It's not a game, Gyps. Let's go." Edwin turns to begin his retreat.

"Wait a minute, handsome. You know I love it when you're all sweaty." I kiss him softly and rub his back. This always wins him over. "Your muscles are tense. When we get home, I'll give you a back massage. You had a strong climb today." He smiles at me, and I can see that his ego is being restored. I'm going to make certain I slow my pace and lag behind Edwin on the way down the mountain. I can't stand anymore of his whining.

On the drive back to his condo, Edwin wants to stop at the grocery store to pick up some ingredients for his famous homemade chicken soup. He only makes his special soup when he's feeling victorious, and I ask him to pick me up a six-pack of Guinness Draught while I wait in the car. I'm going to need a buzz if I have to listen to his bragging all day. He is determined to beat me at something, and cooking is his thing; on that I will succumb.

"Hey Gyps, I was thinking tonight let's go to Club Barcelona. Their martinis are excellent, and they have a live band. I want to get some drinks in you and see if you're still as aggressive as you were when we first met."

"You always bring that up. I was just trying to be friendly." He always brings that first meeting up. Always.

"You wanted me, and who can blame you? I'm a good-looking man."

"Okay, whatever, pick me out something to wear, please. I'm going to jump in the shower."

"You want one of your beers now?"

"Yes, please."

Edwin loves dressing me, and he's pretty good at it, too. Hopefully, he'll forget about that stupid massage I promised him on the mountain top. I take a cool shower and primp in Edwin's master bathroom while he takes a bath in the guest bathroom. Our plan is to make it to Club Barcelona early, before the booths are all taken.

Inside of Barcelona the ambiance is inviting, and the architectural design coupled with the landscaping makes it feel as though we are in a lush tropical oasis in the desert. Cascades of sky blue water streaming down the sides of the faux mountain, which serves as the entrance, puddle under the thick grass needles pushing against the base of the mountain, and buds of yellow flowers sprouting out around the Barcelona sign nestled in the black soil give way to a tulip garden leading up to the doorway.

I'm wearing my white Bebe miniskirt that Edwin picked out with the palest pink, very feminine ruffled sheer blouse. I'm also rocking a pair of white BCBG stilettos that I adore. These heels make my narrow calves appear shapelier and sexy. Edwin loves this outfit on me so much that he can't keep his hands off. I swear every seven minutes he kisses my neck or my lips. Any part of my body that's in his reach he caresses, and he's constantly asking if I need anything from the bar. He's trying to hide it, but I know this man is hopelessly in love with me, and he thinks he's slick, trying to get me drunk so I will be more submissive to him tonight when we get home.

Edwin called on the drive and reserved one of the large open booths that outline the club. Our booth has enormous burgundy tied drapes that may be untied for privacy and seats up to ten people comfortably. Each booth is situated around the perimeter of the bar area, which commands attention itself with large floor-to-ceiling mirrors posing as a backdrop for the sumptuous brands of liquor standing flush against the ever-changing mirrored wall of fruit-flavored colors:

- Stormy blueberry blue to penetrating purple plum
- Brilliant banana yellow to sunset cantaloupe orange
- Delicious strawberry red to dazzling kiwi green

This is extreme clubbing at its best. The fabulously fierce light show changes with each beat of the techno-infused music, and the hyper DJs are going bananas with the re-mixes. Whoever thought of the idea to add a skin-baring female co-DJ is a genius—what a unique twist to keep the guys' attention and make the women compete when choosing which flirty outfit to wear to Barcelona's. Every girl here has a daring, sexy look. Edwin invited several of his friends to meet us, and many of them are pilots from other airlines, and I see a couple from Encompass, but one unfamiliar face stands out amongst the others. Edwin's Euro-dressed friend Seth joins our party and captures my attention immediately. He has two exotic women dressed in black on each arm, and they both seem spellbound by his charm—either that or they are high on X (Ecstasy) . . . I can't really tell. However, I have been flying enough years and have fine tuned my gaydar and I can sniff out a poser in a heartbeat. I tend to automatically judge every male flight attendant (and some pilots) at first sight. Is he gay or is he straight? It's in a flight attendant's nature to question the sexuality. Even the male flight attendants do it, and it helps avoid being rejected or embarrassed by someone you're trying to pursue. Imagine being turned down by a man who you didn't know would rather be the catcher and not the pitcher. I myself don't care if he's gay. I just like to be in the know, and speaking of the know, I recognize Seth from somewhere.

Anyway, as the evening progresses, Edwin and I have a ball. We dance and kiss and dance and drink all the way up until Edwin feels it is time, time to take me back to his place and finish the night. I air kiss the girls and give Seth a gentle wink and blow him a long-distanced kiss. I can tell he is relieved I kept his secret. I think he recognizes me also. Edwin shakes his buddies' hands, and we are off to break more speed limits, ecstatic to be going home knowing that the best part of the night is yet to come.

In the blink of an eye, we're back home at the Desert Mountain Condominiums. Edwin pulls his truck into his reserved covered parking spot and runs up the concrete flight of stairs to apartment 2B. By the time I reach the taupe-colored door of Edwin's apartment, I am pleased to see that he has already stripped down to his skivvies and is standing deliciously in the moonlit living room. As soon as I enter, Edwin's self-regulating left hand springs to the zipper of my miniskirt and begins un-zipping before I have a chance to resist—not that I was going to—and the right hand starts undraping my ruffled blouse, and my breathing increases as I stand there submissive-like in his living room in my undies, waiting for the fantastic finale that always follows these kinds of nights out on the town. Edwin sweeps me up into his strong arms and carries me into the kitchen. He places my hot body on the cool surface of the limestone counter. Loving the contrasting feel of the cold against my skin, I wait for nature to take its course. My mind becomes dizzy with excitement. I anticipate the delicate head of Edwin's penis being installed into my body by the self-proclaimed certified expert, not unlike his counter tops, which had also been previously installed in his kitchen by the same known professional.

Just as I'm awaiting the warm feel of Edwin's massive manhood, he changes his mind and scoops me up from the counter, and he rushes through the threshold of the bedroom with me in his arms and positions our bodies in the center of his king-size bed. Edwin then masterfully guides his thick sex into my wetness. With each potent inch, my breathing increases, almost matching the rhythm from our climb earlier today. Brute noises flee from deep inside Edwin's chest and his climatic thrusts push me into orgasmic heaven, opening the dam gates from within me and letting a river of gratitude flow. Edwin's firm body grows tense and freezes into a sweet silence; a wave of uncontrollable trembles follows and takes over his control. He collapses on top of me, sexed and exhausted, and dozes off to sleep. Extremely pleased by his performance, I begin to drift away too, with Edwin still in place.

Sunday morning we fall right back into the norm:
Early morning coffee
Workout with weights (and trash talking from Edwin)
Mid-morning breakfast
I love you(s) at the airport

"Gypsy, sweetie, remember to call me when you get home. I will be leaving for Holland tomorrow, and I want to hear your voice before I go."

"Okay, I'll remember. Scout's honor." I put up a peace sign to show my pledge.

Damn, I'm going to miss this man. I haven't reached the gate, and I already miss him.

Again the crew is waiting on the plane for me and sitting in first class, pregnant Amy and Vaseline Stacey.

"Hey everybody, sorry I'm late." I manage to make it onboard ten minutes before boarding this time. "Hey, Bob, what is the flight time to DTW?"

"3:15." He forces his answer.

"Can you shave off fifteen minutes? I have plans when I get home."

"I'll try."

Bob is staring at Stacey's lips with a look of disgust plastered on his face. He goes back into the cockpit pulling his bag behind him and pushes the door closed. I know Stacey noticed Bob's awkward glare because Stacey now seems annoyed. He turns away and switches his little tail at Bob and the closed door in a come-and-get-it way and mumbles a few words I refuse to repeat.

"I knew it," I whisper. "He's a poser."

"Who, Bob?" Amy asks.

"Yeah. His bag tag. The picture of his son."

"That's not his son. That's Seth, his boy-toy," Stacey interjects.

Amy and I look at Stacey, and I point toward to cockpit door.

"I thought I knew him from somewhere," I say. "I saw that guy on his bag tag at the club last night."

"Bob is just a hater who is stuck in the closet, girls. Look at the other side of his bag tag."

Amy and I glance at each other and get up to peer into the crack of the flight deck door to study that sinful bag tag Bob has on his luggage. We suppress our laughter when Bob looks up over his shoulder from his captain's chair with the gayest rainbow grin on his face and asks us if we want something. We smile politely, shake our heads no, exit the flight deck, leaving Bob wondering, and walk back into the forward galley. Bob's sly smile confirms what Stacey has known from the start of the trip.

"You were right, Stacey. He plays for your team," I say.

"Told you girls, didn't I?"

Stacey marches back to the aft galley, pleased that he has revealed Bob's undisclosed preference and displays a slick smile of his own.

"I can't wait to end this trip. I don't feel like working, and I really don't feel like dealing with Americans and having to host another 'stupid passenger day' aboard Encompass Airlines. Ever since the low-cost airline carriers invaded the industry and forced lower fares, we have been getting all of Mega Bus's regular passengers." I pour myself a cup of coffee and add some cream with two sugars.

"Well, get used to it because there is no turning back," Amy says.

The gate agent comes running down the jet bridge in hysterics. "I need to begin boarding the flight in three minutes."

"What? I haven't had my second cup of coffee yet. These passengers are in for it if you insist on boarding before I have my proper dosage of caffeine!"

"And first class is full," he smirks at me and rushes back up the jet way.

Figures. Encompass upgrades anyone for any reason. If your overweight body is spilling into the next passenger's seat, no problem, you're upgraded for extra comfort. If you have a close connection, don't worry, Encompass Airlines will put you in first class for free so you will be closer to the door to make your escape. All you are required to do is whine a little, complain a lot, and we will reward your bad behavior. Furthermore, why do passengers seem to believe that first class arrives first, when actually it's the back of the plane that touches ground first upon landing; add to that the taxi time to the gate and the parking of the jet by the ground crew and deplaning of the passengers. Now that twenty-minute connect time you gave yourself has been eaten up by the mean ol' airlines. I always tell passengers, "Never schedule flights too closely, and remember to allow an hour between flights whenever possible." Okay, enough of my pet peeves. In three hours and fifteen minutes, we will be back on the ground, and in approximately four hours, I'll be at home lounging in my lofty loft. Okay, let's do this. Where did I put my fake smile?

We arrive in DTW, and I bid farewell to Amy and Stacey whom I probably will never see again because we have over 10,000 flight attendants system wide. On my walk over to international arrivals, I feel as though I should be doing the queen's wave. Everyone is watching me, especially the Japanese tour group who probably has never seen a professional uniform skirt as short as mine, unless they saw my friend Becky somewhere. I text Kat to make sure she is waiting outside to pick me up. I'm ready to go home and enjoy the next ten days off from work, which I will use to heal my grouchy soul. I'll need that much time to psych myself up for my next trip to India. Those flights really test my nerves. Uggg.

"Hi Kat!"

"Hey Gypsy, guess what? I'm the featured model in the Invisible Darkness fashion show tonight."

"And . . ."

"And it doesn't start until eight. You will have time to take a quick power nap before the show."

"You have it all planned for me. I appreciate that, though next time ask me if I'd like to attend first, please." I feel my cell vibrating, and I take it out to look at the screen. "Hold on. I have a call."

"Who is it? Edwin?"

"Yep, it's Edwin. He typically gives me a one-hour grace period after returning home before he calls. Hello . . ."

"Gyps, you didn't call."

"I know. I must have dementia."

"Don't say that, Gyps. I leave for Holland tomorrow."

"I know this, Edwin."

"I want you to meet me in Aruba."

"Aruba? Why Aruba?"

"I told you I applied for the vacant instructor position to conduct training on the simulator there for the next twenty-six months."

"Yeah, but you said beginning next year."

"They moved training up six months, so I have to go. I'm obligated."

"I'm not complaining, Edwin. It just leaves me with only two weeks to get into superstar shape."

"You're already a superstar."

"Only you can see that, Edwin."

"Just don't get too skinny. I like my women with a little meat."

"Okay, I'll call you when I get home and we can talk about it then."

Edwin only complains when I lose weight. He doesn't like

women smaller than a size two. When I started training to be a spin instructor, Edwin said I was losing too much weight and so he hired me a personal trainer to add muscle to my small frame. His last girlfriend, Jessica, was a personal trainer, and I know she lives somewhere in Aruba. He told me that he met her on his first tour out of training and that she, too, is a size four. I didn't see how this related to me, but he continued his pathetic attempt to explain the reason for bringing her name up anyway. He said it was his leg to fly while the captain took a break. Edwin said the jet was in his control and had suddenly hit clear air turbulence, and then the plane dropped a few hundred feet. The aircraft shook violently for about three minutes, which is an extremely long time when you think you're going to plunge to the ground or slam into an ocean full of concrete water, and then tilted aggressively toward the starboard side making the right wing nearly point "straight to hell." He said he had never been so scared in his life. Jessica was a flight attendant on that flight, and after Edwin regained control of the aircraft, Jessica had stormed up to the flight deck to see what had gone wrong. Edwin was so frightened, even after the captain took command of the controls and landed the airplane safely, that he invited Jessica out for drinks. He said he was flooded with emotions he never had before and needed a woman's company to help calm his nerves. Three weeks after the supposed near-death experience, they moved in together, and to this date, he continues to bring up that girl's name and that stupid flight, which I don't feel is all that monumental. Who hasn't had a few bumps during an airplane ride?

Sheila, Nina, and I enter the fashion show's sexy atmosphere, and a beautiful six-foot male model dressed in all black greets the three of us at the door and offers the champagne that is sitting pleasantly on his serving tray. Thanks to my running late again, we almost missed Kat's performance, who by the way seems to be stealing the show rocking a black billowing miniskirt that makes for a clever contrast against her slender long legs, and she's strutting ostentatiously in a pair of extremely high fantasy heels that she had to practice walking in for a week. Kat is gliding across the stage while masterfully keeping a small sheer piece of fluorescent chiffon over her girls and not missing a beat, high-stepping it down the catwalk. The music is super hot, and the emcee is doing a famous job of entertaining the crowd as he describes the fashions my little sis is wearing to the onlookers. She has become quite the fashion model, and I love watching her head up the finale and showing the new models how to walk the runway. The establishment has the less-experienced models posing as mannequins in the storefront windows and a few others stationed around the catwalk delivering programs to the patrons.

When the lights come up everyone stands and raves about Kat's performance, clapping and demanding an encore presentation of her Naomi Campbell walk. Some designers are asking the director of the fashion show for Kat's agent's name. They're interested in her modeling at the next event at the Fox Theater. I love watching my sister perform, and I always support her shows, but I am exhausted!

"End of the show, thank God. I am so ready to go back home."

"Are you ready yet, Gypsy?" Sheila asks.

"Yes, I just said that. Aren't you?"

"Definitely. Brandon is waiting for me. Let's find Kat and see if she minds our skipping the after party." Sheila has a devilish look about her tonight.

"Here she comes now. Hey Kat!" I spot my little sister walking by the bar area.

"Oh hey, favorite. Did you enjoy the show? You guys want another glass of champagne?"

"Do we have to wait for you to finish schmoozing with your fans?" I ask with a twisted look on my face. Kat is really hyped up tonight.

"No, go ahead, and Sheila, thanks for coming. Gyps, I'll catch up with you later. You must be tired." Clearly distracted, Kat spoke quickly while she watches Nina interact with that gorgeous six-foot model.

"Okay, you're coming home tonight, right?" I don't think she is listening to me so I wave my hand in front of her face. "Kat! Are you coming home? Yes or no?"

"Yeah, no. Go ahead."

Everyone else is trying to get her attention, too, but Kat is headed unswervingly in Nina's direction where we can hear Nina's loud voice bragging about not having a man and not being required to be home by a set time. Nina decides to stay behind to mingle with the beautiful model who greeted us at the door. Clearly she has no idea that she's the target of Kat's infrared beam. I'll pass on this episode.

"That show was live, wasn't it?" I say as I walk Sheila to her car.

"Yeah, what's going on with Kat and Nina?" Sheila slings her purse in the backseat of her car and turns to face me.

"Looks like pretty boy may be causing trouble," I say.

"More Nina drama, huh? I'll call you tomorrow, Gypsy." Sheila slides into the front seat of her Mini Cooper and starts the engine.

"When I get to my four-poster bed, I'm going to pop a sleeping pill and drift off into utopia for the next twelve hours, so don't call too early," I say as I turn to walk away. "Be careful driving home."

How does ten days off fly by so fast? I'm back at the airport checking in for my trip to India, and no, scheduling didn't have to wake me for the start of the trip this time because I woke up on my own. I also remembered to set my alarm clock in case I didn't wake up naturally. I really enjoyed my time off at home hanging out with the GNO crew, but I was ready to get back to flying. Ten days without leaving the country is hell on Earth for me. I don't know how regular people can stand not leaving the U.S. at least once a month, and definitely don't understand not leaving the state once a week, minimum. I had plenty of coffee this morning to ensure that there will be no repeat of that time when I snapped at a first-time flyer for not knowing how to open the lavatory door. She had grabbed the square ashtray located on the back of the door instead of the round door handle. These passengers can relax. I will be nice and breezy today.

This trip is on a B747-400, the big dog of aircrafts. On large planes like this one, the crew is required to have a flight attendant briefing in a special room, ironically named the briefing room. All sixteen flight attendants (ten women, six men [four gay, two straight]) and the three pilots (all straight) gather in to discuss flight operations. This is also the time where we decide on the scheduled rest periods—the most important info ever, as far as I'm concerned. Upstairs in the back of the plane are eight crew bunks for flight attendants to rest in, and my name is on one of them for the second break period. Hopefully, the purser will get this briefing started soon so that I have time to shop at the gift shop before boarding. I saw a girly key ring at She-She I want to pick up for Nina.

"I love this new hotel," I say to no one particular crewmember while waiting for the briefing to begin.

"The hotel in India?" replies a spotted-faced, fast-speaking flight attendant sitting next to me.

"Yeah, I love *the* king-size sleep number beds. I keep mine on sixty-five, and I set *the* mini-refrigerator to the coldest setting possible. I'm all about extremes, and *the* one-cup coffee maker is constantly brewing. I like to have a hot cup in my hand and lounge around in *the* complimentary robe and slippers." I lower my voice as the purser clears his throat to get our attention.

"Don't forget *the* large marble bathroom and *the* walk-in shower located across from *the* oversized tub. I can soak in that thing for hours," the Dalmatian flight attendant says, mocking my use of the word *the*. "After I visit Dr. Bombay, I plan on spending the rest of my layover in *the* tub."

"And *the* most important hotel feature of all is an outlet located on *the* nightstand lamp so we don't have to search for an available one to plug our cell phones into." I'm speaking fast, matching Dalmatian's pace, and we give each other a high five and laugh loudly, interrupting the briefing. She must have had some bad work done in

India to cause that facial discoloration—maybe she should consider skipping Dr. Bombay's appointment.

"I do love our international hotels, and I'm super-obsessed with ultra-modern airports like the mega-structures in China, with those massively high ceilings and vast glass windows serving as walls." I spread my arms open wide. "Colossal steel pillars, towering beams, and state-of-the-art people movers. Love it. Love it."

"Stop, you're making me wish we were there already."

"Excuse me ladies, we are having the briefing now. Care to join in?" The purser says.

Once the briefing is over and the purser dismisses us, Dalmatian and I continue to dwell on the more glamorous aspects of our lifestyle as we stroll through the terminal to our gate. On the walk to the aircraft, we touch on what we consider to be the most exotic island location, the Maldives. Places to shop in Singapore for bags—she found an area where they sell last season's purses at a deep discount. The many great restaurants in Rome near the Spanish steps, and how magnificent the view of Saipan is from the sky—you never get tired of looking down on its beauty, no matter how many times you visit.

Both Dalmatian and I are junior on the crew list, and we are stuck working together in the back galley, the kitchen, which I actually prefer better than working first class or main cabin on these India flights. The passengers can get too demanding at times. Mostly Eastern Indians travel on our flight to Mumbai, bobble-heads we call them. It's comical to watch them because they don't distinctively shake their heads "yes" or "no." Instead it is more of a bobble-head action, which is hard for the crewmembers to decipher, kind of nauseating, too.

Our fifty-ton aircraft jumps the pond (the Atlantic), travels over Europe, crosses the Indian Ocean, and lands in Bombay (recently renamed Mumbai) fifteen hours and forty-five minutes later. The eager crew is in a hurry to catch our van to the hotel, but I need to stop at the money exchange booth in the airport first.

"I'm going to exchange my U.S. dollars for Rupees before taking the van to the hotel," I call out to the crew. "I have a lot of shopping and pampering to accomplish during our layover. I'll only be a minute. Don't leave me!"

I'm usually the last one to get to the van. In order to sneak ink pens to the begging children outside of the airport terminal, I lag behind on purpose. The crew hates when flight attendants do this, but the kids love getting the pens I collect from different hotels. The crew thinks it's not the pens themselves they like but the value of the pens on the streets. I say, if they can profit and use the money to help feed their families, then whatever, I've done my civic duty, and this way I don't feel bad about spending so much money shopping for silk pashmena scarves and 500-count sheets in Mumbai.

A few flight attendants are going with Dalmatian to see Dr. Bombay for Botox injections and other vanity facial procedures. The fees are minimal in India so I guess that makes it worth the health standards risk. Others are having a spa day, the massage, mani-pedi, and waxing thing, and me, I'm doing it all! I'll even hit the streets and try to blend in with the locals on my way to eat at Leopold's restaurant downtown. I'll have to order a glass of milk with my meal though because the food is too spicy for me. What's really odd is that most of the crew won't leave the hotel seeing that it's monsoon season. The rain falls hard like hurricane storms throughout the entire day for months. It's an awesome sight for visitors to see. I love the way the rain pours out of the sky like bath water and drenches the city streets.

During my layover, I will only communicate with Edwin via email or text messaging. My international layovers are used for quiet time, time for meditating and reflecting on my past. Actually, I really don't know how to quiet my mind. What I end up doing is sitting for five minutes, and then my ADHD kicks in, and I turn on the TV to channel surf. See, it's like this: thinking about how to go about clearing my head only puts thoughts right back up there in my mind, so mostly I end up using my five minutes trying to think of ways to stop thinking. Reflecting on when I first applied for this flight attendant position back in 2000 is one way I distract my mind and relax.

I remember watching Reese to the Rescue, an undercover whistleblower agency, catch the Encompass interviewers on a secret video trying to employ their own family members for the airline in order to dominate the much-sought-after skilled positions in the sky. Encompass was refusing to hire candidates regardless of their experience and schooling or how well suited the individual was for the job. Rude, so that same group of candidates filed a class-action suit against Encompass and won. I was among the group of 200, and sometimes when I arrive at work I look at the names on the crew list to see if I recognize any of the family members who we pin named the flying cartel, the interviewers who tried to steal our careers. I haven't run into any of them yet, but I know they're out there somewhere, and I keep a watchful eye. Maybe that's why I get grouchy occasionally, because this kind of thinking surely doesn't do much to relax me. No, the Greyhound passengers irritate me too, not just the cartel. I need to just stop thinking because now I'm getting upset. The quieting of the mind is something I will struggle with forever, I guess.

Okay enough reflecting. It's too crowded on this elevator ride to think about relaxing anyway, and everyone is piled into the hotel's lift so tightly that there isn't ample room for all my thoughts to spread out and be free.

"Gypsy, tonight the crew is planning to meet in the lounge on the tenth floor. Are you coming?" Dalmatian asks me.

"Yes, I'll be there. I like to see which Air France pilots will show up—the very handsome or the extremely sexy ones. It's always a toss up."

"Unlike our very old or extremely fat ones."

"I know, right?!" I like Dalmatian, she gets me.

We both laugh and ignore the odd look we receive from the conservative Indian elevator operator.

Oh, I found out that Dalmatian's name is really Michelle. I looked at her name tag on her uniform jacket during the elevator ride. Nice name, Michelle.

Typically, several airline crews gather in the lounge, which is actually for airline personnel only. There are several comfy chairs and a few small round tables in the bar area, a pool table situated near the rear of the room, and over by the computers in the corner is a satellite TV with the station set to the video music channel playing top '40s. Most times, we end up closing the bar around 3:00 a.m. A couple hours of winding down before going to bed helps us get on the country's time zone. Tonight I'll have to make sure I go to bed earlier than normal because an Encompass flight attendant from my flight asked if I would like to trade trips. Her early morning flight stops in AMS for a twenty-four-hour layover, and my flight goes directly to DTW. This is perfect. With this trip trade, I can pay Edwin a surprise visit and help him pack for his move to Aruba. He's going to be so thrilled when I call. He'll want to come immediately to the hotel and pick me up. I'll need to sleep when I get there so I better call him later, after I've had my nap and freshened up a bit. First things first, I'm going to go to my room now and change out of this sweaty uniform, then relax for just a few before meeting the crew in the lounge.

"Ms. Moon, this is your wake up call. Have a good flight."

"What? Oh, sorry, thank you. Thank you very much, ma'am."

Dang. I slept through my entire layover. When I receive the call from the front desk it is the next evening and time to meet downstairs for my flight to Amsterdam. I missed all the fun, the crew lounge, going shopping, eating, the whole bit. Dang.

"Surprise, Edwin! I'm in town. I traded trips so I could come and help you pack for your big move!" I'm so excited my words burst through the phone line.

"Err . . . Gyps, most of my packing has already been completed. The only thing really left to do is the taping of the boxes," Edwin says. "And I've already made special plans to meet with some friends in the red light district at one of the coffee houses."

"Oh, good, come and get me. I want to check out the new

live sex show and maybe have dinner at that transgender restaurant near the canal," I say, feeling a little unwanted.

"Um, what time are you leaving for Detroit tomorrow?"

"What? Ten in the morning. Why?" He better not say his friends are waiting. I'm getting irritated.

"That's early. Why don't you wait and join me in Aruba?"

"Wait for what? I traded my trip so I could come here to see you and help pack." I'm really irritated now.

"Gyps, I will have to turn around and come all the way back across town. Do you know how long that would take?"

I am truly stunned. This Dutchman knows good and well I flew eight hours to get to Holland, and he's complaining about driving an extra thirty to forty minutes? "Edwin, what are you saying?"

"Gypsy, I already know what you're going to say. You have been making the sacrifices lately, traveling from Detroit to Phoenix on your days off. I would love for you to join me, but I don't have time for the commute. The traffic is heavy this time of day." Edwin is pausing and waiting for a response from me before he continues. "I don't take for granted the energy and discipline you have for our relationship."

"Edwin, did you say you don't have time for the commute?" Man, I am not prepared for this response. I allow my mind to open up to more possibilities.

"What I meant was I haven't the time. I need to drop my buddy off downtown and then after a couple of drinks I have to head to the airport. The company called and added an Africa trip to my schedule."

"What? You can't drink and fly."

"I know. They're sending me on another business trip. I won't be working a live flight until the next day."

His voice does sound sincere.

CLICK.

I hang up anyway.

Early morning, I receive a call from a lady at the front desk with a Dutch accent. Sometimes these accented calls are my only clue as to which country I'm waking up in.

"Hello Ms. Moon, this is your wake-up call." Her high-energy singing voice awakens me.

"Thank you," replies my low, groggy voice.

Today, I am going back to Detroit and I will meet downstairs with a different crew to take the van to the airport and I'll have to endure another briefing with the fifteen other crew members and three pilots. We haven't worked together before, and the company feels it's necessary to talk together as a group about what we already know as individuals. The purser informs us that flight time from AMS to DTW is going to be a long eight hours. I hope no one on the crew asks what I did on my layover because, if someone does, I may burst into tears like I did last night after I hung up on Edwin. I spent my entire layover with a box of lotion-infused tissues wondering what Edwin was doing and with whom.

We land at Detroit's Metropolitan Airport an hour late because of a weather delay. I bid farewell to the hygiene-challenged mostly European passengers and officially title this flight as "candid passenger day." The Dutch say exactly what's on their mind at any given moment, and many said that they will never fly this airline again if they miss their connections, but they lie. They'll be back. Edwin lies, too. I don't believe he got called out to fly to Africa. Forget him. I better hurry. I have Kat waiting outside for me at international arrivals.

I quicken my pace and smile at the sight of my little sister waiting.

"Are you hungry?" Kat asks me. She hardly ever asks questions about eating.

"Yes, always."

"Let's go to J. Alexander's for lunch. I'm dying for their salad."

"Figures, I want the prime rib and a cool glass of white wine. Chardonnay. What are you going to drink, Kat? Water?"

She pinches my arm and smirks a bit, but I know she is going to order bottled water.

Over lunch, I break down and tell her about the Edwin fiasco.

"Gypsy, maybe he did have a trip to Africa."

"Humph," I manage to utter.

"Listen, you love him, right?"

"Of course, but at the same time I feel I need to protect myself. I'm not sure if I can trust him with my emotions."

"Do you plan on going to Aruba?"

"I had planned on going when I had faith in him, but now I'm thinking about staying home and supporting you. What time is your fashion show tonight?" I swiftly try to change the subject.

"At eight, but I don't feel like modeling. I wish we could trade lives for one week. I would love to be leaving for Aruba."

"Yeah, and I would love to be modeling Studio Couture's spring collection. You have the best life and the best closet."

"Okay, stop. We are not going to have that 'who has the better life' conversation again."

"No, we're not because we already know who the winner is."

We talk for a while longer, and after we finish our lunch we jump in the car and turn onto I-94 East toward downtown. I am jet-lagged and ready to retire for the night on my own mattress. My body's clock is time advanced and believes it's early in the evening instead of mid-afternoon, so I'm going to have to take a sleeping pill before climbing into my four-poster bed and trying to continue forgetting about Edwin, Africa, and the Aruba trip.

Edwin has been in Aruba for two weeks now, and I still haven't made an appearance, nor have I made myself available to any of his persistent phone calls. My phone has been purring all morning long, and my caller ID suggests that I have somehow missed six calls. I probably should not have taken two sleeping pills last night.

"Hello."

"Gypsy, sweetie?"

"Hello, Edwin."

"Did you change your mind about coming to Aruba?"

"No, I'm still coming." Think fast, Gypsy. Think. Think.

"When?"

"Matter of fact, I just called to check the passenger loads to see if there was any room on the flights to Aruba. Most of them are oversold."

"Try calling Southern Airlines. We can use the jump seat if there are no empty seats available."

"Oh, we can? That must be something new. I'll call and book it then."

"I can't wait to hold you again. I miss you so much."

"I miss you, too. I'll call you back after I make my reservations."

"Okay, honey, I'll see you soon?"

"Yeah, I'll call you back and let you know what time to pick me up from the airport. Love you."

"Love you too."

Dang, I'm not sure if I'm ready to see him yet. I have been avoiding his calls and delaying my trip to Aruba hoping that I'll figure out what he's up to. I want to believe he had a trip to Africa, but the logical side of me is wary, and now I must face reality and confront Edwin. Sadly, what motivates me more is knowing that Jessica the ex still lives in Aruba, and the thought of Edwin alone with size four on a beautiful beach is giving me acid reflux and burning a hole in my esophagus. I know he better not get lonely and decide he's going to have another flood of emotion and need the company of a woman again, and he better not rush into her waiting arms to disclose any more secrets of his, or any of my shortcomings to her, and he better not give her any-more praise for being what he considers a loyal friend. I can hear him now telling her how she is a much better listener or that she is more patient than I am. I don't know why they ever broke up if she's that great of a person. Let me hurry up and make those reservations.

"Hello."

"Hello?"

"Hello, Melody. My phone didn't ring. In fact, I was trying to make a call."

"How are you doing, little sis?" Melody asks.

"How are you? How is the missionary work going?"

"Good, good. I will be coming to the States at the end of the month."

"When you get home, you're going to have to fill me in on everything you did in Africa, and don't leave out any details. I can't wait to see you."

"What are you talking about? You saw me last month, Gypsy."

"Web cam doesn't count. I want to see you in person. I need a big hug."

"What's wrong?"

"I need some major counseling. I think Edwin's cheating on me."

"Really? I wish you would have told me that when I last spoke to you."

"Not much you could do about it, Melody."

"Yeah, right. When I saw him at the Diamond Factory, I would have given him a piece of my mind."

"You saw Edwin in Africa?"

"Yes, and I wouldn't hesitate to say to him 'you dirty bastard, my sister is in love with you and this is how you treat her.'"

"Oh my God. Melody, I love you. You just saved my life."

"What?"

"I have to go now, but I love you and I can't wait to see you."

"Wait. What's going on?"

"I'll fill you in later, I have to go now, bye."

I quickly hang up the phone on Melody and dial the airline's 800 number to book the jump seat to Aruba.

Lush vegetation and eerie rock formations outline the picturesque island of Aruba as we descend onto the tropical desert. I see the crystal-clear water's edge kissing the white sand beach, and I can smell the warm air seeping into the airplane's cabin. I close my eyes to give thanks to the creator for the Divi Divi trees located everywhere and for the oxygen they help provide. I give advance thanks for the salt water as it will heal my dry skin during my romps in the ocean and a bunch of thank yous for creating the developer of Victoria's Secret's sizzling bikini catalog. I bought four new bikinis specifically for these romps in the ocean.

Standing outside of Queen Beatrix International Airport, I see Edwin, my loyal Dutchman, holding a single rose.

"Edwin!" I run to his waiting arms and deep kiss him like a hormonal teenager.

"Gypsy, I'm glad you're here. I have good news," Edwin says as he walks me to the passenger side of his Jeep.

"What news is that?"

"The company has offered me a chief pilot position. The pay is almost double what I'm making now."

"Oh Edwin, that's great news. Now you can buy the beach house here that you've been renting."

"Yes, and wait until you see what I have already purchased."

"Don't tell me you went furniture shopping without me."

"Yes, I did. You keep calling my bed the Jessica Bed. I had to get rid of it."

"But still, I love furniture shopping and I'm so good at it. I'm mad now."

"You were supposed to be here two weeks ago. I was sure you had changed your mind about coming."

"No, I was upset about not spending time with you in Amsterdam. You know how my mind creates havoc when I don't get my way."

"You thought I was cheating again, didn't you?"

"Again. What do you mean again?"

"Again you thought I was cheating, not cheating again."

"Right. Yes I did."

"That's why you rushed out here. The flights were never oversold. I've been checking them hoping you would be on one of the many empty flights from Detroit."

"Oh, right. You are able to check. Silly me."

"When we get to the house, I want you to close your eyes. You're going to be proud of how well I redecorated."

"Okay. I hope you saved your receipts."

Edwin guides me into the beach house with his large hands covering my eyes. He doesn't trust that I will keep my eyes closed until we get to the bedroom, and he insists on putting his calloused hands on my freshly made-up face.

"Here we are. Open your eyes."

I hold my breath and open my eyes to the sight of the Jessica Bed, sitting in its original position. Angrily, I turn to face Edwin.

"Why did you lie . . ."

Edwin's shaking hands are holding a two-carat, princess-cut diamond ring in a black velvet box. I gasp at the stone dazzling in the sunlight shining bright, and Edwin's lovable smile is just as bright.

"Edwin."

"Gypsy, my love, will you do me the honor of becoming my wife and accept this ring as a symbol of our commitment?" Edwin is holding my face in his right hand and the sparkling ring in his left.

"Oh, Edwin."

"Please, share your life with me."

"Edwin, yes, I will marry you."

"You will?!"

"Of course I will. I'd love to be your wife."

"What a relief. Can we plan to marry next year?"

"Next weekend." I say as I hold my left finger out to receive the ring.

"I'm sorry. What did you say, Gyps?"

"I said next weekend. I want us to be blissfully married by next week."

"Why the rush?" his voice speaks with celebration.

When I arrived in Aruba, I felt my emotional wall lowering—the same wall I build each time I think Edwin is being a cheat. I need to put an end to this nonsense and let him into my heart and begin to tear down the wall of destruction once and for all.

"No rush, I'm very happy and what I need is for you to be spontaneous and agree to next weekend."

"Okay, if you are sure then I can arrange it."

"A wedding on the beach," I insert.

"Okay, sweetie."

"Barefoot, at dusk." More insertion.

"Yes, anything for you."

"And get rid of this Jessica Bed, please."

"Here, take my AMEX and choose whichever bed you like."

"Ooh, will I get one of these with my own name on it?"

"Everything will have your name on it, including the beach house."

"Gypsy Moon." Edwin lowers himself down on one knee. "Will you marry me?"

"Yes, my love, I will." I say in a soft voice.

Edwin places the delicious ice on my finger and I sink into the comfort of his embrace.

The next Sunday morning, I awake as Mrs. Edwin Egypt in our new bed. How cool is that? Gypsy Egypt. Everyone in the States is going to be upset with me for not inviting them to my unplanned wedding. Edwin suggests that I compose a detailed email offering up the best reasons for our sudden nuptials. Why with so many of my family and friends sprinkled throughout the universe, Melody is in Africa, Summer in Atlanta, Nina and Sheila at home in Detroit, Kat on the road with the auto show in California, and all of my flight attendant colleagues scattered around the world, how could I have possibly arranged a wedding? Sounds good.

After typing my favorite reasons and asking for forgiveness, I promise to plan a fab reception later in the year to celebrate with my loved ones. I cross my fingers and hold my breath as I push the send button on my Vaio computer. Staring at the blank screen and not sure of what to do next, I decide to call Encompass Airlines and request the one-year leave of absence the company is offering. It's time for a change. It seems I've been flying all my life, and now that I'm a newlywed I feel I should focus on my family life and build a strong foundation like Mom had with Daddy. Edwin flies enough for the both of us anyway so the money won't be a problem, and soon he'll be making more than our current combined income, humph. I wonder what the start-up cost to form a foundation is. I hear you don't have to pay taxes on those.

"What do you think you might want to do if they grant you the leave, Gyps?"

"I don't know. The hotels and resorts in Aruba are always looking for spin instructors. I figure I could put that certification to use and spin for a year." I smile at Edwin. "After my one-year leave of absence has expired, I can apply for an extended leave if that's okay with you and we can start a foundation, or I could finish taking lessons for my private pilot license. Or how about my becoming a local soap opera actress? My acting skills far exceed what I have seen on some of these channels in Aruba. You think Encompass will ever relocate you back to the States? I can continue my career as a flight attendant if they do."

"Foundation, you're kidding me. I like the other options better, especially the pilot instructor one. You could also be a stay-at-home mom."

"What pilot instructor? I said pilot. And a stay-at-home mom with a body like this won't do, either. I'm not taking chances on ruining this figure just so you can run back to size-four Jessica." I give Edwin a quick wink. "We will revisit the mommy theory in a year or two."

"You would make a good mother."

"Well, we will discuss those options later."

"What's wrong with now?"

"Or now. Since we are on the subject, let's start with names."

"Start with names, Gyps?"

"Yeah, names. We could name the girl Tiffany."

"What if it's a boy?"

"Then he'll get teased a lot in school."

"He will be a junior named after me, of course."

"Oh, of course."

"My wish is for us to have twins. One boy and one girl."

"Okay, but we need to agree to wait at least one year. I want you to myself a little longer. Agreed?"

"Agreed. Now come over here, Mrs. Egypt, and let's start practicing."

"You haven't listened to a word I said."

"No, because you talk too much sometimes. Now come here."

"Oh boy, here we go. As if our new bed hasn't been christened enough, Edwin."

The future is unknown, but I trust that I'll be prepared for whatever it brings. I am a lucky woman, and I have an extremely loving man by my side to support me in my endeavors. I made a wise decision when I married Edwin last weekend, and another fabulous decision in my nine lives was made on that AMS to DTW flight when I decided to wake and enchant the sleeping stranger seated in the first-class cabin fifteen months ago. I did apologize to Edwin about my accusations right before we got married. I remember when I, too, had my trip instructions changed like Edwin's Africa trip (okay, so I jumped to conclusions). That was the best schedule change ever because I met my husband on that flight. I laminated the changes, and now they are pressed between the pages of our wedding album alongside my flowers.

Acknowledgments

My parents' spirit can finally rest in knowing that their daughters are all living beautiful lives, my oldest sister Melody is a responsible adult and continues her life of good will by helping those in need. After grandma settled into an assisted living community, I inherited my little sister, Kat, she has now become a successful model in her own right, which was my indication that the time had come to let go and allow her to spread her wings and fly. I'm in a good place in my life as well, and I feel I have truly lived nine separate lives with my first life being the greatest because my parents were the main ingredient, and then came the in-between yet fundamental lives: a gullible teen, a juvenile wife, a divorcee' and a career girl. Now in what I believe to be my finale life, I am a happily married and complete woman who has indeed been blessed with the knowledge and experience from living a colorful life. I now feel like I, Gypsy Moon-Egypt, have come into my own. I am a self –assured, confident woman, and I will use my positive energy to promote great changes in the world.

Deepest love and sincere thanks to Teshe' Vassell, thank you for all your support, input, guidance, and, most of all, thank you for believing in me. You hold a special place in my heart right next to my mother, Judith Bracey. I also want to thank all the true characters in my life, the premium fuel that stimulated me to create and move forward in my venture to write my life's story.